I0629825

You Should've Just Let Me Go

Bailey Thomas

Bailey Thomas Books, LLC

Copy Editing by Hannah G. Scheffer-Wentz, English Proper Editing Services

Life's too short. Don't settle.

Contents

1. Hailey   1

2. Logan   7

3. Hailey   13

4. Logan   19

5. Hailey   25

6. Logan   31

7. Hailey   37

8. Logan   43

9. Hailey   49

10. Logan   55

11. Hailey   61

12. Logan   67

13. Hailey   73

14. Logan   79

15. Hailey   85

16. Logan   91

17. Hailey   97

18. Logan   103

19. Hailey   107

20. Logan   109

21. Logan   111

22. Hailey   117

23. Logan   123

24. Hailey   129

25. Logan   135

26. Hailey   141

27. Logan   147

28. Hailey   153

29. Logan   159

30. Hailey   165

31. Logan   171

32. Hailey   177

33. Logan   183

34. Hailey   189

35. Logan   195

36. Hailey   201

37. Logan   207

38. Hailey   213

39. Logan   219

40. Hailey   225

41. Logan   235

42. Hailey   239

Hailey

I hated social events.

Well, not necessarily the events themselves, but the preparation it took to attend one. I was never the type of girl who got all dressed up, wore heavy makeup, or perfectly styled my hair. First of all, I spent most of my college days attending online classes, so it wasn't like I even needed to look presentable. And once I graduated and started my job as an accountant, I was only required to work from the office once a month. It was the perfect hybrid schedule, although I still dreaded that one day a month where I had to actually find a way to appear professional.

My makeup skills were far behind my peers, but even at the prime age of twenty-three, I still had stubborn acne that needed to be somewhat covered up. Despite the ugly bumps on my face that were honestly probably caused by stress at this point, the real challenge was trying to tame my wild curls. I used to be jealous of the girls with pin-straight hair who could run a comb through it without a hitch, but I eventually grew to love the natural state of my hair. Many of my hair ties had fallen victim to the thick mane that ended up snapping most of them in half, but when styled properly, my curls were the source of many compliments.

The struggle of getting ready didn't stop once my hair was done and my makeup was complete. The whole look had to be put together with an outfit that never seemed to please me. It wasn't like I didn't have any clothes. My entire closet was stuffed with items that I wore in high school to items that still had the price tag on them. I definitely did not fall short of options, but somehow, when it was actually time to go somewhere, none of them sounded appealing. Usually, I would go shopping a few days prior to an event so that I wouldn't run into this problem, but dating a real estate agent meant that there were a lot of social gatherings that would pop up at the last minute.

My boyfriend, Logan Tate, entered the world of selling residential homes at the beginning of the summer. He had only been in the industry for a few months, but it didn't take long for me to realize how much image played a role in his new job. I fully embraced the idea of him dressing to impress, but it took a turn when he went from buying new suits to buying a new car. Logan was already struggling financially, which was why I let him live in my apartment for free, so I was really surprised when a new vehicle pulled into the complex parking lot. He wasn't drowning in debt or struggling to eat, but his account usually hovered around fifty dollars once he paid all of his expenses. Logan assured me that once the housing market started to recover and he was able to sell a few homes, then we would move out of my small apartment and into our own house. We had been dating for six years so I more than trusted him, but at this point in our relationship, I was just looking forward to the day when we didn't have to split the check on dates.

"Hailey, why don't you just wear the dress I bought you?" Logan offered when he witnessed the clothing explosion.

I was simply looking for something suitable to wear to his open house, but I ended up covering the entire bedroom floor with the clothes that were once hanging in my closet. Logan had to step over numerous piles just to reach me. The open house was a big step in Logan's career, and I wanted to do everything I could to help him sell his first home, even if it involved looking my very best. I hoped that each event would be one step closer to allowing Logan to not have to rely on me as much for financial reasons. I didn't mind helping him. My salary was pretty generous and I knew it would take him a while to start seeing an income. But sometimes, it would've been nice to have some help.

"Hmm, I think I want to wear something else," I reluctantly responded.

The dress Logan had bought me was nice, but I didn't think it was suitable for a work occasion. It was pretty short and slightly revealing. I had worn it on a few of our date nights, but I wasn't sold on wearing it as professional attire.

"See, this is why I don't buy you nice clothes," Logan stammered. "You never wear anything I get you."

He stormed out of the bedroom and presumably returned to the kitchen to wait for me to finish getting ready. I understood he was under a lot of stress with the pressure of his new job, but I hated when he took his frustrations out on me. I was used to it for the most part. He had always done that throughout our entire relationship, but I had been spared from it for a few years when we attended separate colleges. Logan went to a school in Fort Collins, Colorado, which was only an hour away from my university in Denver, but we didn't live together and usually only hung out on the weekends. I used to miss him a lot when he wasn't around, which was why I offered for us to live together when we graduated last year. It was supposed to be a step that would grow our relationship, but ever since he moved in, we started arguing a lot more. Sometimes, I wondered if we were truly meant to be together because we would constantly fight, and I honestly felt the most sense of peace when he wasn't home. Nonetheless, we had been together for six years and had so much history together. There was no way either one of us was going to give up on the other person and start over with someone else. I couldn't even imagine dating again.

After trying on a few more outfits, I eventually caved and settled on the dress that Logan had bought me. I still wasn't comfortable with the amount of skin it showed and truly did not feel that it matched the occasion, but at least I had chosen an outfit. Logan was either going to bother me about not listening to him sooner, or appreciate that I decided to take his advice. He wasn't a fashion expert by any means, but he definitely was into clothes way more than I was, and as a result, he dressed significantly better than me. I never wore designer brands, and sometimes I didn't even match. When I put effort into what I wore, I thought I looked pretty nice, but most of the time, I just threw on whatever I pulled out of my drawers first.

My lack of style bothered Logan, and it used to be the cause of many of our fights. He argued that since I was his girlfriend, I was a direct representation of him. Wearing mismatched clothes and baggy outfits indicated that I did not take care of myself, which apparently told others that my boyfriend also did not care for himself. I didn't think anyone noticed if I wore tattered sweats to the grocery store, but I tried to take his feelings seriously and step up my fashion game. It was a real pain to wear heels to the gas station and dresses to the coffee shop, but I did it because I wanted to please Logan. He appreciated my efforts, but still wasn't satisfied. Apparently, it was a crime to wear the same outfit twice in the same week, even if it was dressy. I wasn't sure how he came up with the money, but one day I came home from work and there were bags of new clothes waiting for me on the bed. It was a really nice gesture, but Logan and I had different tastes. I wasn't a fan of revealing clothing or expensive fabrics, which was all that was inside the shopping bags. The outfits were super itchy and uncomfortable, but I sucked it up and wore them for him. After a few weeks of wearing only the items that Logan had purchased, I resorted back to my original outfits. When he noticed my shift in style, he ended up returning all the clothes that he had bought me. I tried to explain the type of style that I gravitated toward, but he just called me ungrateful and didn't talk to me for an entire week. Needless to say, he doesn't buy me nice clothes anymore.

I looked in the mirror and was satisfied with the completed look. My hair was controlled, my makeup was smoothly applied, and I finally had a dress to tie it all together. I added the few pieces of jewelry that Logan had gifted me in order to further show that I appreciated when he bought me things. Receiving gifts wasn't one of my love languages, but giving gifts was Logan's. The only catch was that I had to also buy him something in return. It took the thoughtfulness out of the gift when I knew that it was now my turn to surprise him. Unfortunately for me, he was never fully appreciative unless the item was expensive, which didn't work out in my favor since our exchanges usually consisted of me receiving new hair ties and him receiving a new golf club.

Logan wasn't all bad, though. Yes, he was obsessed with appearance and one-sided gift exchanges, but overall, he was a really nice guy. I was tired of dating narcissistic men, and when I met Logan, he was a breath of fresh air. A little over six years ago, I saw him walk into the restaurant where I was a waitress at. He was actually on a date with his girlfriend at the time, but she ended up breaking up with him over the course of the dinner. When she left him alone at the restaurant, I consoled his broken heart and we ended up hitting it off right away. I wasn't proud of the fact that he and I started officially dating only a week after his most recent relationship, but we were meant to be. Honestly, the toughest part of it all was that he remained friends with his ex, and she was still a part of his life to this day. I tried not to get jealous over his ex-girlfriend, Ivy, but Logan would always drop anything he was doing to answer her calls. He even visited her in Oregon when she was sick. Logan assured me many times that he had no romantic feelings toward her. He simply claimed that once he loved someone, he always carried some type of love for them, even after the relationship. I tried to argue his logic many times, but he said his relationship with Ivy was nonnegotiable and if I didn't like it, then I should just leave him. Obviously,

I chose to accept it considering we had been together six years now, but I didn't think I'd ever fully support their relationship.

I finished putting on the jewelry and hoped that by wearing a dress and a few bracelets, Logan would shower me with compliments since he had practically bought my entire outfit. He mentioned before that since we were dating, I should already know that he thinks I'm pretty, but I still liked hearing compliments in the rare instances that he gave them. Usually, they only surfaced when I would wear something that he picked out, so I hoped that this ensemble would be the cause for a few positive remarks.

I looked in the mirror one more time before finally navigating through the piles of clothes that impeded my pathway to the door. It was going to take me an entire afternoon just to get everything back into my closet. I should've just listened to Logan from the beginning about what to wear.

2

Logan

"You look nice," I commented as Hailey made her way down the stairs.

She was wearing the dress I had gotten her a few weeks ago. My best friend, Dalton, had originally purchased it for his girlfriend, but it was too big for her, so I took it off his hands and gave it to Hailey. I didn't always give her clothes from Dalton, but she never tended to wear anything that I personally bought for her. Money was tight, especially after quitting my job to follow my dream of becoming a real estate agent, so I couldn't always afford to gift her a new dress. One time, I had used the last couple hundred dollars that my mom had given me for my birthday to buy Hailey a whole new wardrobe. The clothes consisted of fancy apparel and accompanying accessories. It made me so happy to see her wearing items that actually accentuated her beautiful figure, but she reverted back to her old outfits a few weeks later. She sometimes struggled with self-confidence, so I thought she would've been grateful for the clothes, but it took her over a week to even notice that I took them all back to the store. All I wanted to do was make her feel as beautiful on the outside as she was on the inside. I haven't bought her any new clothes since then.

"Aw, thank you," Hailey responded with her pretty smile. "So do you."

She grabbed her purse and we made our way to my car, which was conveniently parked in the garage. Her apartment only had a one-car garage, but Hailey graciously let me use it while she utilized the complex's open lot. My mother had given me a loan to buy a new vehicle after I was practically on my knees, begging her for the money. All the other real estate agents were driving the hottest cars on the market. They warned me that if I didn't drive a model that was manufactured within the last two years, then no client would ever want to work with me. Although the purchase wasn't my smartest financial decision, I was hoping that it would gain me the clientele

I needed to finally move out of Hailey's tiny apartment and buy us our own home.

I constantly met with local Denver agents for advice on how to make it in the business. They told me what to drive, what to wear, and even how to style my hair, which disappointed me when I had to chop off my curls. I really wanted to fit in the industry, but it proved to be more difficult than I had originally thought. It was tough being a biracial man in the business of selling homes, let alone being biracial in the state of Colorado, but it was something that Hailey and I always bonded over. We had a lot in common, and our ethnicity was one of them. She was my biggest supporter and number one cheerleader. If I ever felt alone, I knew I could always turn to her and she would be there for me. Our relationship had its flaws, but overall, the past six years had been the best six years of my life. I met Hailey, graduated from college, and started my path in real estate. I couldn't wait to finally sell my first home and eventually be able to afford us a bigger space. Hailey paid the rent and most of the utilities. I pretended it didn't bother me, but I was counting down the days until I could properly contribute to our finances.

The entire drive over to the open house was filled with the sounds of the radio. It was a normal occurrence for our relationship. Usually, I wouldn't complain about music, but it made me miss the times when Hailey and I would jam out in the car together. We stopped singing songs together and dancing along to the beat a while ago. Ever since Hailey started her job as an accountant, her focus had been more around her work than me. I was proud of her for landing a role with one of the top firms in the world, but they didn't believe in a forty-hour work week. She usually went to bed after me and woke up before me, which left little time to actually hang out as a couple. Because of her busy work schedule, it meant even more to me when Hailey and I would hang out on the weekends and attend events together, but I didn't believe they meant as much to her as they did to me. We would always show up later than projected because she always took so long to get ready, and she never seemed too excited about the details of the real estate industry. I knew it wasn't the most exciting career path in the world, but I just wanted my favorite cheerleader by my side supporting me.

It was sad, but not unexpected, to finally pull up to the house that I was showing without having spoken one word to each other. I knew it was probably in my best interest to bring this issue up to Hailey, but she usually got defensive if I mentioned something that was wrong in our relationship.

She would take it personally, and would end up getting mad at me. Maybe I would bring it up later, but today I just wanted to focus on my open house. The commission on the sale would most likely go toward paying my mom back for the car loan, but each sale was one step closer to giving Hailey the life she deserved. All I had to do was sell a few houses. With my new car, new suit, and new haircut, I was pretty confident that it wouldn't take long before I bought Hailey a car of her own.

"Can you help me get rid of some of these weeds?" I wishfully asked Hailey when I got out of the car and observed the unkempt yard.

The house needed to look as presentable as possible, but there were a few eyesores tainting the beauty of the house. There weren't too many rogue weeds, but enough where I needed a second pair of hands to dispose of them before the open house began.

Hailey nodded and began ripping at the unwanted plants. Engaging in some last-minute yardwork further confirmed that the real estate business was truly about appearance. The house, the yard, the agent, the agent's girlfriend—everything needed to be in pristine condition or the client would take their money elsewhere. In all honesty, the house needed a lot of work done internally. The structure wasn't sound and the plumbing needed fixing, but externally, it was a gem. A fresh coat of paint and a dusting of the furniture made a huge difference. Surface-level beauty was the theme of the industry. As much as I hated the superficial parts of my job, I had to play the depthless game. It was the only way to get by.

"Logan!" Hailey shouted, "I think you have your first customer!"

She quickly threw the plucked weeds into the trash, wiped her dress clean, and put on her best smile. I appreciated her eagerness, but when I saw the car that was pulling up to the house, I immediately recognized it as Dalton's. I was really proud of this open house, so I had to invite my best friend and his girlfriend, Piper, to it. Hailey was slightly disappointed that the occupants of the car were our friends and not a potential buyer, but nonetheless, she was happy to see them.

Dalton and I had been best friends since middle school. We were always on the same sports teams growing up and only separated when he went to college in Idaho. He moved back to Colorado after he graduated, and now spends his days as a manager of a bank. Because of his elite position, Dalton was constantly around wealthy individuals, which made him the perfect person to earn referrals from. I had only been in this field for a few months, but I was confident that I was going to sell my first home soon with all of the free marketing he was doing for me.

"Hey, man," Dalton greeted as he exited his car, "the house looks good."

"You want to buy it, D?" I joked as I met him in for a brotherly hug. "It's only worth a quarter of a million dollars—way within your budget, Mr. Bank Manager."

"Absolutely not," Piper chimed in. "He needs to buy me a ring before he buys us a house."

Piper was a pageant queen among civilians. She always had to look perfect. Her blonde hair was never out of place, and her blue eyes always matched the sky. A day never went by when she didn't have makeup on. Although most of the time that Piper and Dalton had been dating was in Idaho, in their three years together, I had never seen Piper's natural face.

I watched as Dalton rolled his eyes to his girlfriend's remarks regarding a proposal. Every time she brought it up, he would always brush it off and pretend to ignore her, even though he was planning on popping the question soon. Little did Piper know, Dalton had already been shopping around for the perfect ring for her—a ring that I would have to sell at least five houses to afford.

"Hi, Hailey!" Piper exclaimed when my girlfriend joined the group. "Wow, that dress looks so good on you. Dalton bought me that same one, but it was too big for me. Anyway, it looks way better on you."

Hailey blushed while Dalton and I exchanged mischievous looks. We were the only ones who knew that the dress Piper was referring to was the same dress Hailey was wearing.

"Yeah, it looks really good on you," Dalton agreed.

He and I continued to exchange smiles, but the girls were oblivious.

"Are you here to help us pick weeds?" Hailey eagerly questioned.

Even though she didn't complain about the task, I was sure she was open to the idea of some help.

"Sorry, but I just got my nails done," Piper answered as she held up her newly painted fingers.

I never understood why girls opted to get their nails so long. Piper's fingers looked more like pink claws to me.

"Why don't Logan and Piper tidy up the inside," Dalton suggested, "and Hailey and I will fix up the yard."

"Deal!" Piper exclaimed before I even had a chance to respond.

She grabbed me by my wrist and pulled me toward the front door of the house. I didn't want to leave Hailey behind, but I was relieved to be able to escape the Colorado sun. Besides, she was in good hands. Between her and Dalton's strength, the weeds would be gone in no time.

I unlocked the door and let Piper and me inside. The house was quiet, but more importantly, it was clean. There would only be some minor staging needs done; opening a few curtains, fluffing a few pillows, adjusting some furniture, but nothing too time-consuming.

I opened the blinds in the living room, and peeked out the window to watch Hailey and Dalton continue to tend to the lawn. They had already eliminated most of the weeds and had moved on to picking up the surrounding garbage that had tangled itself in the grass. It was a beautiful sight, watching the house slowly transform before my eyes into a home that was ready to be sold. I had my closest friends with me, working together to help me achieve my dream. The best part was knowing I was going through this new career journey with my amazing girlfriend by my side. Hailey and I made a great team.

3

Hailey

Dalton and I made a great team.

The weeds were gone in seconds. We even had enough time to pick up some of the trash that had been scattered around the yard. We only had a few more minutes until the start of the open house, but I was confident that the exterior would be ready way before anyone showed up. Dalton and I had decided to split the lawn in half and comb through our designated section, removing any garbage or additional weeds that we missed. He purposely took the side of the yard that needed the most work done because he didn't want me to constantly be bending down in a dress. It wasn't the most fun task in the world, but he made it entertaining. He sang every tune that popped into his head, and he even added in a few dance moves. I was so distracted by his awful dancing that I forgot I was even working. Dalton was the perfect teammate.

Logan introduced me to Dalton early in our relationship. They had been best friends longer than I had even known Logan, so it wasn't surprising that Dalton was always around. He and I had developed a friendship of our own over the years since we were both so ingrained in Logan's life. I always thought it was so ironic how close they were because Dalton Riddler was the complete opposite of Logan Tate. Outside of their love for sports and growing up in Colorado, they couldn't be more different. Dalton was six-foot five with emerald green eyes and chestnut brown hair. He was a large man, especially compared to Logan's five-foot eleven frame, but he was still able to fill out every inch of his height with pounds of muscle. Dalton lived in the gym, and had a passion for fitness. Logan and I would occasionally lift weights with Dalton and Piper, but eventually our group of four turned into a duo. Now, only Dalton and I went to the gym. Because of how much time we spent together, away from our significant others, I couldn't help but sometimes wonder what it would've been like if I was dating him instead. I loved Logan with all my heart and would never step outside of our relationship, but Dalton and I just seemed to click better. We were both super active and really into our careers. I was an accountant at a top firm, and Dalton was the manager of a prestigious bank. Logan never took much interest in hearing about my workdays, but Dalton and I could go on and on about budgeting and numbers. He matched my energy a lot better than Logan did, and he never seemed to care too much about superficial things. I bet the way I dressed didn't even bother him.

"Do you think if I bought this house, I could fit a pool in the front yard and a pool in the backyard?" he jokingly commented once we finished cleaning.

"Why don't you just build one giant pool that flows between the yards?" I sarcastically returned.

"See, this is why I keep you around, Ms. Ross." He chuckled.

We took a seat on the stairs of the front porch to admire our work. If the inside looked even close to as good as the outside, the house was going to be sold in seconds, and I would be one step closer to living the life that Logan had always promised me.

I watched a bead of sweat drip from Dalton's face, and realized that we probably smelled like the weeds and trash that we had just discarded. It was already November, but the sun was beating down on us as if it were the heart of summer. It didn't help that we lived in a city that was a mile closer to the sun.

"Do I look as bad as I smell?" I asked as I sniffed parts of my dress.

I noticed some dirt had smeared along the bottom of the dress, and sweat was starting to soak the areas near my armpits. Logan probably wouldn't be happy if I welcomed potential buyers with a dirty outfit, but it gave me an excuse to wear something else. I was pretty sure I had a pair of sweatpants and an extra t-shirt in Logan's car.

"You look absolutely beautiful," Dalton responded as he smiled down at me.

Even sitting, he still towered over me. His giant body made me feel protected, and his kind eyes made me feel safe. We were already positioned next to each other, but he scooted over to be even closer to me. He leaned his face closer to mine, and for a second I thought he was about to risk both of our relationships and kiss me, but my mind was suddenly directed elsewhere when his nose began to sniffle.

"But you smell like my gym bag," Dalton eagerly added.

He pinched his nose and created more distance between us, abruptly leaning away from me. I started to become self-conscious of my body odor until he started obnoxiously gagging, which was when I realized that he was just messing with me.

"I smell that bad, huh?" I playfully uttered.

Dalton aggressively nodded his head, still acting as if he was going to be sick at any moment. His obscene dry heaves made me thankful that he worked in finance and not in Hollywood.

I took the opportunity to wrap Dalton in a giant bear hug and rub my musty scent all over him. He squirmed beneath my arms, but it didn't take long for his strength to outmatch mine, allowing him to free himself from my grip. I started laughing at my attempt to transfer my dirty smell onto him, until he gladly returned the favor and pulled me toward his sweaty chest. I was nowhere near as strong as him, so I wasn't able to escape him as easily as he was able to do to me. I struggled to get away from his sticky skin, as I was firmly pressed against his chest. Dalton held on to me tightly, and I wasn't even close to breaking free, although, I didn't think I was putting in my full effort. There was something comforting about being that close to him. I was kind of enjoying the close proximity to him, and I think he enjoyed it, too. He showed no signs of letting me go, and I was only eventually released from his hold when the front door opened.

"Thought you two could use some water," Piper offered with two ice cold bottles in her hand, "but it looks like maybe a shower would serve you better." She looked at us in disgust as she handed us both the waters. She immediately returned inside, and I would have bet my life savings that she ran and told Logan about how repulsive we looked.

"I guess we do look as bad as we smell." Dalton laughed.

He didn't seem too worried that we were at a professional event covered in sweat and dirt, but I knew that if I didn't fix the situation, Logan would blame me if the house went unsold. I quickly pulled out my phone and texted my sister, Megan, and asked her to bring me a change of clothes. She still lived with our parents, roughly fifteen minutes outside of Denver, and was about the same size as me. I had extra clothes still lingering in the closet of my parents' house, but she had great style, so a dress from her wardrobe would be just fine.

"Do you want my sister to bring you one of my dad's shirts?" I asked.

Dalton wasn't nearly as dirty as I was, but I could still see the sweat seeping through.

"Nah, that's okay," he kindly declined. "I like the smell of hard work."

He winked at me as he continued to drink the water that Piper had brought us.

I was jealous of Dalton. Even smelly and sweaty, he still maintained his gorgeous appearance. In the rare case that his looks did falter, I bet he had a supportive girlfriend that wouldn't blame her failures on him. I wished I had a boyfriend that offered me the same grace.

***

Twenty minutes later, Megan showed up with a new dress and a bottle of perfume. She saved me from enduring any more of the disgusting scent, and from the wrath of Logan Tate. The open house started ten minutes ago, but nobody had shown up yet, so I was spared Logan's disappointment. He had given me a look of frustration when he noticed my tattered clothes, but when I had told him Megan was on her way, he eased up. Dalton also had my back and had told Logan to relax, which was probably the real reason why Logan hadn't yelled at me. Either way, I was just glad I wasn't going to ruin the event.

Although five years younger than me, Megan was a spitting image of me. We had the same curly hair, long legs, and stubborn acne. In public, we often got mistaken as twins, which made me wonder if I looked her age or she looked mine. As my only sibling, I was very protective of her. In fact, I was very protective of my parents, too. My family meant the world to me, and I usually visited them every weekend. It was easy to see them since they lived so close, but Megan had been preparing to apply to Princeton and would have to move if she got in. I never wanted her to leave the state of Colorado, but I could never let her turn down such an elite school. As long as my family was happy and my career was on track, life was good.

"Wow, cool house!" Megan complimented when she met me at the stairs of the front porch.

"You won't find a single weed in the yard." Dalton smirked as he gave her a hug.

Piper and Logan were still getting the inside ready, and it was Dalton's and my job to alert them if anyone showed up. So far, not even a single car drove by, but we were only ten minutes into a four-hour showing.

"You might be able to afford it someday if you get into Princeton," I proudly mentioned.

"Woah, Princeton?" Dalton gasped. "You must get your intelligence from your sister."

He kindly smiled at me, and I was thankful that my tan complexion was able to hide most of my blushing. I still wasn't used to compliments because Logan rarely commented on my appearance, and he definitely never said nice things about my brain. I worked for such an elite firm and graduated with a 4.0, yet he still never mentioned anything about how smart I was. Dalton, on the other hand, was always trying to find a way to make me smile.

"I want to major in Political Science," Megan pleasantly informed him. "I am going to be the President of the United States of America one day."

"Well, you've got my vote," Dalton encouraged.

As we were discussing the details of Megan's future political campaign, a white car pulled into the driveway.

"Should I grab Logan?" Dalton frantically asked.

"Yes, and please be fast," I relayed.

In any other case, Logan would have been disappointed to know that the owner of the vehicle that parked in front of the house was not a client. We still weren't even an hour into the open house, but I was starting to get a little nervous that nobody was going to show up, which meant that Logan was also probably getting nervous. He most likely would get excited at the sight of Dalton and assume that someone had shown up, but it would be a false alarm. Normally, getting his hopes up for them to eventually be let down would upset Logan. However, this time, his excitement wouldn't be crushed. Although the woman walking toward me had no intention of putting in an offer on the house, her presence was still going to make Logan very happy.

4

Logan

My mother showed up about a half an hour into the open house. Piper and I had just finished the final touches on the interior, and we were patiently waiting for the first potential buyer to walk through the doors. My nerves were starting to take over, so I was grateful when Dalton notified me of my mother's arrival. Throughout my childhood, she had always been there to support me. She showed up to every one of my sporting events, and she never missed a game. I always had a fan in the crowd, no matter the circumstances.

My mom had to play the part of a maternal and paternal figure, as my father walked out of my life when I was only seven. I didn't remember much of him, but apparently he had a whole other family with another woman and decided to be with them instead. With no father and no relationship with my half-siblings, my mom was my rock. She was the only thing in my life that came before Hailey. I would give up my friendship with Dalton, sports, and even my real estate career to be with my amazing girlfriend, but my mom came first. She was number one.

"Oh, baby, I'm so proud of you," my mom greeted when I met her outside. "The house is beautiful." She gave me a few kisses on my cheek and squeezed me as hard as she could.

"Thanks, Mom," I stammered under the force of her hug. "Dalton and Hailey fixed up the outside, but wait until you see the inside."

My mom released me from her arms and looked Hailey up and down. She was still covered in dirt from her recent gardening venture and was holding a new outfit to change into that Megan had brought her.

"Oh," my mother began, "is that why she looks like she hasn't showered in weeks?" My mother glanced over her one more time with a disgusted look on her face.

"She was busy helping your son prepare for his open house," Dalton interjected.

Dalton was such a softie. Growing up, he had always been afraid of my mother. She used to discipline him harder than his own mom did, and would even occasionally put him in timeouts if he broke our house rules. One night, when Dalton was over for a sleepover, she caught him sneaking ice cream out of the freezer after midnight. My mother was strict about how many sweets we ate, and it was against her rules to have any dessert unless she gave us permission. After she caught him with the tub of ice cream in his hands, she made him do our yardwork for a week straight. I didn't think Dalton ever told his mom the real reason why he would return sweaty and covered in grass stains every time he left my house, but I guess that was how he was able to clear the weeds so easily for the open house—he already had a lot of practice.

"Are you not working today, Hailey?" my mom continued.

"It's Saturday, Ms. Tate," Hailey politely informed her.

"Well, my son is working today. Maybe if you worked as hard as he did, you could afford yourself a dress that actually covered your legs," my mom calmly suggested.

I could see Hailey's eyebrow twitching, which meant she was about to explode in anger. She still hadn't gotten used to my mom's tough parenting style. I promised Hailey that despite her delivery, she always meant well and just wanted the best for her. Despite her coming off as abrasive, she loved Hailey and had approved of our relationship from the very beginning.

"Mom, why don't I give you and Megan a tour of the house?" I proclaimed in an effort to diffuse the situation.

An awkward silence filled the air as my mom and Megan looked at each other.

"I'm actually about to head home," Megan informed me. "I have some college applications I need to finish."

Megan walked off the porch, waving everyone goodbye as she headed toward her car, while I guided my mom into the house giving the rest of the group strict instructions to notify me if someone showed up. Once inside, my mom was amazed at the beauty of the interior of the house. I used her as practice and showed her around the home as if she was an actual client. Each room was carefully staged, and I was able to successfully describe every detail of the house and answer every one of her questions. I already knew I was prepared, but giving my mom a tour solidified my confidence. I was ready to sell the house and pay her back for the car. When I finally finished showing her around, we returned to the kitchen where I was surprised to see Hailey, Dalton, and Piper all gathered around the refreshments that were set out for the guests.

"Colorado sun got to us," Dalton initiated, "but we can see the front door from here."

Dalton took a bite of a cookie and washed it down with a cup of lemonade. He was the only one who dared to touch the snacks, but I guess he deserved some relief from being outside most of the day and completing yard work. My mom and I joined them around the kitchen counter where we patiently waited for the first buyer to show up. There were still three hours left in the open house, but I was starting to get worried that nobody was going to show up.

"So, what's everyone doing tomorrow?" Hailey chimed in. I think she could sense my apprehension and wanted to distract my thoughts.

"Probably just going to hang out around the house," Dalton answered. "You guys are more than welcome to come over."

"We'd love to!" Hailey excitedly exclaimed.

As much as I wanted to spend another day with Dalton and Piper, I actually was busy. My Sunday plans were going to upset Hailey, but I had been so focused on the open house that I forgot to tell her that I was meeting Ivy for lunch. I knew Hailey didn't like when I met up with my ex-girlfriend, but she was only in town for the weekend, and I had to spend today at the open house.

Ivy was my middle school sweetheart. We met in sixth grade and dated all the way up until my junior year of high school. I initially thought that Ivy was my soulmate, but my young heart was just happy to be in love. We were always together, well, as much as our parents would allow at that age, and I had envisioned a forever future with her. Our relationship was full of fun and laughter in the beginning, but once we got older, things changed. As soon as we reached high school, Ivy's priorities shifted, and she no longer had time for me. We both were athletes, but I was able to finish my schoolwork, attend practices, and still find time to see her. Ivy wasn't as great at time management as I was, and I slowly fell down the list of things that were important to her. Because of all the love and respect that were between us from dating so long and basically growing up together, we decided to go on one more date before we eventually agreed to end the relationship over dinner. Hailey happened to be our waitress at our breakup date, and although it wasn't the greatest idea to date her only a week after Ivy, the relationship had ended far before the title had.

"Thanks for the invite, D, but I'm actually meeting Ivy for lunch tomorrow," I hesitantly responded.

Dalton was friends with Ivy while we were dating, but their friendship ended when our relationship did. He was now on Team Hailey, but Dalton was just an overall supportive guy. I was sure that if Hailey and I ever broke up, he would move on from her and become best friends with the next girl I dated. Though his loyalty would always remain with me, I could still see the look of concern on his face for Hailey. He knew how upset she got over even the slightest mention of Ivy.

"Oh, I love Ivy!" my mom happily cheered. "Tell her I said hi!"

My mom also knew how irritated Hailey became when I hung out with my ex, but she didn't mean any harm by her excitement. Ivy and my mom were best friends when we dated. She was the daughter my mother never had, and they would constantly hang out, even without me. Hailey and my mom were also friends, but they didn't get along as well as my mom had with Ivy.

"Um, when were you going to tell me about this?" Hailey questioned as calmly as she possibly could.

"Relax, Hailey," my mom interjected. "It's okay to still be friends with your ex. Once my son loves someone, he will always have love for them. You will find that out when you guys break up."

I could tell Piper wanted no part of the conversation as she slowly began to step away from the kitchen counter and fade into the background, but Dalton was itching to save Hailey before she burst into a blaze of flames that engulfed the entire kitchen.

"Ms. Tate, Piper and I wanted your advice on something," Dalton stated when he decided that he couldn't hold his tongue any longer. "I was wondering if I bought this house, could I fit a pool in the front yard and the backyard? Do you think you could evaluate the size of the yards with me?"

My mother enthusiastically agreed to Dalton's proposal, as she loved giving her opinion on things. She eagerly followed Piper and Dalton outside, leaving Hailey and me alone to discuss the Ivy situation.

"Hailey, I know how upset you get over me seeing Ivy, but tomorrow is her last day in town and I haven't seen her in a while," I passionately defended once we were finally alone. "I don't have any feelings for her anymore, and you know that."

I watched as Hailey's eyebrow continued to furrow as she contemplated the idea of me going to lunch with my ex. "I just don't understand why you insist on keeping a relationship with her when you know it upsets me," she whimpered.

"I only see her like once a year," I argued. "She's a very important person in my life, and I told you that from the beginning."

Tears started to form in the corners of Hailey's eyes.

"I know it causes an argument between us," I continued, "but I'm okay with fighting about this with you if it means I get to have a friendship with her."

My last comment was the final blow to the barrier that was keeping the tears from falling down Hailey's sweet cheeks. In a matter of seconds, her face was drenched from painful cries over the thought of me spending an afternoon with someone who I considered a friend. I hated watching Hailey cry, but I didn't understand why she was so upset. Yes, Ivy and I had dated a long time ago, but I truly just considered her a good friend. Hailey couldn't expect me to completely cut Ivy out of my life—that would be so controlling on her part. Despite my lack of understanding, I still made my way over to Hailey and put my arm around her in a comforting embrace.

"There is no one in this world that I rather be with than you," I softly whispered to her. "She is just a good friend, nothing more."

She continued to cry in my arms, but there was nothing further that I could do at that point. I had already made the decision that I was going to see Ivy tomorrow, and it was too late to back down now. I knew Hailey had her insecurities, but she had nothing to worry about. I hoped someday she would eventually be able to get over her issues surrounding my friendship with my ex-girlfriend, because Ivy truly did have a meaningful impact in my life, and I didn't want to let her go.

Sadly, Hailey continued to cry in my arms for the rest of the open house. For three hours straight, she soaked my nice suit in the dampness of her tears. Even when Dalton, Piper, and my mom returned from detailing the dimensions of the yards, Hailey continued to bawl. I was worried that a potential buyer was going to walk in and discover a hysterical girl in a dirty dress crying on the real estate agent, but Hailey was able to freely express her sadness the entire time because nobody showed up. My girlfriend was crying on my shoulder, and my open house had been a complete failure.

5

Hailey

"I can tell that you're getting stronger," Dalton kindly noted. "I think you should add more weight next time."

Dalton and I were seated in the outdoor patio area of our favorite smoothie spot. After every lift, we would enjoy a post-workout beverage and discuss how the session went, what our fitness goals were, and update each other on the current events in our lives. Most of the time, our conversations were centered around our relationships, but it was nice to be able to vent to someone other than Logan.

"If I add any more weight, I'm going to fall on my butt," I reassured. "I'm already squatting almost double what I did last month."

Dalton laughed, but he probably was just reminiscing about how far I'd come in my fitness journey. When we used to lift with Piper and Logan, I never pushed myself in the gym. I spent most of our sessions gossiping with Piper over the latest pop culture drama, but now that it was just Dalton and I, I took it more seriously. My goal was to have a body as ripped as Dalton's, but I didn't think even the best personal trainer in the world could get me there. Dalton was on another level.

"Then, at least squat lower," Dalton instructed. "It's sunny outside."

"What's that supposed to mean?" I questioned.

"Sun's out, buns out," Dalton pleasantly informed.

I rolled my eyes at his comment, giving the appearance as though I didn't find him funny at all. In all honesty, I was trying my hardest not to laugh. His joke was stupid, but I still found it hilarious. I attempted to hide my suppressed laughter by taking a sip of my smoothie, but I failed miserably. As soon as it hit my throat, the berry drink that was intended to be swallowed made a reappearance through my nose. I frantically grabbed some napkins to cover my face and hide the disastrous mess, but Dalton was already rolling out of his chair, laughing hysterically. Sun's out, smoothie out.

"If this was a first date, I would for sure never call you back," Dalton croaked in between laughs. "Sorry, but I prefer girls who can handle their smoothies."

"Yeah, and I prefer guys who can bench press more than I weigh," I rebutted, still trying to clean up the fruity explosion.

Dalton looked surprised, but at least he stopped laughing at me. He took one more sip of his smoothie before setting the record straight.

"Ms. Ross, I can bench press double your weight." He gave me a sly smile.

I hated to admit it, but he was right. Dalton Riddler could probably lift triple my weight with one arm. He was so strong, and watching his muscles flex after each movement was just another perk of being his gym partner.

"Well, since you're so strong," I smugly began, "the next time Logan tasks us with performing manual labor on his open houses, you're on your own."

"Speaking of that," Dalton started, "has he said anything about the open house yesterday? I know he was pretty bummed that nobody showed up."

I wasn't surprised that he was concerned over Logan's feelings in regards to the underwhelming event, but the truth was that Logan wasn't as disappointed as he should've been. I loved that he was able to put the unsuccessful event behind him and move on to the next one, but I was more upset about it than he was. It was only his first open house, but I was tired of his confident promises that we would be out of my small apartment and into a place of our own in no time. I trusted him, but I was starting to lose faith in the life that he had envisioned for us.

"I think he is just ready to finally sell his first home," I relayed to Dalton.

There was no point in explaining my frustrations regarding Logan's new job so early in his career. I knew it took years for real estate agents to actually see a meaningful profit, but Logan was a hard worker. And even though I was losing confidence, I still had a tiny bit of hope that he was going to be one of the lucky ones that would make it in the industry.

"Well, then, how are you feeling about the other day?" Dalton continued to question. "You took a lot of heat from Ms. Tate."

I gripped my smoothie a little tighter at the mention of Logan's mother. Logan swore that she loved me, but she had been nothing but rude to me ever since I'd met her. She constantly threw out passive-aggressive comments, and she never apologized for her rude behavior. I understood being protective over family, but Logan's mom took it to another level. I didn't think she liked that her only child was spending more time with me than the one who birthed him. She loved being at the top spot in his life, and my presence threatened her position as number one.

"All I can say is that I don't know how such a crazy woman raised such a kind man," I answered, still gripping the life out of my smoothie.

Dalton grabbed my hand and held it in his to save my cup from faltering beneath the strength of my fingers and initiating another liquid berry explosion. Although his gesture was innocent, I felt guilty for allowing Logan's best friend to caress my hand. It wasn't so much the physical sensation that warranted the alarm bells in my head, but the emotional connection I felt. I knew that holding hands with Dalton made me feel things that I didn't feel with Logan. I quickly retracted my hand, leaving the warmness of Dalton's grip.

"Are you sure you're okay?" Dalton cautiously questioned.

"Yeah, I'm fine. I've just been under a lot of stress today," I reluctantly vented. "Logan's at lunch with Ivy right now."

Despite me crying my eyes out at his open house, Logan still insisted on following through with his plans to see her. We barely spoke to each other this morning because we knew it was going to end up in a fight. Logan and I just went about our day as if I wasn't hurting inside. Sometimes, it was just easier to deal with our relationship problems internally than to hash them out. When we tried to communicate, I would end up crying and Logan would end up shutting down. Our arguments were not productive, and we never solved anything. There were years and years of problems that I had constantly pushed down. They sometimes made their way to the surface, and I found myself in random bad moods, but I was usually able to push them back down until they popped up again. One day I might explode, but it had been six years and I was still holding it together.

"Oh, I'm sorry, Hailey," Dalton apologized on Logan's behalf. "I know there's nothing I can say that will make everything better, but I do know that Logan really loves you. I know it sucks that he is still friends with his ex, but trust me, you are his world."

I really wanted to believe Dalton, but I felt if Logan truly loved me, then he would have respected my wishes and not continued to have a close relationship with Ivy. I clearly got the short end of the stick as Logan had nothing to worry about on his end. My dating history could fit on a napkin.

I had flings and minor crushes, but nothing serious. Logan was my first serious boyfriend, which meant that he didn't have to deal with any past relationships hitting me up and inviting me to lunch.

"Do you think he's cheating on me?" I blurted out. My question almost made Dalton choke on his smoothie, but I just wanted reassurance that Logan only had eyes for me.

"There is no way he's cheating on you, Hailey," Dalton strongly confirmed.

"How can you be so sure?" I fired back. I knew Dalton was Logan's best friend and they told each other everything, but Dalton seemed overly confident in Logan's faithfulness.

"Because Logan's not stupid," he replied, "and it would take a very stupid man to ruin a relationship with a girl like you."

He took my hand into his again, but this time I let him. I needed the comfort. It was tough dating a guy who blatantly disregarded his girl-friend's feelings in order to please an ex. If we ever broke up, I couldn't imagine sitting down for lunch with him years later in a totally platonic manner. There would always be feelings present, and that's what I feared was going on between Ivy and Logan. It had to be impossible for them to just enjoy a lunch as friends. They had a serious relationship, and those memories just don't go away. I imagined them reminiscing over the good times that they had shared, and discussing all the things they did together as a couple. I wondered if Logan would remember all the good times with Ivy and realize that the relationship with her was better than the one with me. I wouldn't be surprised if he came home from the lunch ready to break up with me and retry things with her. I truly believe Logan loved me. I just wasn't sure if he loved me as much as he loved Ivy.

"What can I do to make you feel better?" Dalton sympathetically inquired.

There was nothing Dalton could truly do to make everything right, but I wasn't going to pass up the opportunity that he was presenting.

"Hmm, well, I wouldn't mind seeing a smoothie come out of your nose this time," I sarcastically requested. "It's only fair."

Dalton looked at me quizzically but wasted no time in pouring the remnants of his smoothie all over his face. Before I could even react, his face was covered in a dark green liquid.

"I wasn't sure how to make it come out of my nose, but I hope this counts." He smiled through the mess on his face.

"That is definitely a close second." I enthusiastically laughed.

Since I led Dalton into the mess, it only made sense for me to help him get out of it. I retrieved a few napkins from the dispenser and made my way over to him. The smoothie was starting to drip all over his shirt, so I quickly smashed the pile of napkins onto his face. By the way he was mumbling under the wipes, I figured I was doing more harm than good.

"Maybe a little gentler next time." Dalton chuckled as he took ownership of the cleaning responsibility.

"Sorry," I proclaimed. "I forgot I'm stronger than I used to be."

I giggled at the sight of Dalton wiping away the rest of the smoothie that he purposely dumped on his face to make me feel better. It was safe to say that his tactic had worked.

"Are we even now?" Dalton chuckled. He stuck out his hand for me to shake, signaling a truce.

"We're even." I smiled as I emphatically shook his hand.

I wasn't sure what the average length of a handshake was. My best guess would have been around two or three seconds; or maybe it was measured by shakes instead of time. In that case, I believed one or two would suffice before the individual parties let go. Whatever the average length of a handshake was, ours clearly surpassed it. I believed at one point we stopped shaking, and it eventually just turned into us holding hands. Logan had my heart, and I loved him very much, but for a moment, I thought there might be a possibility that I could love someone else even more.

6

Logan

I arrived at the café a little early, so I grabbed a table in the far corner. The place was unusually quiet, especially for it being the prime of lunch hour, but I was grateful that Ivy and I wouldn't have to scream across the table to hear each other. I purposely chose this place because they served the best turkey sandwiches in the entire state of Colorado. It was a hidden gem, roughly ten minutes from the apartment. The quick-service restaurant made it the perfect establishment to have a casual lunch. There wasn't the pressure of fancy waiters trying to encourage you to order expensive menu items, but rather it was a simple eatery where you ordered your favorite sandwich without breaking the bank. I would've easily chosen a nice steakhouse over a café that served deli meats, but I really wanted to show Hailey that this lunch was not even close to a date. I truly did not have any romantic feelings left for Ivy; it was merely just two friends catching up.

Ivy Sanders moved to Oregon our senior year of high school. We had already broken up at that point in time, but it was still sad to see her go. She had a going-away party a few days before she left, which almost the entire school attended. Ivy had always been super popular and well-liked among our peers. Her wavy blonde hair was the envy of most of the girls at our school, but it was really her kind energy that made people attracted to her. I was always drawn to her outgoing personality and infectious smile, as was everyone else. I had considered myself an extrovert, but I was nothing compared to Ivy. She was the source of fun at every event. The Earth, along with the rest of the planets, would have wasted no time in abandoning their usual route around the sun to orbit around her. When we became a couple, I was automatically put into the spotlight with her. At first, it was uncomfortable receiving so much attention and having everyone know your name. As much as I loved being the life of the party, being the only kid of color at my school made me want to hide in the shadows. I tried really hard to not stick out as much as I already did, but dating Ivy forced me to come out of my shell and embrace the popularity.

Being with Ivy severely increased my confidence and self-esteem, but there was a reason why we weren't together anymore. Our relationship wasn't all sunshine and rainbows, and we endured problems even before she removed me from her priority list. High school exacerbated our relationship flaws, and even though her lack of ability to make time for me ultimately led to our downfall, our fate to break up was inevitable. Ivy was a great girl, but she wasn't great at being a girlfriend. She never remembered anniversaries, hated affection, and didn't possess a romantic bone in her body. The entire time we were dating, it felt like we were just best friends that decided to slap on a relationship title. Granted, we became official in middle school, so there wasn't much of a difference between dating and friends at that age, but she still never fully assumed the role of a girlfriend when we entered high school, either. We were never meant to be anything more than just platonic. I figured that's why I was so adamant about keeping a friendship with her all these years. Despite dating for such a long time, the entire relationship was basically just an exclusive friendship. I didn't even view her as an ex-girlfriend because of how casual our relationship was.

Dating Hailey was completely different than dating Ivy. Hailey and I were actually old enough to know what love was, and we could positively identify that we had that feeling for each other. We went on real dates, shared romantic moments, and made plans for our future. Even though I was Hailey's first relationship, she had totally embraced her title as a girlfriend and prioritized the relationship. Well, at least at the beginning. I believed she was uncomfortable with me seeing my ex because she thought that I felt the same way for Ivy as I did for her, but that couldn't be further from the truth. I had tried to explain to her multiple times that I loved Ivy as a friend and nothing more, but Hailey didn't understand. I hoped that she would one day become comfortable with our relationship because I wouldn't want to be put in the place where I had to choose one over the other. I loved Hailey, but it wouldn't work out in her favor if she gave me the ultimatum. It was discussed at the beginning that I was still in touch with my ex, and Hailey agreed to it. If she made me decide between her and Ivy, then she was clearly not the one for me. It would have nothing to do with Ivy, but everything to do with the fact that Hailey would even think to put me in that position.

I continued to reserve the table in the back of the cafe until wavy blonde locks and a petite frame walked through the door. Ivy scanned the restaurant looking for me, but I put an end to her search when I removed myself from the chair and met her at the front of the establishment. I greeted her with a friendly side hug before we made our way behind the few customers in line to place our orders.

"It's so good to see you!" Ivy exclaimed. "I can't believe it's already been a year since the last time we saw each other."

Because of how much of her life that she had spent in Colorado, Ivy usually took a trip back at least once a year to see her friends who still resided here. I tried to make an effort to see her every time she was in town, but sometimes it didn't work out. The most recent time she came to visit, Ivy spent a majority of her time skiing in the mountains, so I didn't get a chance to hang out with her. The last time we saw each other was the previous year, when I went to Oregon for the weekend to camp with some of my friends. While I was there, she ended up being so sick that she went to the hospital for a few days. I used my last day of camping to check on her and make sure she was alright. Hailey wasn't too happy that I visited Ivy in the hospital, but if Hailey and I had broken up, I would have done the same thing for her. I didn't see any harm in tending to my ailed friend, but when I returned home, Hailey was mad at me for an entire week until she eventually got over it. I tried to put myself in my girlfriend's position, but I became really irritated when Hailey tried to fight me for being a caring person.

"Glad we are meeting up at a sandwich shop and not a hospital this time," I casually uttered.

"Oh my gosh, do you remember that? I was throwing up every hour," Ivy reminisced. "Stupid food poisoning."

I decided to not carry on the topic of Ivy vomiting, considering we were about to eat lunch, so I pretended to study the menu as if I didn't already know what I wanted while I let Ivy go in front of me to order. Once Ivy completed her transaction, I ordered my usual turkey sub and handed the cashier my credit card. As soon as the cashier swiped my card, the machine reacted with an overwhelming beeping noise.

"I'm sorry, sir," the cashier sincerely apologized, "your card declined."

"Can you try it again?" I frantically pleaded.

My card was met with another wave of beeps, and I could tell that some of the customers behind me were starting to get annoyed.

"Here, you can use mine," Ivy politely offered. "Sometimes the machines don't read the cards right."

I knew Ivy was just saying that to make me feel better. It was just in her character to try and save me from further embarrassment. As much as I appreciated her kind gesture to pay for my meal, I didn't want to give Hailey any reason to think there was anything going on between Ivy and me. If she knew Ivy had paid for my meal, she might overlook the casual lunch and view it as something more. Thankfully, I had a twenty-dollar bill in my wallet, so I kindly declined Ivy's offer and paid for the food with cash—crisis averted.

It didn't take long for our sandwiches to be prepared, so by the time we returned to the counter from filling up our drink cups, our lunch was ready for us. We took it back to the table that I had reserved earlier, and dove into our beautifully crafted sandwiches.

"Wow, this is so good," Ivy complimented with a mouthful of bread.

"Best turkey sandwiches in the state," I cheerfully added.

We continued to eat our sandwiches in the comforting presence of each other. It was nice to be around a familiar face that I had known since middle school. I was proud of Ivy and the woman that she had become. She seemed to have her life together, and it was nice to see that she had matured over the years. I was eager to catch up with her and hear about how her life had been, but I couldn't help but think about how Hailey was doing. I knew she went to the gym with Dalton, but we didn't talk much this morning in an effort to not turn a conversation into a full-blown argument. I was still glad I had followed through with the lunch with Ivy, but I definitely could've handled the situation a lot better.

"So, how's life?" Ivy asked after taking a giant gulp of her drink. "Are you a rich real estate agent yet? Have you sold any mansions?"

Ivy smiled, waiting for an answer. I didn't think she realized that my card declining was a direct reflection of how my career was going. Forget selling a mansion, I couldn't even get one person to show up to an open house.

"I'm still learning the business," I finally answered. "There's a lot to know."

At the conclusion of my response, I took a nervous sip of my own drink, hoping that Ivy would switch topics away from my career.

"What about Hailey? How's she doing?" she followed up.

"Hailey is great." I smiled, both relieved from the change in subject and from the chance to talk about my girlfriend. "She is working at a top accounting firm."

"Oh wow. I always knew she was smart," Ivy commented.

"What about you?" I asked in return. "Dating anyone yet?"

Ivy let out a deep sigh. I could already tell what her answer was going to be from her defeated reaction.

"Still single," Ivy uttered, "but ready to mingle. My mailman is pretty cute. He brought me flowers one time, though, and it ruined it for me. I don't like flowers."

I laughed at Ivy's little crush on her mailman, and her resistance to romantic gestures. No matter how much Ivy grew over the years, some things never changed.

We spent the rest of the lunch updating each other about our families and upcoming plans. After about a half an hour of conversation, we both said our goodbyes and went our separate ways. It felt nice to hang out with an old friend again, but I was so ready to get back to Hailey. Seeing Ivy again made me realize how much I was truly grateful for my current relationship. I had myself a really great girl. The entire drive home was spent smiling because I couldn't wait to see my beautiful girlfriend again.

7

Hailey

Logan returned from his lunch date with Ivy in an overly excited mood. He must have really enjoyed his time with his ex-girlfriend by the way he was smiling from ear to ear. I couldn't remember the last time I was the one responsible for his sudden burst of happiness, but of course an hour with Ivy was enough to have him frolicking around the apartment like a little girl. I refused to speak to him or give him the time of day. He clearly thought my feelings were not as important as Ivy's since he had no problem going against my wishes. However, his glowing energy and cheery attitude were eventually crushed under the weight of my irritation. I was so upset that he followed through with the lunch plans that my intentions of not talking to him for the rest of the day turned into a whole week. I even tried to stay in a separate room from him unless we were sleeping. My apartment had two bedrooms, but I had turned one of them into an office since I worked from home so often. Every night, I contemplated sleeping there so that I wouldn't have to share a bed with Logan, but I wasn't willing to sleep on the air mattress that was tucked away deep inside the closet. If anything, Logan should've been the one to sleep in the office. I was the one who paid the rent, anyway.

The only reason I agreed to get into a car with him that following weekend and travel twenty minutes across the city was because Dalton and Piper had adopted a new puppy. They found a post online advertising a new litter of Cocker Spaniels and eventually decided to adopt one. Although they had only been together for three years, they seemed to be moving a lot faster than our six-year relationship. They rented a house together, adopted a dog, and were already talking about marriage. From what Logan had told me, Dalton was already ring shopping. Even though we were all only in our early twenties, marriage was on the horizon. I didn't understand how, after six years together, Logan didn't even think to ask me about what kind of ring I wanted. Dalton had been with Piper half the amount of time and already knew she was the one.

After a silent car ride, Logan pulled into Dalton and Piper's driveway. I was super excited to meet the new puppy, but I wasn't thrilled at the idea of having to hang out with Logan.

"Can we at least just get through this day without arguing?" Logan pleaded before getting out of the car. "Let's just pretend everything is fine for now."

"Isn't that what we always do?" I frustratingly pointed out.

I exited the vehicle and put on a happy face. It wasn't genuine, but it would get me through the time that I had to be around him. Logan and I were always on different pages, but one thing we did agree on was not letting others know when we were fighting. We could be on our way to a dinner at my parents' house, screaming at each other the entire time, but would smile and laugh as soon as we were around my family. It was a way to avoid unwanted criticism from outside perspectives, but it also was a coping mechanism. When we were forced to play nice and pretend to like each other, we often just stayed that way, even when we were alone again. It took a lot of energy to be mad. Neither one of us wanted to be angry at the other person, so we usually calmed down after about a week. After today, I'd probably end up getting over my anger, especially after being around a cute dog. Unfortunately, this would eventually just be another issue that I would push down with the rest of them.

I walked alongside Logan toward the front of the house. He knocked on their door in which we were eventually greeted by Piper, Dalton, and a tiny creature that was cuddled up in Dalton's arms. The overload of cuteness made me immediately drop the grudge that I was holding against Logan. My whole focus was on the tiny Cocker Spaniel puppy resting on Dalton's bicep. They let us inside, and Dalton eventually put the dog down to let him roam around the area of the house that was protected with pee pads and littered with dog toys.

"What's its name?" I excitedly questioned as I watched the little pup stumble over its own feet.

It was the cutest animal in the world. Its copper coat was shiny and beautiful, and its adorable face made me want to kiss it endlessly.

"Rooster," Dalton pridefully answered, "because he has reddish fur and wakes me up early in the morning."

He laughed, but Piper didn't seem too amused.

"We flipped a coin," Piper confessed. "I wanted to name him Max."

Logan and I could take a lesson out of Dalton and Piper's relationship handbook. They never seemed to have any problems, but maybe it was because they solved all their arguments with a coin flip.

"I like Rooster better, anyway," Logan boldly agreed.

Piper and I rolled our eyes in unison. Sometimes, we thought Logan and Dalton shared the same brain cell because they seemed to agree on everything.

"Can I hold him?" I kindly begged. Rooster looked so soft, and I couldn't wait to have the lovable puppy in my arms.

"Absolutely!" Piper cheerfully confirmed.

She carefully lifted the dog from the ground and placed his tiny body into my lap. He was so warm and fuzzy, but barely weighed a thing. I stroked his luscious coat and took in the presence of the lovable animal. I brought his face closer to mine and let him give me kisses on the cheek. Piper and Dalton thought it was the cutest thing ever, but Logan didn't seem too fond of watching the puppy lick me. I placed Rooster back in my lap and continued to pet him. I was hoping that Logan wasn't going to ask to hold him next, because I wanted to spend the rest of the day holding on to him. He was such a sweet boy and was so well-behaved. I loved how cozy he felt in my lap, but the area where he was laying was starting to feel unusually warm. It got to the point where I started to seriously question how much heat puppies were capable of radiating, until I finally lifted him up. A giant wet spot was soaking my leg in the exact area where Rooster was laying.

"Umm, I think Rooster had an accident," I calmly announced.

Piper took the dog from my hands and observed the dark stain on my jeans.

"Oh my gosh, I am so sorry, Hailey! Bad dog! Bad Rooster!" Piper scolded.

"Don't yell at him, Piper. He's just a baby," Dalton corrected. "He doesn't know any better."

Piper responded to Dalton's comment with an annoyed glare. They rarely ever showed signs of arguing, but it made me feel better when they did. It confirmed that all couples had their own issues, and it showed me that it was okay to have disagreements.

"We have some paper towels in the kitchen, Hailey," Dalton noted. "I'll help you clean up."

I followed Dalton to the kitchen sink, eager to dry the pee stain on my pants. It would've been more convenient to change into an extra pair of Piper's pants, but she was about half a foot shorter than me and roughly fifty pounds lighter than me. I would have been better off with my soiled bottoms than trying to squeeze into something that she owned.

"Sorry about that," Dalton apologized on behalf of his new pet while he dampened a few sheets of paper towels. "He isn't trained yet."

"Don't worry about it," I sympathetically relayed. "I could never be mad at something so cute."

I smiled softly at Dalton, revealing that I truly wasn't upset about the wet spot on my thigh. Rooster didn't do it on purpose.

Dalton returned with a kind smile of his own as he placed the towel over my leg. He dabbed at the pee spot in an effort to dry it.

"I think the paper towel needs to be wetter," I advised.

As much as I wanted the stain to go away, I didn't want a smelly leg. It made more sense to try and dilute the pee stain with water before attempting to dry it. I decided to take matters into my own hands, so I reached over to turn on the kitchen sink. I didn't realize how strong I had turned on the faucet until my force on the handle had released the water on full blast. The strong stream hit the pile of dishes at the bottom of the sink, making the water splash back onto Dalton. Panic took over, and I froze as the stream continued to flood the kitchen. I eventually snapped out of my shocked state and turned off the sink. Surprisingly, in the short amount of time that I had been too stunned to move, I managed to drench the paper towel Dalton was holding, as well as the clothes he was wearing. The small stain on my pants was nothing compared to the wet t-shirt that was clinging to Dalton's body.

"Oops ..." I hesitantly muttered.

Dalton stared back at me as water dripped onto his face from the tips of his hair.

"First, you encourage me to dump a smoothie on my head, and now you soak me with the kitchen sink," he exclaimed. "I am going to start bringing a towel every time I'm around you, Ms. Ross."

I laughed at the sight of him dripping wet in his own kitchen. He looked as though he had just gotten off a water ride at an amusement park. Thankfully, he found it as funny as I did, and we both started laughing at each other's misery. One of us had a pee stain, and the other was drenched in water.

"I'm so sorry," I finally managed to say after recovering from laughing so hard. "I didn't know your water pressure was so strong."

"No worries," Dalton acknowledged. "I could never be mad at something so cute."

He winked at me as he removed the soaked shirt from his body, and I couldn't help but stare at the chiseled abs that were in front of me. I bit my lip to prevent my jaw from dropping to the floor, but there was nothing I could do about the redness that swarmed my cheeks. Dalton grabbed a dish towel to dry himself off, and I watched him rub it all over his body. I wanted that towel to be me. The rag he was using to dry himself off with was so lucky to be so close to him—to be touching his skin.

My heart started to thump against my chest, and I didn't think my eyes had blinked yet. I was in a complete trance over the sight of his bare chest.

"What happened in here?" Piper shouted when she noticed her drenched boyfriend and the puddles of water on the floor. Logan had accompanied her into the kitchen and was also surprised by the mess.

"We had a little mishap," Dalton warily responded.

"Ugh!" Piper scoffed. "This is why Rooster isn't trained. His own dad can't even work a sink right."

Piper grabbed another dish towel and started assisting Dalton in his mission to dry himself. She didn't even think twice about what she was doing. The privilege of being able to freely touch Dalton's body didn't even cross her mind. She just wiped at his skin as if the sight of his naked chest was nothing to stop and stare at. Piper was so lucky, and she didn't even realize it. If I ever got the chance to touch Dalton in that way, I would make sure to savor every moment. He deserved all the appreciation in the world.

8

Logan

Right when we got home, Hailey immediately jumped into the shower. It was a usual part of her bedtime routine, but this time she was extra motivated to wash off. Dalton had tried to help her clean Rooster's pee off her leg, but he ended up flooding the kitchen. Of all the people I had met in my life, Dalton was definitely the smartest. Unfortunately, he was only able to develop an intelligence that stemmed from attending lectures and reading books. He wasn't blessed with common sense. He was a great guy, but severely lacked in the street smarts department. Good thing he was already basically married to Piper, because I wasn't sure if he would be able to find another girl that was willing to put up with his idiotic behavior. I mean, the guy couldn't even work a kitchen sink properly—classic Dalton.

While Hailey showered, I made my way into the bathroom to brush my teeth. My nighttime festivities were light work compared to hers. I only needed to clean my teeth, splash a bit of water on my face, and change into an old pair of basketball shorts. It wasn't a giant ordeal to get ready for bed. My girlfriend, on the other hand, took up most of the bathroom counter with all the products that she used at night. There were lotions for her face, creams for her skin, and sprays for her hair. I wasn't sure how she kept track of everything. It almost took her longer to get ready to go to sleep as it did for a formal event.

"So, what did you think of Rooster?" Hailey shouted from behind the shower curtain. "He's so adorable, isn't he?"

It was a nice feeling to hear the sound of Hailey's voice after not talking for a week. The puppy must've made her forget about our fight earlier, because ever since we had left Dalton and Piper's house, she could not stop talking about their new dog.

"He is very cute," I joyfully admitted. "We should get one of our own one day."

"Maybe," Hailey solemnly answered.

"Just maybe?" I responded, fully expecting her to leap at the idea of getting a pet together. However, my response was met with only the sound of running water.

"What do you mean by 'maybe'?" I repeated. "I thought you would sound a little more excited."

"I am excited, it's just ..." she began.

"Just what?" I interjected, eager to hear what possible reason could have prevented Hailey from jumping out the shower right now and heading to the pet store.

"You can't even take care of yourself, Logan," Hailey eventually spoke up. "So, how do you expect to care for a dog?"

Her explanation was completely false, and honestly, totally uncalled for. It definitely caught me off guard and was enough to alter my entire mood for the night. This time, it was her turn to be met with silence.

"Besides, they cost a lot of money, anyway," she casually added, trying to sugarcoat the insult she just threw at me.

I wasn't sure if Hailey attacking my ability to care for myself or my financial situation hurt more. Either way, both were unnecessary.

"Maybe once I sell a few houses we can get one then," I managed to mutter between my teeth. "I have another open house tomorrow."

I wanted to call her out for her rude remark, but I didn't want to cause another argument. We had just gotten over the fight in regard to me having lunch with Ivy, so I was in no position to start another disagreement between us.

"Sorry, Logan. I can't go tomorrow," Hailey informed. "I promised Megan I would help her with her Princeton application."

"That's fine," I declared. "I'm working with another agent on this home, so I'll probably be busy the entire time, anyway."

I really wanted Hailey to attend, but I was super excited to have another real estate agent in the agency accompany me on an open house. Her name was Skylar, and she was one of the top agents in the business. She had only been selling homes for about three years, but was already making six figures. The Denver real estate agent community was relatively small; everyone knew everyone, and gossip traveled fast. Therefore, when Skylar heard about my failed first attempt at showing a home, she offered to help me on the next one. Tomorrow's listing belonged to her, but I was eager to learn from her. Skylar was going to be the key to my first sale.

The water came to a squeaky halt, and Hailey stepped out of the shower to wrap a towel around her wet body. Her skin glowed, and she looked clean and refreshed. Her exposed skin excited me, sending chills throughout my body. I wanted to see more of her. She looked so perfect, and I couldn't believe that the gorgeous girl in front of me was mine.

"What are you looking at?" Hailey asserted when she caught me staring at her.

"Just my hot girlfriend," I sensually noted.

I seductively inched my way closer to her and started kissing her neck. Her skin was still wet and slippery from the shower, but it was warm and soft.

"Can you stop doing that?" Hailey countered as she jerked her body away from me. She stormed out of the bathroom and headed to the closet to change into her pajamas.

Hailey and I hadn't talked for a week because of our most recent fight, but it had been even longer than that since she allowed me to touch her. I believed our intimacy issues started to surface shortly after I quit going to the gym with her. She didn't seem unhappy with the extra pounds I had put on, but she definitely noticed them. I didn't have a six-pack like Dalton, but I was still in shape.

She also wasn't too fond of my personal hygiene habits, and often commented on the number of showers I took. Just because I didn't wash myself twice a day like she did, didn't mean that there was a problem with my cleanliness. I was twenty-three years old, which meant I was old enough to know when I needed to shower. The crazy thing was that none of these complaints were brought up at the beginning of our relationship. Hailey had no problem when I skipped a day at the gym or had an issue with the way I smelled when we first started dating. Now, all of a sudden, she had a list of issues with me.

"Do you think I'm ugly or something, Hailey?" I snapped when we finally finished our nightly routines and joined each other in bed. "I don't understand why you won't even let me touch you. Every time I get near you, you look at me in disgust. You're my girlfriend, and I want to show you how much I love you, but you don't even want me by you."

Even in the dark, I could sense Hailey's attitude. I was trying my hardest to not initiate any more arguments, but I hadn't been able to be affectionate with my own girlfriend in a while. She would only let me if she was in a really good mood, but that only occurred roughly once a month.

"I don't think you're ugly," Hailey hissed. "I'm just not in the mood."

"You're never in the mood," I declared. "Whether you want to admit it or not, I don't think you're attracted to me anymore."

Hailey rustled the blankets as she sat straight up in the bed.

"I'm very attracted to you, Logan," she sternly disclosed. "I don't know why we are having intimacy issues."

"We?" I questioned. "This sounds more like a 'you' problem. I obviously find you very attractive, but you're the one who can't stand to be around me. You need to figure out what the solution is. I can't help you understand why you won't ever touch me."

A few moments of silence passed until I heard Hailey start to sniffle and then dive under the blankets to muffle her cries. I gently placed my hand on her to show that I was there to comfort her, but at this point, I was tired of her making everything about her. I never got the chance to express how I felt because she always ended up crying. I would then have to abandon everything on my mind in order to tend to her. Sometimes, I thought she just cried on purpose to escape a conversation with me.

"Please don't cry, Hailey," I begged.

"We are supposed to be a team," she sobbingly croaked. "We are supposed to handle our relationship problems together."

"I want to handle this together, but there's nothing I can do to help. I've done all I can," I relayed.

"Like what?" she bellowed. "All you do is blame everything on me."

I had enough arguing for the day, so instead of continuing on with the back and forth, I simply turned my body to face away from her to assume a more comfortable sleeping position. Obviously, nothing was going to be fixed tonight. We were probably going to spend another week in silence until we eventually got over it. This was why I never felt comfortable enough to share my feelings with her. It always ended in a fight. She would either claim that she did nothing wrong, or fix the issue for a few days and then revert back to her old habits. I had brought up the intimacy issue many times before. We'd probably had this exact same disagreement at least eight times in the past. Evidently, nothing was resolved. I guess I would just have to wait for the next time that I caught her in a good mood.

I had no problems falling asleep in the midst of an unresolved issue. It was not hard for me to push the conversation out of my head and clear my thoughts for the night. However, Hailey did not have the same ability. I wasn't surprised when I heard the sound of her sit back up in bed and bring back up her intimacy issue again.

"I think I'm just stressed about the long hours I've been working," Hailey hesitantly whispered. "I use all my energy during the day and have nothing left in the tank at night. Even on weekends, I'm just exhausted from the long work week. I'll try to be better about it."

I turned back around to face Hailey. I sat up next to her, swallowing her body into my arms. She nestled her face into the base of my neck, wiping her tears on me in the process.

"It's okay, Hailey," I murmured, "I understand. I'm tired, too."

I kissed the top of her head and continued to hold her. A few more warm tears escaped her eyes and dampened my neck, but they seemed more like cries of relief knowing that she could finally escape the hustle of the day and relax. I squeezed her a little tighter to let her know that she was safe and secure, and then we both laid back down. Obviously, our issue was not resolved. I was still very upset with her, but I knew I wasn't going to get any sleep unless Hailey's mind was satisfied with how the conversation ended.

I wasn't sure if the exhaustion of the day or of the fight got to her first, but she was sound asleep a few minutes later. In order to not wake her up, I slowly removed my arm from under her, so that it wouldn't go numb under the weight of her body. I wrapped the blanket tightly around us before eventually passing out next to her.

We both had our own complaints about the other person, but at the end of the day, we were a strong couple. Hailey and I didn't last six years for no reason. We both were committed to the relationship and to the work it took to keep us together. The bad times were awful, but the good times were incredible. We fought hard, but we loved harder. I loved Hailey, and I couldn't imagine being with anyone else. Our relationship wasn't perfect, however, we were perfect for each other. She fit seamlessly into my life and was present during the most important times. I couldn't have asked for a better support system, and I was lucky that I was able to cheer her on as much as she cheered for me. The open house tomorrow would be another opportunity to get myself back on the right track for the betterment of my career and our relationship. One sale equaled one step closer to giving Hailey her dream life. It would only take one.

9

Hailey

Logan tried to initiate intimacy again this morning before I left for my parents' house, but I wasn't having it. It's not that I wasn't physically attracted to him anymore, but it was hard to engage in such a personal act with someone whose bills you were paying, and messes you were cleaning up. He felt more like my child than my boyfriend at times, which often led me to being completely turned off by him. During the entire drive over to see my family, I kept asking myself how he didn't notice how worn out I was from taking care of everything. I didn't understand how he could expect me to pay rent in the morning and then cuddle him at night. Logan treated me like his mom when he needed something, but his girlfriend when he wanted something. The sad part was that sometimes my body would just automatically reject his touches without me even realizing. When he would lean in for a kiss or invade my personal space, I often steered away from him as if it were an automated response. I wasn't trying to make him feel undesired, but it was exhausting trying to meet his basic needs—and his physical ones, too. It was already hard enough to care for myself while working a demanding job, so adding on the responsibility of another person meant some area of our relationship had to sacrifice.

Logan didn't really help much around the apartment either, which made things even worse. It was one thing to clean up your own messes, but to clean up someone else's was a whole other feat. He clearly didn't appreciate how much work I did around the house because he never said thank you and always found a way to further contribute to the mess. There was always a sock left behind, shoes in the middle of the living room, or trash scattered around the counter. I couldn't even get him to take the trash out or clean his dirty dishes. I once went on a strike and didn't do any chores, but after a few days, it drove me crazy before it even phased Logan, so I ended up continuing to assume all the responsibilities.

Despite all the dish soap and cleaning supplies I went through to keep up with the messes of two people, the worst part was the laundry. Our laundry basket was combined, which added another task to my list. When I lived by myself I washed my clothes about once a week, but with Logan, I was doing a load almost every other day. Logan had an outfit for his morning meetings, and then another for his afternoon showings, before changing into another set of clothes for an evening event. I couldn't keep up with how fast our laundry basket filled up, and sometimes had to do two loads. If a shirt Logan was looking for was still crumpled up at the bottom of the bin and wasn't cleaned yet, he would claim that his day was ruined and that I would be the one responsible if he didn't make a sale that day. I tried to confront him about how difficult it was to fit laundry into my schedule, and suggested that he start taking over the responsibility, but he explained that if he was taking time away from his job to do chores, then it would take longer to sell a home, and thus we would be stuck in a tiny two-bedroom apartment longer than anticipated. I didn't understand his logic, but I didn't argue it, either. My job afforded me the luxury of being able to rent a two-bedroom apartment, but I was making nowhere close to what I would need to actually purchase a home. The earning potential for Logan's job was endless. Even one sale could provide him with the commission needed to finally allow us to leave the apartment life behind. I couldn't wait for the day that he finally made his first profitable sale, or at least got his own laundry basket.

I pulled into the driveway, excited to see my parents and help Megan with her college applications, but I was even more excited to not be driving anymore. It gave me too much alone time to really reflect on my relationship with Logan. Often times, it left me thinking about how life would be like without him, but I knew those thoughts were irrational. When I was in the car by myself, I didn't have anyone to snap me out of my spiraling thoughts, so I never trusted the conclusions I came to. Logan was a great guy. I just needed to be more grateful for him. He wasn't perfect, but he wasn't horrible, either. In six years, he never cheated on me, hit me, or committed any other elaborate offense. There were definitely worse guys in the world than him. I didn't even want to entertain the idea of entering the single life again. The caliber of men out there was low, and spending my nights alone was something I did not want to do. Logan and I drove each other crazy sometimes, but at least I wasn't lonely. I would deal with the occasional arguments in exchange for reliable companionship.

My father greeted me with a gentle hug when I entered the house. He led me to the kitchen where I found my mom standing over Megan's shoulder. Megan was seated at the kitchen table in front of her laptop that was surrounded by a bunch of college brochures. Princeton was her number one choice, but she was very aware of the low acceptance rate, and her need to reach out to other colleges. She had some interest in a few in-state schools, but most of the places she wanted to go to were out of state. Despite narrowing it down to eight universities that she was willing to apply to, I didn't think Megan really had a second preference. It was Princeton or nothing for her. She wanted to attend the school of her dreams, and anything other than that was a failure in her eyes. I never knew that a random family trip to New Jersey that resulted in us touring Princeton because my dad saw an ad for it online, would leave such an impression on my sister.

"Hi, Hailey!" my mom shouted as she left Megan's side to greet me. "Good to see you!"

"Good to see you too, Mom," I returned as I slightly bent over so that she could give me a kiss on the cheek.

Megan and I clearly got our height from our dad. She and I each stood around five-ten, while our mom was five-six on a good day. I really had to lean over when giving her hugs, but I was sure it was even more of a difficult feat for my dad. He was six-three, so he really had to hunch over to hug her.

"Hey," Megan welcomed while trying to force a smile.

I could tell she was stressed about the number of colleges that she was planning on applying to, especially since they didn't pique her interest like her dream school did. They were all just backup options.

"You seem busy," I joked as I observed the scattered brochures, "but I'm here to help."

I offered her a gentle smile, but she still appeared overwhelmed. There was no way she was going to be able to apply to colleges, let alone Princeton, in her current state.

"I just want to get this over with," Megan frustratingly explained, "but I don't even know where to start."

Megan continued to groan in disappointment as she stared at the blank computer screen.

"You should've started by not waiting until the week they are due," my dad interjected.

My mom gave him a menacing glance, knowing that his comment wasn't helpful at all. Megan wasn't typically a procrastinator, but she uncharacteristically left her college applications until the last minute. I believed she was just intimidated by the fact that these applications were the door to her future.

After some quick thinking, I briskly walked toward the table, closed my eyes, and shuffled through the brochures. I pulled two of them off the table, one in each hand, and held them up for display.

"Why don't you just focus on applying to these two schools right now?" I offered. "Then we can take a break."

I could sense some of the stress leaving Megan's body.

"We will get through them all. Don't worry," I confidently confirmed. "One by one."

Megan breathed a heavy sigh, "Fine. I'll just knock them all out."

I handed her the brochures, but she ignored them.

"I at least want to do Princeton's application first," she declared while she started navigating to their website.

I smiled, knowing that Megan was finally making progress. I knew my dad was messing with her about waiting until the last minute, but it wasn't because she was disorganized. Even with all the brochures scattered around the kitchen, Megan knew which school she wanted to apply to first. She just needed a little bit of encouragement, but that's what family was for. When anyone of us was going through a hard time, we were always there for each other. Family was everything.

"So, how's your job going?" my mom asked when it was clear that Megan was in a good headspace.

"Fine," I answered. "It's demanding, but it pays well, and I am learning a lot."

My job did require long hours and tedious tasks, but I had always understood accounting fairly well. It didn't take me long to start figuring out how to do the work without having to spend most of my days asking a million questions. The firm was one of the best in the world, and I wanted to work my way up the corporate ladder and really make my mark on the company.

"Well, don't work too hard, honey," my mom chimed in. "There are more important things in life than your career."

"I know," I reluctantly claimed, "but the bills have to get paid somehow."

My mom always found a way to turn every conversation into some sort of lecture.

"What about Logan?" my dad interjected. "Isn't he helping contribute financially?"

My eyebrows started twitching, as they always did when I got nervous, and I refrained from making eye contact with my parents. They knew Logan had recently made a career switch, but they didn't know I was basically letting him live with me for free.

"He does what he can," I solemnly admitted. "He's still trying to figure out his new job."

When we first moved in together, Logan and I had agreed to split the bills evenly. Initially, he was a customer service representative, and though it wasn't his dream job, it provided the money he needed to go half on all of our shared expenses. He was even able to pay for our dates at the time. He didn't come home happy, and he dreaded going into work every day, but at least he had a decent job. Once he quit to pursue real estate, I graciously gave him the month off from contributing financially. I knew that it was going to be an adjustment going from a steady income to only getting paid when he sold a house, so I tried to relieve him at least a little. It also allowed him the opportunity to use his money to buy more suits and fancy shoes. Unfortunately, that one month off from paying bills turned into two, until he eventually just never pitched in again. Logan occasionally bought the groceries, and he sometimes sent me some money for utilities, but I was easily paying over triple of what he contributed. I used to bring up this issue often, but I felt bad seeing my boyfriend of six years admit his financial struggles. I really wanted him to follow his dream, and I knew that one day he would be the breadwinner. There would be a moment in time where Logan would be the financial provider, and would cover not only his portion of the expenses, but would also be able to take me out on fancy dates. One day, Logan would be able to take care of me, and all the stress I had accumulated from carrying the burden of the bills would disappear. He just needed to sell a house.

10

Logan

I wasn't able to sell the house, but the event was still a success.

Not only was there a great turnout at the open house, but I even got some of the email addresses from the people that showed up. Everyone really liked the property, but it didn't have a pool, so some were not interested. However, I got their information to contact them further if I found a place that was better suited for them. Despite the lack of a pool, there was a lot of positive feedback, and I got to build relationships with potential future clients. Additionally, I thoroughly enjoyed working alongside Skylar and watching her interact with potential buyers. She was truly a natural, and it wasn't surprising that she was one of the top agents in Denver. Her delivery was flawless, and she was super honest and charismatic in her explanations about the details of the house. Skylar had a few more years of experience in the business than I did, but I still felt like I was decades behind her in terms of knowledge. Although the home was her listing, I studied the property, but even then, she was able to answer questions that I didn't even have a clue as to what the correct response was.

Skylar was who I aspired to be in the real estate industry: professional, knowledgeable, determined, but most importantly, successful. Thankfully, she agreed to help me navigate this new career path and teach me everything I needed to know about the real estate business. I was excited for this new mentorship, but I was even more excited that I was one giant step closer to selling my first home. With Skylar assisting me, I was for sure going to make it in the industry, and maybe one day, become as successful as her.

I desperately wanted to spend the rest of my Sunday researching homes for the people whose contact information I received, but my mom insisted that I stop by her house for dinner. Whenever she asked me to come over, it was more of a demand than a question. She loved spending time with me, and would get pretty upset if I ever turned her down. I felt bad because

I knew how lonely she had been ever since my dad left her, so I only ever declined her requests if I absolutely had to. Her mom had passed away a few years ago and she never met her own father, so I was the only family she had left. I was the man in her life, therefore, quality time with me was very important to her.

It had been about sixteen years since my dad walked out of our lives, and she still hadn't even been on a single date. I wasn't sure if she was still upset over how things ended or just had no interest in being in another relationship, but my dad had for sure moved on. We didn't have his new phone number or anything, but after the split, with the help of the internet, we were able to find him on social media pretty easily. He seemed happy in his new life, which probably upset my mom even more. I also wasn't thrilled at the idea of my biological father raising a family that didn't include me, but I didn't even remember him that well to begin with. I vaguely recalled a time when he had helped me learn how to hit a baseball, but that was pretty much the extent of the memories that I had of him.

When I was in high school, I started becoming increasingly curious about what my father was like and even wanted a chance at rekindling a relationship with him. I tried reaching out to him online, but he never responded. After that, I just figured my life was better off without him. Unfortunately, I didn't think my mom had reached that conclusion yet, and I wasn't sure that she ever would. It was no secret that my mom and I loved hard. Once we truly loved someone, it was really hard for us to let them go, even if it was for the best. However, I was also like my dad in a sense too—once I was done with someone and completely moved on, I wanted nothing to do with them, either.

"Hi, honey!" my mom yelled from her driveway when I parked my car.

Because of how eager she was to see me, she often couldn't wait until I made it to the front door and usually just greeted me outside as soon as I pulled up—this time was no different. When I got out of the car, I was immediately wrapped in a motherly embrace.

"Hello, Mom," I responded while being hugged a little too tightly.

"Glad you could make it for dinner," my mom announced while we made our way inside her house and toward the kitchen. "I am making your favorite dish, macaroni and cheese."

I thanked my mom for the kind gesture, even though macaroni and cheese stopped being my favorite when I was around ten years old. As a twenty-three year old man, a nicely prepared steak was my new preferred meal, but I didn't have the heart to tell her that my taste buds had matured over the years, and they no longer desired noodles smothered in cheese. Nonetheless, every time she made it, I still finished my bowl in its entirety with a smile on my face. My mom had gone through enough in her life. One more inconvenience, such as her only child no longer craving such a nostalgic dinner, would probably be the last straw that would finally crush her already injured heart. She would most likely always live in such an emotionally fragile state, but I didn't blame her. Biting my tongue to the comments she made to Hailey and pretending to like her cooking were just some things I had to do in order to prevent her from completely falling apart. Though it took a lot of energy to tiptoe around the hurt that she was obviously still carrying, I dedicated myself to protecting her. I was her son, the only male figure in her life, so I took it upon myself to make sure she lived the rest of her life as comfortably as she could.

"How was the open house?" my mom questioned as she stirred the pot of mac and cheese that was bubbling on the stove. It smelled stale and processed, but I was already fully dedicated to eating it.

"It was great," I answered. "I didn't sell the house, but I did a lot of networking. I'm even working with another agent who is going to help me complete my first sale."

"Oh, that is just wonderful, honey," my mom commented. "We will have to celebrate when you sell your first home." She scooped up a hefty portion of the cheesy noodles out of the pot and served us each a bowl. My mom took a seat across from me and dove into the hot meal. Sometimes I wondered if she also was pretending to still like macaroni, however, if she was, she was a great actress.

"We will definitely have to celebrate," I agreed. "And as soon as I get the commission from it, I promise I will pay you back for the car." I stared back at the steaming bowl in front of me and slowly took a bite. It wasn't horrible, but it wasn't delicious, either.

"Don't worry about that, sweetie," my mom asserted. "Consider it a gift for starting a new job."

"Wow, thank you so much, Mom," I graciously remarked.

My mom smiled as she continued to dive into the noodles. I followed suit, as being suddenly relieved from a loan that I wasn't confident I would be able to pay back in a reasonable amount of time anyway, made the meal a lot more appetizing. My mom wasn't rich, but she had mentioned before that she had earned a generous settlement in the divorce. Apparently, my dad wanted to leave the marriage so desperately that he gave her the house and a hefty lump sum in order to avoid a drawn-out legal battle. My mom was pretty generous about the money when it came to spending it on me. The only caveat was that I had to promise her that I wouldn't put her in a nursing home once she got too old to live on her own. She definitely had at least another good thirty years of life left before having to consider moving in with me, but I wanted my first home to be my forever home. I hadn't verbally expressed it to Hailey yet, but once I was able to afford a real house, I wanted my mom to be able to move in with us immediately. I was sure Hailey wouldn't mind, considering that it was my own mother, but I was fully planning on getting a house for all three of us.

"So, how is Hailey doing?" my mom asked through mouthfuls of macaroni.

"She's good," I offered. "It's our anniversary next week."

"Wow, how long have you guys been together?" she questioned. "It has to have been at least five years, maybe even six."

"It will be seven tomorrow," I proudly announced.

I knew Hailey and I had been dating for a while, but saying it out loud made it sound even longer. It was crazy that a relationship that started when we were both so young was still going strong.

"What are your plans for it?" she asked.

"Probably just going out for dinner," I relayed. "Nothing too crazy."

After almost a decade together, our anniversaries became less and less special over the years. When we first started dating, the entire week leading up to our anniversary was an ordeal. We gifted each other numerous presents, and it seemed to be the only topic that consumed our conversations. It was definitely more exciting back then. Each annual milestone was a big deal to us, and we celebrated accordingly. The last couple of anniversaries were still special, but they were nothing compared to how they used to be.

"Do you need any money for the dinner?" my mom eagerly offered.

"You don't have to pay for our anniversary dinner, Mom," I calmly relayed. She was always trying to find a way to help me out. I was grateful for it, but sometimes it made me feel like I was less of a man. I wanted her to know that I was fully capable of taking care of myself and my relationship, even if I was short on funds.

"Oh, don't be so ridiculous, Logan," my mom insisted. "I know how hard you have been working. It takes a brave man to switch careers like you did. Take the money so you can focus on your job and not about paying for the dinner."

"Okay," I reluctantly agreed. "Fine." My mom was not one to argue with, so I agreed to her offer, even though she didn't have to twist my arm that hard to accept the money.

In a matter of seconds, she abruptly left the kitchen table and returned with her purse. She started fishing for her wallet until she eventually found it and pulled out a hundred-dollar bill.

"Here," my mom muttered as she handed over the cash. "For my favorite son." She winked as she returned her wallet to its original home inside her purse.

"Thank you," I exclaimed, "for everything."

I smiled at my mom, truly grateful for all that she had done for me. She didn't have to help me out financially as much as she did, but she was such a generous person. I came over to her house in debt and with a low anniversary budget, but left with my loan relieved and money for dinner. I guess I would have to come over more often.

11

Hailey

"Take a couple of steps to your left," Piper directed with a camera in her hand. "Okay, perfect! Don't move."

I heard the shutter of Piper's camera while she snapped a few photos of Logan and me. We were staring lovingly into each other's eyes as Piper contorted her body in different ways to capture as many angles as she could.

She was a photographer on the side and offered to do a photoshoot for us in honor of our upcoming anniversary. The session was supposed to start at five, but I was slammed at work, so we had to push it back until six-thirty. I was actually surprised I was even able to make it at all. Mondays usually weren't that busy, but with the end of the year quickly approaching, I was working overtime. I wasn't always going to be tied to my laptop until almost ten o'clock most nights, but it was a busy time of the year. It definitely hindered the amount of quality time that Logan and I got, so I was grateful to still be able to participate in the shoot.

"Let's get a couple of photos of you two kissing," Piper instructed.

I didn't know why I didn't feel super comfortable kissing Logan at that moment. I wasn't sure if it was awkward because we had never kissed for a photo before or because Dalton was in the corner watching us. Either way, Logan wasted no time grabbing my face and pulling me close until his lips met mine. Good thing he was holding on to the back of my neck because I felt my body pull away from him, as it usually instinctively did. I quickly pulled myself together and smiled against Logan's mouth, hoping that the photo would show a happy, loving couple and not one that was constantly arguing and getting on each other's nerves.

"Aw, these are gorgeous!" Piper complimented as she looked at the photos on her camera. "We only have about an hour left of sunlight if there's anything else you want me to capture."

"Can you get a few headshots of me?" Logan proposed. "And maybe a few solo shots for marketing purposes?"

"Of course!" Piper assured.

I stepped out of the frame and let Logan take the pictures he needed for work. I was happy with the photos we had already taken, but it was slightly annoying that Logan managed to make a romantic photoshoot about his job.

"I think your pictures are going to turn out great," Dalton announced when I joined him behind the camera. "You have such a pretty smile."

I tried not to blush at Dalton's comment, but I felt a rush of warmth flood my cheeks. "Thanks," I answered. "I try." I smiled, even though I still felt awkward for holding a kiss that long with Logan in front of him. "How was work today?" I asked in order to change the subject.

"Busy," he responded. "Everyone is freaking out over the end of year deadlines. The staff and the clients are all stressed."

"Tell me about it," I concurred. "I can't catch a break."

It was nice to be able to vent to Dalton about the craziness of the accounting and finance industries during such a busy season. Logan didn't really understand the work I did, but Dalton could definitely relate.

"Me neither," he declared. "I need work to slow down so I can start focusing on how I am going to propose to Piper."

"Oh, wow," I whispered, careful not to alert Piper. "You're really going to get engaged soon?"

"Yeah, I figured I've made her wait long enough." He chuckled.

I would be lying if I said I wasn't jealous that Dalton was planning a proposal while my boyfriend most likely hadn't even thought about being engaged. Logan was so focused on his career that I don't think taking the next step in our relationship was even on his radar.

"Well, she's a lucky girl," I disclosed in the midst of my envy.

"I'm sure Logan will pop the question soon," Dalton assured. "Just don't forget to invite me to the wedding."

He winked, knowing that he was not only going to be invited to the wedding, but would probably be in it. He was evidently Logan's best friend. I was certain that he would be Logan's best man, too.

Dalton and I continued to watch Piper capture photos of Logan. We watched the session in silence as my mind swirled with thoughts about Dalton's future proposal. I was happy for him and Piper, but was also jealous of where they were in their relationship. It angered me that Logan and I weren't already engaged. I was upset that my boyfriend of almost seven years probably hadn't even looked at rings yet.

I snapped out of my train of thought when Piper and Logan finished their session and made their way toward Dalton and I.

"Everything turned out great," Piper remarked. "You both are super photogenic. I'll send you the photos as soon as I'm finished editing them."

She started to put away her camera equipment until I suddenly interjected. "Do you want me to take some photos of you and Dalton?" I politely offered.

The sun was rapidly going down, but we still had a few minutes of light left. Besides, I was sure that they wanted pictures of their own, too, especially since it sounded like they were going to be together forever.

"That would be awesome," Piper chanted. "Thank you, Hailey."

She handed me her camera and gave me a brief overview on how to work it. As soon as I got the hang of it, she grabbed Dalton, and they started posing in front of the emerging sunset. It was such a beautiful background for such a beautiful couple. Logan and I needed a lot of directing, but Dalton and Piper were naturals together—they were made for each other. After a few more poses, the sun finally disappeared, and we were left in the dark. I handed Piper her camera back, and let her go through the photos I had taken of them.

"I think they turned out pretty well," I mentioned to Logan while Piper was scrolling through the pictures. "I'm definitely not as good as Piper is, but I think I got some good shots."

"I'm sure they turned out just fine," Logan responded.

I watched Dalton and Piper smile over the pictures that I had taken of them.

"You know, Dalton said he's going to propose soon," I mumbled, so that Piper wouldn't be able to hear me.

"Yeah," Logan answered, "I'm happy for them."

"They were definitely meant to be together," I noted. "I can't wait for their wedding."

I truly was happy for them, but I was trying to show Logan that I also wanted an engagement for myself.

"It will definitely be a fun time," Logan commented.

He clearly did not get the hint.

"When do you think we could possibly get engaged?" I questioned directly, since he wasn't picking up on the fact that I was waiting for a ring, too.

We had discussions in the past, but there was always an excuse. At first, it was going to happen once we finished school, but once we graduated, the timeline pushed until he got a job and was able to afford one. I never pushed the conversation any further since I was perfectly fine with his reasoning, but after over six years of dating, I was tired of waiting.

"I don't know, Hailey," Logan confessed. "I just started this new job. There's a lot on my plate right now."

"There's always a lot on your plate, Logan," I explained. "I understand your situation. I don't need a ring right now, but maybe a general timeline would be nice."

Logan was silent.

"Or at least give me the confirmation that you're thinking about it," I stammered.

"Of course I'm thinking about," Logan fired back. "I just can't give you an answer as to when. Things change."

I was frustrated with Logan's avoidance. I wanted a real answer.

"Can you at least give me a rough estimate?" I begged.

"I don't know, Hailey," he groaned, clearly not wanting to engage in the conversation anymore. "Maybe like two or three more years."

"Two or three more years?" I shouted.

"I don't know. I'm just guessing," he retorted. "I can't predict the future."

My eyebrows started twitching, and I wanted to explode. There was no way he could expect me to wait that long for a ring—that was completely insane. I wanted to take my frustrations out on him, but Piper and Dalton had just returned from giggling over the photos I had taken.

"The pictures are perfect!" Piper shouted. "Thank you so much."

"You're welcome," I mumbled.

I tried not to reveal how angry I was, but I had been faking a smile all day. I wasn't sure how much longer I could force it.

"Need any help bringing the equipment back to your car?" I offered eagerly. I was looking for any excuse to give myself a break from Logan before I was stuck in a car with him on our drive home.

"Don't worry about it, ladies," Dalton chimed in. "Logan and I can carry it."

The boys picked up some of the camera equipment and started taking trips back and forth to the car. Piper and I stayed behind. She still had her camera on her, so she was letting me have a sneak peek at our photos before she edited them.

"This one is my favorite," Piper squealed as she showed me her camera.

It was the photo of me smiling against Logan's lips. It was a beautiful picture. We looked really happy and totally in love, but that was theme of our life—everything we did was to impress the outside perspective. Our relationship appeared perfect to the public, but behind closed doors, it was falling apart. Just as Logan put on a show for his clients in order to sell a house, we put on a show in front of others to sell the validity of our relationship.

"That one is my favorite, too," I lied.

Piper continued to scroll through the pictures while Dalton and Logan packed the car with the equipment.

"Piper, how'd you know Dalton was the one?" I randomly asked. "Like how did you know you were truly meant to be together?"

Piper put down her camera as she contemplated her answer. After a few short moments, she spoke up.

"Well, I always had a good feeling about him," she admitted. "He always treated me right, and he never gave me a reason to doubt him."

"That makes sense, I guess," I affirmed.

"Why? Are you questioning your relationship with Logan?" she added.

I was close with Piper, but I never usually confided in her about my relationship problems. However, I was sure that Dalton had probably already mentioned a few things to her.

"I love him, but sometimes I just wonder if we were truly meant to be together," I relayed. "I don't want to be with anyone else, but our relationship just isn't what it used to be."

Piper took a minute to think about what I had just said before finally responding.

"I think if you're questioning it," she began, "then it's probably not meant to be."

Her answer hit me hard. I wasn't ready for the reality check that she had just given me. "But I want it to work," I pleaded. "We have been together for so long, and I'm not ready to lose him."

"Then fight for the relationship," Piper suggested. "If you really want it to work that bad, then fight for him."

I appreciated Piper's advice, and I really considered what she had to say. In all honesty, she was right. If I truly wanted to be with Logan, then I needed to fight for him. I needed to be the best girlfriend I could be, even if that meant waiting a few years for a ring. I would have to get over the comments his mother made about me, and remove any doubts I had about Logan's new career path. If I really wanted this to work, I needed to give it my all. The real question was, was the relationship worth fighting for?

12

Logan

"Well, that's the last of it," Dalton confirmed as he closed the trunk. "I would say that the photoshoot was a success."

Dalton and I finished loading his car with Piper's camera equipment in only a few trips. It probably would've only taken one if the girls had helped, but Dalton so graciously volunteered just the guys. I didn't mind, though. The girls were busy smiling over the photos taken, anyway, and I needed an excuse to escape the marriage conversation with Hailey. I wasn't against discussing the topic, but she always pressured me for an exact timeline, and I didn't want to give her any false promises.

"Yeah, Piper is really talented," I exclaimed. "I'm sure all of the photos will turn out great."

The photoshoot was actually really productive. We got enough couple photos to last us a lifetime, and I even got some great professional shots. I would probably need Skylar's help in picking the best ones to go on my business card, but she would have plenty to choose from.

"She's got a good eye for photography," Dalton added. "I hope we will be able to find a wedding photographer at least as half as talented as she is."

"Woah, already thinking about a wedding photographer?" I asked. "Are you planning on popping the question soon, D?"

"Yeah, man," Dalton confessed. "I already got the ring and everything. Just gotta plan something romantic. Maybe I'll find a way to get Rooster involved. It wouldn't be a proper proposal without including the little guy."

"Well, if you need any help, let me know," I remarked. "I'd be happy to help."

"Thanks," Dalton replied. "I just want to give Piper the proposal she deserves."

"I'm sure she will love whatever you come up with," I assured.

Dalton was a certified lover boy. In my opinion, he was moving too fast. He had always loved the idea of marriage and was excited at the thought of having a wedding one day. Three years was a decent amount of time to date someone, but I figured he may have just felt the pressures of society to propose. People always asked me when I was going to take the next step with Hailey, and I was sure Dalton got the same question. Unlike him, I was able to ignore them and decide for myself when the time was right.

Marriage was never something I took lightly. The aftermath of my parents' divorce greatly affected me, and I promised myself that I would not rush into anything. I didn't want the fate of my parents to also become my own. Dalton, on the other hand, came from a loving home. His mom and dad were still happily in love, so I didn't blame him for wanting the same thing for himself. He just hadn't seen the ugly side of love that I had. I hoped that he was making the right decision because the last thing I wanted was for him to experience how bad love can actually hurt.

"What about you, man?" Dalton continued on. "You guys have been together for a while. Thinking about proposing soon?"

"I don't know, D," I admitted. "I've got a lot going on right now."

I never really told Dalton where Hailey and I stood. It was hard admitting the faults in our relationship. I let him know about our major fights, but never really volunteered the details of our everyday arguments. He had no idea Hailey and I were slowly drifting further apart. I liked to hide the bad parts of us. Sometimes it was just easier to pretend that everything was alright. I wouldn't be dating Hailey if I didn't see a future with her, but it was no secret that our relationship was not in a great place. We argued more than we ever had, and it was clear that we were never on the same page. Our priorities never aligned; I felt that she was pretty high on my list, but I was low on hers. Of course, my mom came first, but Hailey followed right after. She focused on her family, her career, her future, and if there was any energy left over, then she would prioritize me. Lately, there hadn't been much left over for me. We barely spent any quality time together, and when we did, it usually just consisted of us fighting.

"Everything okay with you two?" Dalton asked.

"Everything's fine," I answered. "Just not feeling the spark as much as we used to."

The truth was that I hadn't felt the spark with Hailey in years. I hadn't truly felt the butterflies and fireworks in a very long time. I wanted to marry her, but not in the current state of our relationship. I was hoping that after two or three years of working on us and saving enough money, then an engagement would be on the horizon. Until then, I thought a lot of work was needed to be done before we took our relationship any further.

"Oh, that's normal," Dalton proclaimed. "I'm sure after almost seven years together, Piper and I will also start to get under each other's skin, too."

"It's more than just that," I assured. "We don't feel connected at all."

"Don't worry about that," Dalton preached. "You just gotta find a way to keep the love alive."

He was always optimistic about romance, and he very much believed in happily-ever-afters. I needed him to spread some of that positivity amongst Hailey and me.

"When Piper and I are craving some quality time together," Dalton began, "we usually just cook dinner together. It really bonds us. Why don't you try doing that?"

"Hailey is always so busy," I pleaded. "She probably won't even have time."

"I bet she will make time if you ask her to," Dalton argued.

He had a point. Hailey was always busy, but she did try to make time for me when she could. Maybe doing an activity together, like cooking, would ignite some type of flame between us.

"It doesn't have to be anything fancy. Piper and I have made steaks and fancy pastas together before, but honestly we have the most fun when we cook something casual," Dalton insisted. "One night, we just made a pizza. It was simple, but we really enjoyed making it together."

"Alright, D. I'll take your suggestion," I promised, "but if it doesn't work, then I don't know what I'm going to do."

I was hopeful that the quality time would be a way of bringing Hailey and I closer together. It felt like we lived separate lives, but maybe a cooking date would intertwine us again. Tomorrow night could be a pivotal moment in our lives. It would be an attempt to see if our relationship was truly salvageable. If the date went wrong, I wasn't sure if there would be any hope left for us. I loved Hailey, and I never wanted to let her go, however, if she didn't feel that love back for me, I didn't know how much longer I could fight for our relationship.

"Well, if it doesn't work," Dalton uttered, "at least you can say that you tried." He gave me a hopeful smile. "Sometimes trying is all that you can do, man," he explained.

I knew he wanted things between Hailey and I to work out, but I also knew he just wanted the best for me. If moving on from my current relationship was in my best interest, Dalton would be there to support me.

Our brotherly conversation came to a sudden halt when the girls started to approach us.

"Thanks for putting away all of my equipment!" Piper shouted as she and Hailey rejoined us at his car.

"This is why I work out," Dalton declared while he greeted Piper with a kiss on her forehead, "so that I can easily carry your photography equipment."

"Your muscles never cease to amaze me," Piper admired.

"I can show you more of them tonight." Dalton winked.

Dalton and Piper giggled, and it felt as though Hailey and I were interrupting a private moment between them. They were clearly still as in love as the first day they met.

"Well, we better head home," I announced, eager to leave Dalton and Piper to be mushy without Hailey and I in their presence. "Thank you again, Piper, for the photoshoot. You did a really great job."

"Thanks, Logan!" She beamed. "I hope we can do it again for your next anniversary."

She winked at me, and I returned to her a forced smile. As much as I hoped she was right, at this rate, I didn't know if there was going to be another anniversary.

Hailey and I said our goodbyes to them, and we made our way toward my car. When we got in, I pulled out of the parking lot and headed in the direction of our apartment. My mind was clouded with thoughts about the fate of my relationship, and the reality that we could possibly be done was starting to set in. I never envisioned my life without Hailey, but I wasn't able to sacrifice my happiness in order to stay with her anymore. Things just weren't how they used to be.

"Did you enjoy the session?" she asked shortly into the drive, interrupting my train of thought.

I appreciated her actually initiating a conversation between us. We usually drove in silence, and I wasn't sure how she was feeling after the discussion we just had about marriage. I assumed this was her attempt at letting me know that she had moved on from it.

"Yes, it was awesome," I replied. "Piper is good at what she does."

"She's the best," Hailey added.

I continued to drive in the darkness toward our destination. The car fell to its usual silence, besides the radio that hummed a few tunes. This time, it was my turn to break the silence. I was building up the courage to finally ask her on the cooking date that Dalton had kindly suggested, but it didn't take long for me to realize that the longer I waited, the less confident I became.

"What time are you off tomorrow?" I eventually asked.

I assumed my question caught her off guard because it honestly caught me off guard, too. I couldn't remember the last time I had tried to make plans with her after her workday.

"Probably around six or seven," Hailey confessed. "Why?"

I didn't know why I was so nervous to ask my own girlfriend on a date, but I could feel my forehead starting to sweat.

"I was wondering if you wanted to cook dinner together tomorrow?" I offered.

"Like to celebrate our anniversary?" Hailey questioned.

"No," I politely responded. "We can still celebrate our anniversary this weekend. I just thought it would be nice for us to do something together for a change."

My heart started to pound as I waited for her answer. I wasn't sure if she was open to doing something like that with me. We hadn't really gone on a date in a while, let alone cook a meal together.

"I'd love to!" Hailey squealed. "We can start as soon as I'm off work," she added.

"Sounds like a plan," I concurred. "I can grab some ingredients from the store while you're working. Does pizza sound good to you?"

I knew pizza wasn't the most extravagant meal, but it seemed to work perfectly fine for Dalton and Piper.

"That sounds perfect," Hailey noted.

I breathed a sigh of relief knowing that everything had worked out as Dalton had advised. I immediately felt a sense of hope for our fate. It's possible that I was just overreacting earlier about the status of our relationship. It probably wasn't as bad as I was making it out to be. Besides, Dalton said it was normal to go through hard times while dating, especially after almost seven years together. Hailey and I could've just been on a rough patch. Maybe we were actually meant to be together—maybe everything truly wasn't as bad as it seemed.

13

Hailey

I slammed my laptop shut as soon as my last meeting of the day concluded. Thankfully, my hard work on Monday had paid off for today, and I was able to log off around five. It was the earliest I had finished my workday in a long time, and I was grateful for it. I had plenty of time to enjoy the cooking date with Logan that he had so thoughtfully planned out. Considering I was having serious doubts about whether our relationship was worth fighting for, the quality time that he had scheduled for us was even more meaningful. Logan and I had some serious downfalls, but maybe the dinner would be the very thing that would bring us back together. I was willing to keep an open mind and was hopeful for the outcome.

Since our date would remain in the comfort of our apartment, I didn't feel the pressures of dressing up or perfecting my hair. I changed out of my work clothes and threw on a cozy t-shirt and some tattered shorts that I only wore in the privacy of my own apartment. I spritzed my curls with some water to liven them up a bit, but other than that, I didn't bother taming the mane any further. As for makeup, I didn't even bother putting any on. The imperfections of my skin were pretty well hidden through the graininess of the computer screen, so I never wore any when working from home, even if I did have meetings. Honestly, cooking at home was the perfect type of date for me. I really did feel a lot of stress when it came to picking out an outfit and making myself look presentable. With an at-home date, I was able to just be myself and appear in my natural state.

I headed downstairs to the living room and found Logan scrolling through his laptop. He seemed to be working on something important, as he was so focused on his screen that he didn't even notice me.

"Hey, Logan," I called out, "I'm ready to make dinner when you are."

I could tell he wasn't prepared to see me so early by the way he kept checking the time.

"It's not even five-thirty," Logan relayed. "I thought you said around six or seven."

"I finished early," I informed him as I took a seat next to him on the couch, "but we can wait until you're done." I smiled at him, as it was nice to be the one who wasn't working for once.

"I still have a few things I need to catch up on," Logan admitted. "Just give me a few minutes."

"No worries at all," I responded. "Just let me know when you're finished."

I found the remote and put on a random cooking show while I waited for him. I figured watching someone else prepare food would get me even more excited about our date. I figured I could learn a tip or two from watching professionals. Surely, they weren't making a pizza, but I still believed I could pick up on a few techniques. I intently tuned in to the show, hoping that the chef's skills would magically transfer to me while I was watching. I wasn't a horrible cook, but I had definitely burnt my fair share of meals. I usually just stuck to microwaved meals or frozen food, but sometimes Logan would cook dinner. When we first started dating, he used to live in the kitchen. He loved preparing meals, and I loved eating them. Over time, he stopped doing it as often, and now, I couldn't even remember the last time he had made dinner.

"Okay, I'm ready now," Logan alerted around six.

He ended up taking a lot more than a few minutes to finish his work, but I was focused on the television, anyway.

"What were you working on?" I nosily asked as I took a peek at his laptop.

His screen displayed an average-looking house that was definitely overpriced. I wasn't an expert on the housing market, but even I knew that the listing could use a healthy price decrease.

"I'm trying to find a home for some potential clients," Logan responded. "A lot of the guests at my last open house didn't end up purchasing because it didn't have a pool in the backyard, so I was trying to find them some other options."

I took a deeper look at Logan's laptop as he scrolled through some pictures of the property that he had pulled up.

"But that house is ugly," I proclaimed.

"Well, it's within their budget," Logan explained. "It's hard to find a nice house with a pool in Denver under $300,000."

I took another good look at the featured home.

"Well, that's probably why you haven't sold anything yet," I concluded. "You're not showing homes that have curb appeal. That property is not cute at all. I would never buy that." I was only trying to provide a constructive critique, but by the way Logan slammed his laptop in my face, I could tell that he didn't find my advice too helpful.

"Let's just make dinner now," he announced in an effort to change the subject. "I got the ingredients to make a pizza."

I followed him into the kitchen and examined all of the groceries that he had picked up from the store. There was only one bag on the counter, and it didn't contain the typical ingredients that I expected for a pizza night.

"You bought a frozen pizza?" I muttered as I removed the cold item from the plastic bag.

"And pepperoni," Logan added. "Your favorite."

Pepperoni was my favorite topping, but I didn't understand how we were supposed to cook this together. The pizza was already premade.

"Thank you ..." I hesitantly praised.

"What's wrong?" Logan asked. "Do you not like pepperoni anymore?"

I was appreciative of his efforts, but I didn't think Logan knew what a real cooking date was. I had imagined rolling dough together and spreading sauce over our creation before adding our favorite toppings. Instead, this night was just going to consist of preheating the oven.

"I just thought that we were going to be making a pizza from scratch," I explained. "It's not really a cooking date if we are just putting a pizza into an oven."

Logan looked a little defeated at his failed attempt at trying to plan the date.

"But this still works," I quickly interjected before he felt too bad. "I'm super excited to add the extra toppings to it." I smiled and quickly gave Logan a hug. Although it may have been a pity hug, I was still proud of my body for not automatically jerking away from him. I actually embraced the touch that was coming from the hug.

"Thank you for planning this date night," I added. "It really means a lot." Maybe I was just being too hard on our relationship. Logan tried his best to make quality time for us, and even though it wasn't what I expected, I was grateful for the work he put into it. I was so appreciative that I actually gave him a kiss at the conclusion of our hug. I was once so annoyed by engaging in any type of physical affection with him, but Logan was slowly softening my heart. All it took was a little pizza date.

"You're welcome," he solemnly noted.

I removed the frozen pizza from its box while he preheated the oven. We each took turns placing the extra pepperoni on top, using the entire package. By the time we actually put it into the oven, there was barely any pizza showing because of how many toppings we had added. We chuckled at our insane creation. Only Logan and I would find a way to corrupt a perfectly good pizza.

"That's the best-looking pizza I've ever seen," I complimented.

We decided to leave it in the oven a little longer than directed since we added toppings to it, but we ended up losing track of the time and leaving it in too long. The smell of the burning crust invaded the kitchen, and the dough was now a dark crisp. I didn't find it edible anymore since the outsides were black and the middle was still raw, but Logan still sucked it up and ate it. His taste buds were warriors. Mine, on the other hand, were babies. I opted to make myself a bowl of cereal and milk for dinner instead. Maybe Logan's stomach was strong enough to handle the half-overcooked and half-undercooked pizza, but I knew mine couldn't. I was fine with my cereal, although Logan seemed like he wanted me to join him in his dining misery. However, there was no way I was going to subject my digestive system to that nightmare.

"Maybe we should just order out next time." I giggled as Logan continued to maneuver his way around the raw parts of the pizza.

"Probably would have been a better idea," Logan affirmed.

His mood had drastically become more frustrated after the date didn't turn out as he had planned. I knew he probably felt like a failure, but I was thoroughly enjoying our time together. I didn't need an elaborately planned event to feel connected to Logan. He and I alone together, in the comfort of the apartment, was enough for me.

"Do you have room for dessert?" I offered as I cleared our plates. "I can get you some ice cream out of the freezer."

I gave Logan another kiss on the lips before I brought our dirty dishes to the sink. It was fun enjoying intimacy for once. I couldn't remember the last time I not only wanted to kiss him, but craved it.

"No, thank you," Logan declined. "I think I am just going to wind down for the night."

It was only 8:00 p.m., but he did often go to bed early. I figured the long day had probably just caught up to him.

"What about a movie?" I suggested while wiping down the kitchen counter. "We could watch something before we go to bed."

"That works," Logan casually agreed.

As soon as I finished cleaning the kitchen and clearing the dishes, we headed upstairs to get ready for bed and finish the night off with a movie. I chose something romantic since we had just completed a successful date night. Logan usually preferred action or an intense thriller, but he didn't object to my selection.

During the movie, I kept looking over at Logan and thinking about how I almost gave up on him. He was a great boyfriend, and I was glad I didn't let the relationship go. This night confirmed that Logan was worth fighting for. I was going to dedicate myself to this relationship and really give it my all. I was first going to start off by giving Logan something that I knew he had been waiting a long time for. It had been a while since I gave him any type of affection. I knew I had been holding back, but it wasn't to hurt his feelings. It was truly due to the lack of connection I felt with him throughout the day. However, Logan had been super attentive during our date, and I felt extra bonded with him. I wanted to express my love for him and show him how much I really did appreciate the date he had planned.

In the middle of one of the more boring scenes in the movie, I climbed on top of him and was preparing to absolutely shower him with a ton of kisses, but I was met with tired grumbles. Apparently, he had fallen asleep, and my jumping on top of him was the disturbance that woke him up. I figured he was just exhausted from the long day, so I simply climbed off him. Since he was half-asleep and the movie wasn't even that good, I found the remote and turned off the television. I was a little disappointed that I wasn't able to follow through with my original plan of giving him affection, but I was hoping that I would feel the same way about the idea tomorrow.

14

Logan

I was hoping that I wouldn't feel the same way when I woke up the next morning, but I did. I tried really hard to change my own mind and convince myself that my own thoughts were deceiving me—it didn't work. I still woke up feeling the same disappointment as I had the prior night. The cooking date with Hailey was not what I had expected it to be. I really wanted to rekindle the flame that we had once lost, but the quality time together only pushed me farther away from her. I had really hoped that Dalton's suggestion to save our failing relationship would work, but it was no use. After the date, I was on the brink of being fully convinced that our relationship was doomed.

To begin with, I didn't even think she took the date that seriously. I dedicated time out of my day to plan the special alone time together, and she didn't even bother dressing up for it. I had on a nice, collared shirt with dress pants, but she couldn't even find the time to do her hair. She could have at the very least taken a shower. Just because we weren't going anywhere fancy, didn't mean that it was an excuse to not even put any effort into our appearance. I used my nice cologne and wore one of my favorite watches, while she walked down the stairs in an old shirt and her pajama shorts. I knew she wasn't a fan of dressing up, but I thought that she would have set aside her own reservations and looked nice for me. Evidently, I assumed wrong. Even in our apartment, I still wanted it to feel like a real date, but her casual clothes ruined the vibe. To her, it was just another night.

Not only did she walk down the stairs in a wrinkled outfit, but she didn't even give me a heads up that she had finished her workday early. She had originally told me that she would be done around six or seven, so I planned the date accordingly. As soon as I finished my own work, I was going to dim the lights and light a candle to create a romantic ambiance. There was also a bag of rose petals in my backpack waiting to be sprinkled across the dining table. I wished I could have taken credit for the rose petal idea, but I got it from a movie that Hailey liked to watch. She loved romantic gestures, and I was excited to show her how romantic I could actually be. Unfortunately, I didn't get the chance to set the mood since she galloped into the living room without warning. I was a reasonable man. I didn't expect her to update me on every single aspect of her day, but she could have at least given me the courtesy to communicate that she was going to log off earlier than she had previously mentioned. So much for a perfect date night.

In all honesty, it wasn't the biggest deal in the world. I could get over the fact that she was ready earlier than expected and didn't bother dressing up. She was probably just eager. I tried to give her the benefit of the doubt. Besides, it gave us the opportunity to enjoy some bonding time before the date started. However, when she sat on the couch next to me while I worked, even that proved to be a challenge. She wasted no time in reaching for the remote, finding a channel that she liked, and turning up the volume to an unacceptable level. I liked a little background noise while I worked, but Hailey had her show blasting at almost full volume. She was totally consumed in her own entertainment that she didn't notice that she was disrupting my focus. It was really important for me to try and make my first sale. I thought it was also important to her, too, but in that moment, it seemed like she couldn't have cared less. It was a huge deal that I had the contact information for potential buyers looking for a home with a pool. Their email addresses were the key to completing my first transaction. All I needed to do was find the perfect home for them. A task that was only supposed to take me twenty minutes took me about an hour since I kept getting distracted by the television and Hailey's side comments. Apparently, watching cooking shows was more important than letting me focus on my job. I guess she wasn't that eager to get out of her apartment because if she was, she would have been a lot quieter.

I was becoming increasingly annoyed with her but felt refreshed once I had actually finished. I figured I was just feeling the stress of the workday and was just taking out my frustrations on my girlfriend. Hailey did take interest in what I was working on, which made me feel a little better about the night. I was excited at first, since she never seemed to involve herself too much in the real estate industry, but it quickly took a negative turn. She always thought she knew more than everyone about everything. I wouldn't have been surprised if she went to the doctor's office and told her physician how to do their job. The idea that someone could actually possess more knowledge than her about a topic hadn't crossed her mind. Hailey couldn't possibly fathom someone being smarter than her, therefore, she had wasted no time in telling me how ugly she thought the houses I was looking at were. Obviously, I knew that the listings weren't the most attractive, but sometimes buyers needed to know what the properties within their budget truly looked like. Hailey didn't know that, though. In fact, she actually knew nothing about the housing market, but still felt the need to not only insert an opinion about the home, but about how I was doing my job. If I remembered correctly, I believed she had insinuated that my selling tactics were the reason why I hadn't sold anything yet. It was an ignorant and insulting comment. I wondered how Hailey would have felt if I invaded her space while she worked and criticized every move she made, but like always, she was only thinking of herself.

The night was supposed to be a way to connect and bring us closer together, but instead it was just driving me further from her. The actual date hadn't even started before I was already losing hope. I was so turned off by her lack of effort in getting ready and her blatant disrespect of my working habits, that I didn't even know if I wanted to continue on with the night—I was already wanting it to be over. I figured once we actually started cooking, the spark between us would somehow find its way back into our relationship, but it was becoming a lost cause. Cooking together was our last hope in finally getting us back in the right direction, so I had quickly redirected the night toward our goal of making a pizza.

Hailey usually did the grocery shopping, but I was proud of myself for doing it all by myself for once. I didn't show up with a list because I already knew exactly what I wanted. Fortunately, I remembered how much she loved visiting the frozen section every time I went with her because she couldn't wait to get her hands on a pepperoni pizza. It was one of her usual cravings. I didn't think a day went by where we didn't have at least one frozen pizza shoved somewhere in our freezer. One of the dates early in our relationship actually consisted of us heating up a pizza and watching cartoons all night. Although a casual night, it meant a lot to me because it was the day that I fell in love with Hailey. We stayed up all night just laughing and getting to know each other. I couldn't help but fall for her. I wanted to somehow recreate that night. I even bought the same brand of pizza that we had used that very night many years ago. Hailey loved it, but her one complaint was that it never had enough toppings on it. I thought by surprising her with the extra pepperoni, she would be so thankful that our spark would simply return just from that. I couldn't have been more wrong. When I presented her with the groceries, she looked upset. Since the ingredients weren't what she had originally pictured in her mind, she was obviously disappointed. It was clear that she didn't remember our date from a long time ago or realize my attempt at trying to relive it because she had simply just laughed at what I had bought.

At that point in the date, any hope of bringing any type of romance into our relationship was over. I just wanted the night to end. It was really hard to go through with the rest of the date with a fake smile on my face, but I didn't want to ruin it for her. Unlike me, she seemed to be enjoying herself. She had even kissed me at one point, which caught me completely off guard. I couldn't remember the last time she initiated any sort of physical intimacy. It was something I had begged her for in the last couple of years together. Out of all the things that I had wanted her to fix, her lack of physical touch was the biggest one. I was happy that she finally decided to change her ways, but unfortunately, it happened a little too late—I felt nothing from the kiss.

Honestly, the rest of the night was a meaningless blur. I remembered her continuing in her unappreciative ways by not even eating the pizza we had made together. It wasn't to her exact liking, so she made herself a bowl of cereal instead. So much for our cooking date. Hailey even had the audacity to suggest ordering out next time—another comment to further rub in my face how the date didn't go as planned. I put a lot of time into preparing the night, and she couldn't even thank me. I believed we even watched a movie at some point, but I was so mentally checked out that I couldn't even be 100% certain. My mind had been wandering, looking for any type of escape from the night.

Hailey totally ruined the date for me, but the worst offense was that my own girlfriend didn't even realize how I was feeling. It was pretty obvious that I wasn't in the best of moods, but she didn't even check on me to see if anything was wrong. There was no way she didn't pick up on how upset I was. She could usually detect my mood before I even could. She was probably just too focused on herself to notice. I was glad she seemed to enjoy our time together, but I couldn't have felt more alone.

I didn't know if we had many more dates left in our relationship, but either way, that was the last time I was going to try and plan something special for her. It obviously wasn't meaningful enough. I started the night with an open mind, but my doubts about our relationship were only just further confirmed. For about seven years, I had tried my best to overlook any flaws in our relationship and push down my own feelings in order to please Hailey, but I had finally reached my limit. I could no longer pretend that everything was fine between us. Despite not being able to move forward with Hailey anymore, I was still willing to celebrate our anniversary. Hailey deserved it, and so did our relationship. We spent seven good years together, and that deserved to be recognized. I would go out to dinner with her on Saturday, but I had no intention of celebrating any more with her. I was mentally and emotionally done with the relationship.

15

Hailey

I headed to the gym to meet Dalton on Saturday afternoon while Logan went to a work lunch with some girl named Skylar. From what I had gathered about her from the internet, drama followed her wherever she went. The tabloids didn't have the greatest things to say about her or her rough divorce. However, according to Logan, she was a successful real estate agent in Colorado who had graciously agreed to mentor him while he navigated his way into the industry. Skylar was a lot older than Logan and me, so she must have been in the business for a while. He seemed really excited to learn from her, which was great because he seemed kind of down ever since our cooking date. I figured the pressure of his job was finally getting to him since he hadn't sold a house yet. Our date last night probably reminded him of all the empty promises he had made me about being able to afford us a better life one day. He still hadn't earned any commission to get himself closer to fulfilling any of those commitments, and I was certain that he was starting to really stress about it. I could tell by the way he was focusing so hard on his computer before we started our pizza night. Logan usually wasn't sensitive to my comments, so the fact that he freaked out when I said something about his selling strategy further proved that he was not in a great headspace. I was grateful that he was finally meeting with this new mentor and getting the help that he really needed.

When I finally made it to the gym, I groaned at how packed the parking lot was, but I let out an even deeper sigh when I walked inside and saw that Dalton hadn't arrived alone. I was surprised, and slightly disappointed, to see that Piper was with him. I couldn't remember the last time she joined us for a lifting session, and I was really looking forward to hanging out with just Dalton. He was a great person to vent to, and I had a lot on my mind. I wanted to fill him in on my date with Logan and see if he had any advice on how to relieve some of the pressure he was feeling from his new career.

Piper was a great person, but I didn't know her as well as I did Dalton, therefore, I didn't trust her as much with my relationship gossip.

"Hey," I greeted as I walked over to them.

"What's up?" Dalton returned.

"Hi, Hailey!" Piper bellowed.

I joined them in our usual pre-workout stretch routine. He and I normally spent this time catching up, but since Piper was new and didn't know how to do our stretches, Dalton was preoccupied with helping her out. Needless to say, she took up all his attention. I had nothing but great things to say about Piper, but I really wished she had picked another day to join us at the gym.

"How's everything going?" I aimed more toward Dalton than to his girlfriend, hoping that some of his focus would be directed toward me.

"Great, just ready to pump some iron with this rookie." Dalton laughed while he winked at Piper. He didn't seem as bothered that our gym duo had become a trio.

"Yeah, I was actually surprised to see you here, Piper," I casually pointed out. "It's been a while since the last time you joined us."

"Well, I figured now would be a good time to start going to the gym again," Piper relayed. She started staring at Dalton and giggling a bit before finally revealing the giant rock on her hand. "I want to make sure I look as good as possible in my wedding dress."

My eyes widened at the engagement ring sparkling on her finger. Even someone with horrible eyesight would have been able to spot that diamond. I didn't know much about jewelry, but even I could tell he spent a pretty penny on it.

"Oh my gosh!" I screamed. "Congratulations!"

I disrupted both of their stretches to give them a warm embrace. Piper had been looking forward to the proposal for a while, and Dalton successfully followed through. I was happy for them, even though feelings of jealousy were also brewing inside me—mostly due to the fact that I wasn't engaged, but also slightly because Dalton was officially off the market. I would never cross the line with Logan's best friend. Any slight romantic feelings for Dalton remained only in my head, though being engaged really put a damper on my fantasies about him.

"How did it happen?" I inquisitively asked.

"He reserved the entire rooftop of my favorite restaurant, just for us," Piper began, wasting no time by eagerly jumping at the opportunity to talk about the proposal. "Just as the sun was starting to set, he led me to a private area, covered in candles and roses. Rooster ran out with a sign around his neck, asking me to marry him. I'm not sure how he was able to train our dog to propose before training him how to sit, but it was the most romantic thing ever."

Piper pulled out her phone and started scrolling through the pictures that presumably came from a photographer that Dalton had hired to secretly take pictures of the whole ordeal. Rooster definitely stole the show, wearing his adorable sign, and it was evident that Dalton had put a lot of thought into it.

"I'm so happy for you both," I exclaimed as I hugged them one more time, yet I think my envy was starting to come out in my tone.

"Maybe you're next," Dalton announced, probably sensing my jealousy. "Isn't it your anniversary dinner tonight?"

"Oh my!" Piper screeched. "He's definitely going to ask you tonight!"

Dalton took a quick second to scold his new fiancée. "Don't spoil it, Piper," he muttered.

It all made sense. The random cooking date, Logan's edgy mood, our anniversary—Logan was getting ready to propose. It hadn't even crossed my mind because of how rocky our relationship had been, but the date night together probably gave Logan the answers he was looking for. Our conversation at the photoshoot most likely sparked the idea into his head, and our pizza night confirmed it. I couldn't believe it. I had been waiting for forever for this moment. I never thought the day would actually come, but after tonight, I was going to be engaged.

"I hope so," I responded trying my hardest to suppress the giddy smile that was begging to emerge. "I've only waited seven years for it."

"Just make sure you don't ugly cry," Piper advised. "He will probably have someone recording or taking pictures."

Dalton corralled us to an empty rack so that we could start our lifting session, but Piper kept going on and on about my potential proposal. The reason she stopped lifting with us was because she and I would just gossip the entire time, and she still hadn't changed. I would need this workout too if I was also going to have to fit into a wedding dress, but she clearly was more interested in my anniversary dinner than squatting.

"And make sure you wear a dress color that won't blend in with the tablecloth," Piper rambled, "or else it will blend together and not photograph well." Piper continued while Dalton worked out.

She gave me every piece of advice that she could think of and repeated some without realizing it. I tried to find a break in the conversation so that I could get some reps in, but she didn't even take a second to breathe. Dalton simply ignored her and left us to talk as he continued with his own lifting session. By the time he was done, I hadn't touched a single weight.

"We should do this again sometime!" Piper hollered once Dalton finished his last set.

"Absolutely," I replied as cheerfully as I could despite being annoyed that I missed out on a chance to hang out with Dalton and workout.

We all made our way toward the exit, but I found my window of opportunity right before Piper and Dalton walked out the door. "I'm actually going to head to the bathroom first," I stated, "but I'll see you guys next time."

"Let us know how tonight goes," Piper uttered, flashing me a giant wink. "We can plan our weddings together."

I forced a smile and gave Piper and Dalton a hug before quickly retreating to the bathroom. There were a few people in there, so I stood in a stall for a few minutes until I was certain that Dalton and Piper had left. I didn't actually have to use the restroom, but I figured it would be awkward if I exited the stall without at least flushing, so I gave the toilet handle a gentle tug. Hanging out with Piper was great and all, but I wasn't about to leave the gym without doing at least one exercise, especially knowing that I would have to start preparing my body for a wedding dress.

When I left the bathroom, I noticed that there weren't a lot of people by the rack of dumbbells, so I decided I would just do a few sets of arm curls before officially calling it a day. I couldn't remember which weight I normally used since Dalton typically just grabbed them for me, so I took a few seconds to contemplate the various options before deciding which one to choose.

"There's a lot to pick from," a random male voice commented from behind me.

I turned around to identify the man who was talking to me, but I had never seen him before. It didn't surprise me though because Dalton and I spent a lot of time around the leg machines, and the strange guy was clearly top heavy. His bottom half looked like it hadn't moved a weight in years.

"Yup, there's a lot," I coldly confirmed. I figured my apparent attitude would hint to him that I did not intend on engaging in any further conversation.

"I bet I could squat you on my shoulders," he added.

"Probably," I stated dismissively. He clearly was not understanding that I was not interested.

"Let's test it out," the strange man proudly suggested.

"No, thanks," I answered. "I don't think my boyfriend would like that very much." I turned my attention back to the various dumbbells, hoping that the random man would leave me alone.

"Oh, you're one of those girls," he asserted. "You think every guy that talks to you, wants you."

I rolled my eyes, but I still wasn't facing him so he didn't notice.

"News flash, you're not even that pretty," he added, "and you're even uglier from the back. I bet your boyfriend wishes he was dating someone else."

At the slight attack on my relationship, I quickly whipped my head around to set him straight. "Actually," I began, "my boyfriend thinks I'm the most beautiful girl in the world ... from the front and the back. He's actually proposing to me tonight." I eyed him up and down, but made sure I focused more on his bottom half. "And at least my backside is thicker than your legs." I snickered as I grabbed my gym bag and headed toward the exit.

I was pretty sure he yelled something back at me, but I wasn't really paying attention to any of the other nonsense that was leaving his mouth. He was just another loser at the gym, and another prime example of why I was happy that I wasn't in the dating world. It honestly made me really reflect on how I had been viewing my relationship with Logan. There were obviously things about him that got under my skin, but he wasn't nearly as bad as the rest of the guys in the world. I couldn't imagine being single and trying to find a life partner with the current available options. If the guys out there were anything like the man at the gym, I really felt bad for all the single girls who were still trying to find love. I may not have liked everything that Logan did, but he really was better than all the other men out there. There had been doubts swirling in my head about our relationship, but as of our cooking date, I was fully committed to being with him. No more thinking about what life would be like without him or imaging myself with someone else. I got a glimpse of what the caliber of men out there were like, and I wanted absolutely no part of it. I was happy with Logan, and I didn't want anyone else.

I left the gym after not even lifting a single weight, and entered the busy parking lot. When I made it to my car, I threw my gym bag into the trunk, even though it didn't smell as bad as it usually did since I didn't even break a sweat. I got into my car, turned on my favorite radio station, and pulled out of the lot. I was happy to finally leave my encounter with the jerk at the gym behind, but instead of driving back to my apartment, I took a little detour to the nail salon. I couldn't get proposed to without a fresh set of nails.

16

Logan

Skylar was already seated at a table when I arrived at the coffee shop. Her brown hair was glistening in the natural light shining through the nearby window, which made it appear as though it were a lighter shade. I never really paid much attention to her hair color before, but it was glowing underneath the sun—it actually really suited her. The sunlight didn't stop at just her hair, though. It also highlighted her facial features. As I got closer to the table, I could see freckles dancing on her cheeks, and not a single imperfection on her skin. She was nine years older than me, but I couldn't see a single sign of aging on her face. I would've guessed that she was twenty-two as opposed to thirty-two.

When she felt my presence approaching her, she looked up and made eye contact with me. I could have easily mistaken her eyes for pools of honey by the way their golden tones were glistening. Skylar's physical appearance had never been top of mind to me. Nobody could deny that she was a pretty girl, but I was so focused on her brain that I never really stopped to pay attention to anything else. Sitting across from her at the table with the light shining on her not only forced me to look at her physical features, but to admire them. Pretty was actually an understatement when it came to her; Skylar was beautiful.

"Hey, Logan," she cheerfully greeted. "I got you a chai tea latte." She directed a kind smile in my direction as she nudged the drink closer to me. "I remember you mentioning that it was one of your favorite drinks, so I figured I would just order you one. I hope you don't mind."

I took a sip of the drink, and the liquid ran down my throat in a warm sensation. It was the best chai tea latte I had ever tasted, partly because it was one of my favorite drinks, but also because of the thought that went behind ordering it. She had not only remembered what I liked, but she took it a step further by also ordering it for me. I couldn't believe how thoughtful she was.

"I don't mind at all," I returned. "It's delicious. Thank you."

"Okay, great," Skylar replied. She took a sip of her own drink, which momentarily hid her gorgeous smile. "I'm super excited to help you out with your career," she affirmed. "I wish someone was there to help me out when I first started."

"Well, I'm super grateful for your time," I exclaimed, still admiring all of the parts of her face that the sunlight continued to reveal to me.

She sat there looking picturesque, but temporarily removed herself from the sun's rays to reach over to the side of her chair. Skylar had a large purse with her that she began to shuffle through and pull folders and papers out of.

"So, where did you want to start?" she asked while she organized the documents in front of her. "I have a few ideas, but I wanted to hear your thoughts first."

I quickly snapped out of my daze and reminded myself why I was actually meeting up with her. We weren't sitting at a coffee shop so that I could stare at her all day, but so that I could learn from her. She took the Colorado real estate industry by storm when she entered it a few years ago, and I wanted her to share some of her secrets with me. In the first few months of her career, she sold a $3.1 million dollar home, which put her on the map. I was amazed by all of her accomplishments that I was able to discover online, and almost wondered why there weren't more people begging to learn from her, until I remembered the reputation that she carried with her. Through networking with other agents and after reading a few articles, it was brought to my attention that she used to be married to a really wealthy man, therefore, some dismissed her skillset, and attributed her success to her privileged background.

Apparently, their divorce was super ugly, and a lot of shady things went down. Most of the posts that I read about the situation claimed she had stolen a lot of money from him. I refused to believe that because I also read somewhere that he had cheated on her with multiple women, which proved that there was more to the story. I wanted to ask her about it, but it didn't feel like it was my place. She had a reputation of being an icon in the industry, but she was more known for her public divorce and the allegations in regard to her stealing money from her ex-husband. Despite that sentiment, I still viewed Skylar as an elite agent. I actually got to see her in action and knew what she was capable of. Her rich ex-husband may have opened the door of opportunity for her, but it was her hard work that got her to where she was today.

"I'm willing to start wherever," I noted. "I just want to sell a house."

Skylar giggled a bit, "Don't we all?"

"Yes, but I really want to sell one," I repeated with a little more passion.

I was so thankful that Skylar was willing to meet with me on a Saturday morning to start our mentorship. Hopefully, all would go well and we could start making these meetings a more regular occurrence. I wasn't going to stop until I finally achieved my goal.

"Well, let's start with your motivation then," Skylar suggested. "Why do you want to be a real estate agent?"

I hesitated before I responded, knowing that my answer would be a lot more complicated than it sounded.

"Hailey," I slowly replied. "My girlfriend."

"Oh, that's wonderful," Skylar began. "She motivates you to do better?"

"More like she pressures me to make money," I explained.

I didn't realize how bad it sounded until after it had already left my mouth.

"I mean, I want to sell a house because I want to afford us a better lifestyle," I quickly corrected.

Skylar seemed to accept my second response since her expression didn't reveal any sign of apprehension.

"How long have you been dating her?" she asked.

"Seven years," I answered, although I wasn't too excited about it because of the current state of our relationship. "It's actually our anniversary today."

"Congratulations," Skylar commended.

I smiled in return, but she could tell something was off.

"I remember what it's like to celebrate an anniversary since I haven't been single for that long," Skylar explained. She studied the emotions on my face before finishing. "I guess I just expected you to sound a little happier about it. Is everything okay?"

I took another sip of latte to buy myself more time in deciding how much of my relationship I was willing to divulge. "We're just not in a great place right now," I responded as I chose to just keep my answers general.

"I'm sorry to hear that," Skylar comforted. "Sounds like you may need a new motivation then."

"Isn't that the truth," I agreed. I diverted my attention to the parking lot that could be seen through the window next to our table, trying to escape the conversation at hand. It was hard to stay engaged because I had been hurting inside. Hailey was still my girlfriend, but I was already grieving the relationship.

"Do you want to talk about it?" Skylar asked when she noticed my disengagement. "I totally understand if you don't want to, but I'm here for you if you do want to share." She reached across the table and gave my hand a gentle squeeze.

I was going back and forth in my head about whether I wanted to talk about Hailey or not, but Skylar's presence was already putting me at ease. My biggest complaint was that I didn't feel like a priority in Hailey's life, and yet, there was already another girl willing to take time out of her day to listen to my problems. I was already mentally checking out of my relationship before Skylar had even entered into my life, but I couldn't lie, Skylar was definitely making it a little easier to move on.

"We are just on different pages," I finally admitted. "She takes my love for granted." I took a deep breath before continuing. "She just assumes that I'm always going to be there for her, so she doesn't make me a priority. I'm not expecting her to give me her full attention every second of the day, but she could at least let me know she cares about me more often."

A look of concern flooded Skylar's face. She was already showing more care than Hailey had in the last few years of our relationship. "You are too good of a guy to get brushed to the side," Skylar confessed. "You deserve someone who is going to tell you how great you are every single day."

Skylar's words were more powerful than she realized. She was truly helping me process the end of my relationship, and was comforting me in my time of grief.

"Hailey is just not the girl that she was at the beginning of our relationship," I revealed.

Admitting Hailey's faults were harsh, but they were healing at the same time. I kept on fighting for a girl that I didn't fully realize was not meant for me until saying her flaws out loud. I was confused about whether I should just stay in the relationship or not, but talking to Skylar about it gave me clarity that it was in both of our best interest to just go our separate ways. Hailey wasn't the girl for me, and I was not the guy for her.

"You deserve better," Skylar consoled, "and I can assure you that there is better out there."

I tried to force a smile, but I wasn't able to.

"You are handsome, smart, and successful," she urged while caressing my hand. "Don't let anyone make you feel less than the greatest man on Earth."

That time, I actually was able to smile. Her words validated my feelings. I wasn't crazy for thinking that I deserved better.

Our meeting was supposed to be centered around my career, but instead it was revolved around my failing relationship. I thought I was going to talk about the housing market, but instead, I was on the brink of tears mourning the girl that I thought I was going to marry. My heart was aching, but I was glad to have Skylar there for me.

"So, are you going to break up with her?" Skylar questioned with compassion.

"Obviously not tonight," I affirmed. "I still want to enjoy our anniversary dinner."

I thought about my date with Hailey later that evening. I had just finished basically telling Skylar that I was going to end my seven-year relationship, but what I hadn't told her was all the love that was still there between Hailey and me. It felt good to get my issues off of my chest, but since I had confessed them all, I immediately felt better and was doubting whether I actually wanted to follow through with a breakup. Maybe all I really needed was to just talk to someone about everything.

When I was confessing all my problems, ending the relationship sounded like the obvious decision, but I wasn't so sure anymore. Of course, I still had my doubts, but were they really enough to constitute a breakup? I didn't know what I was going to do, but I did know I didn't have to make a decision today. I'd revisit my feelings about the relationship another time because I just wanted to focus on my anniversary dinner. Hailey and I made it seven years, and that definitely deserved a celebration.

17

Hailey

I acted surprised when the waiter led us to a romantically decorated table in a private area of the restaurant. It was covered in roses, which popped against the black tablecloth, and it even had a complimentary bottle of champagne in the middle. A beautifully lit candle was the focal point of the centerpiece, but the view was what really stole the show. We were seated next to a window that overlooked the city of Denver. I had added in the notes of our reservation that we were celebrating an anniversary, but it was clear that Logan had called the restaurant and notified them that a proposal was also happening that night. The staff was super hospitable and the restaurant was super gracious, but there was no way that our table was decorated to that caliber with only an anniversary in mind. It was clearly prepared to celebrate something even greater.

I removed my jacket and placed it on the back of my chair before I sat down across from Logan. He was wearing a navy polo with black dress pants that evidently needed to be ironed. I would have guessed that he would've worn a suit, especially since he was obsessed with his appearance and there was probably going to be a photographer taking pictures of us, but it wasn't like he was dressed super casually, either. His color scheme went well with my white dress, anyway. It was a special outfit that I had actually saved for a moment like a proposal. When I initially bought it, I imagined myself wearing it to my engagement party, but I was so excited for the dinner that I decided to wear it. I didn't think I was going to be aware of the night when Logan was going to pop the question, but since I was, the dress was perfect for the occasion. Besides, I could always buy a new one for the actual engagement party. It would give me an excuse to go shopping again.

"Welcome to Blue Farm Steakhouse," the waiter announced while he poured us each a glass of water. "My name is Robbie, and I will be your server this evening." He was a tall gentleman with kind eyes and a stoic presence. He appeared very professional in his white collared shirt and black vest. His movements were very sharp and precise, and it seemed as though he had been working in fancy steakhouses his whole life.

"I heard this is a special night," Robbie relayed while gesturing toward the bottle on the table. "Thank you for choosing Blue Farms to commemorate your special moment. Please accept the complimentary bottle of champagne as the restaurant's congratulatory gift. I will return in a few moments to answer any questions you may have about our menu."

Robbie swiftly left our table and disappeared behind some swinging doors.

"I like Robbie." I giggled. "He seems like he's going to take good care of us."

"Yeah. We are in good hands," Logan responded back in an unenthusiastic tone.

I was in a good mood. In fact, I was in a great mood. It was our anniversary, my nails were done, and we were at a nice restaurant. However, it felt as though Logan didn't share the same sentiment. It didn't even seem like he wanted to be there. He refrained from making any direct eye contact with me, and his tone of voice was casual and disinterested. Despite my gorgeous gown and styled hair, his phone still appeared to be more important to look at than me. Maybe he was just incredibly nervous to propose, but either way, he could have at least cracked a smile. I tried not to overthink it because I didn't want to go down that rabbit hole, but even before dinner, he was acting strange. His lunch with Skylar must not have gone as planned because he returned home acting more distant than he was now. I wasn't sure how much damage could be done at a work meeting, but when I tried asking him about it, he refused to engage in conversation. It must have gone really poorly.

I peered over the menu, trying to distract my thoughts that were solely focused on Logan's odd behavior. I was hoping he would be able to get over it soon because I didn't want him to put a damper on the night. Instead, I tried to focus on my own emotions. I wasn't going to let Logan bring my excitement down, even if he was just extremely anxious over proposing or really stressed about work.

"Should we get an appetizer?" I asked.

The appetizers did look good, but I was mostly asking to see if the subtle hints of grumpiness were still present in his voice.

"Whatever you want," Logan answered.

They were still there.

If his concern was truly about the upcoming proposal, he didn't need to be that tense. I thought it was pretty obvious that I was going to say yes—I had made that quite apparent. To try and uplift his spirits, I quickly tried to come up with something else to distract him from whatever he was thinking about, but nothing came to mind. Thankfully, our waiter, Robbie, returned with a delicious bread and butter basket. He set it in the middle of the table and pulled out a pen and a pad of paper.

"Have we had a chance to review the menu?" Robbie asked. "I can offer you some recommendations if you are having trouble deciding."

I looked at Logan, but he was still browsing. Honestly, he hadn't really looked up since we sat down.

"Maybe just a few more minutes," I eventually relayed to Robbie.

"Take your time," he returned. "I will point out that we are running a special on our surf and turf platter, which is detailed on the back of the menu. I highly recommend it."

Robbie pointed to the section of the menu, explaining the terms of the promotion.

"Thank you," I responded.

"I will return in a few moments, but please do not hesitate to reach out with any questions," Robbie affirmed.

He left our table almost as quickly as he had arrived, leaving Logan and I in awkward silence.

"Wow, the bread looks so good," I blurted as I reached for a slice.

It was a random comment, but at least it broke the silence.

"So good," Logan agreed with a dull tone.

He still hadn't removed his eyes from the menu. There were a lot of options, but it didn't take that long to read.

We fell back into a deafening silence, and I made one last attempt to break it.

"Happy anniversary!" I cheered as I raised my glass of water in an effort to finally get him to look me in the eyes.

"Happy anniversary," Logan repeated when his glass met mine.

He seemed less irritated, but I could still tell something was wrong.

"Is everything okay?" I finally asked. "You seem off."

I couldn't take his dreary attitude any longer. It was starting to rub off on me. I was really excited for the night, but he was starting to drag me down with him.

"Yeah, I'm fine," Logan murmured.

"Well, you don't seem fine," I uttered sharply.

Logan finally peered up from his menu. He took a giant swig of his water and breathed a heavy sigh. It seemed as though he was about to deliver some bad news, but at this point, I just wanted him to say something.

"I need to ask you a serious question," he confessed.

This was it. The moment that I had been waiting for was finally happening. His poor mood had almost completely killed my excitement, but I quickly forgave him. I was ready to become his fiancée.

Logan cleared his throat. He didn't stand up or ask me to stand up, but getting on one knee to propose was probably cliché nowadays. I didn't really mind if he asked me sitting, standing, or kneeling. I just cared that he was finally asking. A giant smile was creeping across my lips, but I managed to keep a straight face. I didn't want him to know that I knew what he was about to say. Logan started to open his mouth to speak, and it took everything in me to not immediately scream, *yes!*

"Are you happy in this relationship, Hailey?" Logan mumbled

"Excuse me?" I questioned. I wasn't sure if I had heard him correctly.

"Are you truly happy in this relationship?" Logan repeated.

I had heard him right, and my heart dropped a bit. If this was the beginning of his proposal speech, it was a pretty bad start.

"Yeah ..." I began. "Are you?"

Logan took a deep breath before responding.

"No, I'm not," Logan admitted. "I haven't been happy in a long time, and I don't think you have either."

I definitely didn't like where this conversation was going.

"Well, we definitely have things to work on," I confirmed, "but so does every couple." My eyebrows started twitching, and my hopes of being proposed to were quickly fading.

"I'm just not as happy as I used to be," Logan stated.

Each word that he uttered was another blow to the chest. A few more sentences and my heart was probably going to completely break.

"It's definitely not how it was in the beginning," I admitted, "but I still enjoy being with you ..."

I was on the verge of crying, but I didn't want to burst into a ball of tears until I heard what else he had to say. There was still a little bit of hope left in me that a ring would end up on my finger by the end of the night.

"I just feel like I'm not important to you. I want to be a priority in your life, and I don't think you see me as one," Logan disclosed.

In all honesty, I wanted to comfort him. I wanted to tell him that everything he was feeling was valid and that I would do better. It truly wasn't my intention to make him feel unimportant in my life. I actually thought that I was being a good girlfriend by letting him stay at my apartment for free, cleaning after his messes, and supporting his career. It didn't cross my mind that he was feeling neglected. My focus had been on my own family and my own career, but we were only twenty-three. We had the rest of our lives to put each other first. There was no way I would be able to make him number one in my life if I didn't handle my own responsibilities first. I needed to be in a good place myself before I dedicated my life to his wants and needs. I really was planning on telling Logan exactly how I felt, but my train of thought was interrupted by the ring of my phone. I wouldn't have answered if it was anyone else, but it was Megan, so I had to pick up.

"Just give me one second," I muttered to Logan before answering the phone.

I knew he wasn't going to like the fact that I took a call in the middle of an argument, but my sister needed me.

"Hey, Megan," I began. "I'm at dinner right now, is everything okay?"

"Someone just hit my car!" Megan shouted.

"You're joking!" I fired back.

"What do I do? I've never been in a car accident before," Megan shrieked.

"Calm down," I relayed. "Are you hurt? Are you okay?"

"Yeah, I'm fine. I'm just freaking out," Megan shared.

I listened intently as Megan explained how a car had run a stop sign and slammed into her. Obviously, her phone call came at an inopportune time, but I was so glad that I answered—my sister needed me. Robbie returned while I was still talking to Megan, but Logan rudely dismissed him and instructed him to come back in a few more minutes. I figured Robbie could sense that there was some tension because he didn't seem to take Logan's disrespect to heart.

In total, my call with Megan only lasted roughly ten minutes, but when I eventually hung up once my parents and the police had arrived, Logan's face made it seem like I had been on the phone for three hours.

"What?" I finally blurted.

"You seriously just took a phone call in the middle of an important conversation?" Logan grunted.

"It was my sister," I defended.

"So?" Logan fumed.

"So ..." I started. "Family first."

18

Logan

"Exactly," I responded. "Family first, Logan last."

"You're not last," Hailey argued.

"But I'm not first, either," I snapped back. "Or even close to it."

My voice was starting to raise. It must have startled our waiter because he emerged through the swinging doors again ready to take our order until he heard us arguing. When he realized what was going on, he immediately turned around and left Hailey and me to continue our heated discussion in private.

"I've got a lot going on, Logan," Hailey explained. "I'm working a demanding job, I'm trying to be a good sister, I'm figuring out life after college."

"And I don't have a lot going on?" I stammered. "I arguably have a lot more going on in my life than you do, but I still make time for you."

"That's not fair to say, and you know it," Hailey stated. "I definitely make time for you."

The argument was turning into a pointless discussion. She never could admit when she was wrong or put herself in someone else's shoes.

"When's the last time you really made an effort to make me feel loved?" I hollered. "You don't even touch me anymore, Hailey."

"I literally am letting you live at my apartment for free!" Hailey cried out.

Of course she would bring up finances in the middle of an argument about love.

"I have been working my butt off to try and get us into a home of our own. You know I have been grinding," I fussed.

The back-and-forth finally ceased when Hailey had no response. She probably realized that she was in the wrong.

"I just can't continue in this relationship feeling like this." I sighed.

"How long have you felt this way?" Hailey asked while tears streamed down her face.

I hated seeing her cry. I wanted to hug her and comfort her, but I knew this conversation needed to be had.

"A long time, Hailey," I confessed on the brink of tears myself. "A really long time."

We both just stared at each other in a painful silence. The sounds of the hustle and bustle of the restaurant disappeared, and only the echoes of our breaking hearts and splashes of our tears falling down our cheeks were left to hear.

"I'll be better." Hailey sobbed. "I promise. I'll treat you exactly how you deserve to be treated. I will put you first in my life. I promise, Logan ..."

We were both crying at that point, and it took a lot to even formulate a sentence, let alone express the intense feelings I was having.

"I'm sorry, Hailey ..." I cautioned, "but it's too late."

The next few minutes were filled with both of us sobbing. I had no intentions of bringing up my issues about our relationship during our anniversary dinner, but it sort of just happened. Hailey was the love of my life, and it was hard to break her heart, but I felt it was for the best. We both weren't happy, and we couldn't continue on the path we were on. The longer we stayed together, the more it was going to hurt when we finally decided to separate. It was obvious Hailey and I weren't meant for each other, but we overlooked the warning signs until we were both in too deep. Whether she wanted to admit it or not, it wasn't healthy for us to stay together. I was tired of pushing down my emotions in order to not make her mad. It was frustrating starting a new career without my girlfriend's full support. She didn't even see me as a priority anymore. I tried my best. I really tried my hardest to stick it out with Hailey, but I was exhausted from fighting for someone who wasn't fighting as hard for me.

"So, what now?" Hailey mourned.

"I think I'm just ... done ..." I admitted. Once I uttered those words, I felt a weight immediately lift off my shoulders. I was upset. I was heartbroken. However, I also felt somewhat relieved.

"Wow, Logan," Hailey raged. "So you're breaking up with me on our anniversary?" Her sadness was starting to turn into anger. "How long have you known that you didn't want to be with me?" she shouted. "Why are we even celebrating tonight?"

Her words hurt. I didn't feel confident about the future of our relationship for a while, but that didn't mean I was plotting some sort of epic breakup plan. I didn't even have any intentions of ending the relationship at dinner. I just saw an opportunity to discuss my feelings, and it ended in a breakup.

"I'm sorry," I whispered.

An apology was all I was able to vocalize at that time. My seven-year relationship was crumbling in front of me, and I was pushing the love of my life away. Deep down, I knew it was for the best, but that didn't make it hurt any less.

"I want to go home," Hailey announced. "Take me home, now."

I nodded in agreement. There was no reason to continue fighting in such a public place. I grabbed my keys while Hailey put on her jacket. We made our way through the restaurant, and I made eye contact with our waiter on the way out. I didn't know what to do, so I just forced an awkward grin and waved. Based on how fast he left our table when he heard our argument, I was certain he could've guessed what was going on. He may have even sympathized with me.

When we made it to my car, Hailey assumed her position in the passenger seat and faced the window. I couldn't see her face, but I could hear her sniffles, so I knew she was still crying. As usual, we endured the entire drive home without talking to each other. I usually complained about the silence, but that time, I was actually grateful for it. There was a lot on my mind that I needed to process, and I was starting to wonder if I had truly made the right decision. I wasn't sure what other guy would even think about cutting off a relationship with a girl he had been dating for seven years. She had caused me a lot of heartache, but we also had some really good times together. I had given our relationship more than enough chances to try and turn around, but nothing had ever happened. However, watching Hailey totally fall apart almost made me immediately regret my decision. I knew she had a good heart and always had the best intentions, even if it didn't come across at times. I began to wonder if I had made my decision too quickly. Maybe I should've given Hailey another chance; maybe it wasn't too late to take it all back ...

19

Hailey

If I could precisely describe the pain of heartbreak, then I would. All I can say is that getting hit by a bus would've probably hurt less. I've heard people describe feeling 'empty' inside or feeling that their heart was just ripped out of their chest—they lied. If I were actually hollow inside and my heart was truly removed, then I would've had the luxury of not feeling its pain anymore. However, my heart was very much still in my chest, shooting aches of pain throughout my entire body with every heartbeat.

I've heard about the sadness, the depression, and the intense feeling of grief, but nobody ever talked about the lingering hurt that doesn't go away. I couldn't care less about the endless tears, the pounding headache, or the state of confusion. I could go on in life with puffy eyes and low energy. What I couldn't handle was the constant pain. You can't escape it. It follows you wherever you go. Every thought you have is consumed by it. Every decision you make is driven by it. You are chained to it like a prisoner.

I truly wished there was a string of words that could be put together to accurately depict the feeling you get when someone crushes your heart; when someone robs you of any hope of love—there's not. I could go on and on trying to tell you how it feels, but words wouldn't do it justice. You only know the true damage of heartbreak if you have experienced it.

But for the lucky ones who haven't ... if I could accurately describe the pain of heartbreak for you, I would.

20

Logan

When we got home, Hailey immediately went to our room and started grabbing clothes out of the closet and toiletries out of the bathroom. She rummaged through drawers and cabinets, throwing everything she could get her hands on into the little duffel bag that she had in her arms. She was moving like a machine. There was no emotion behind her action, and she was solely focused on the task at hand. It was her mission to move out of the room as quickly as she could. Watching her pack up her things was almost as painful as the breakup itself.

"We can still talk about this," I kindly offered.

Hailey took a break from collecting some of her belongings. She snapped her neck around and faced me. "What is there to talk about, Logan?" she stammered. "Do you want to continue to tell me about how bad of a girlfriend I've been? I'm sorry, did I not fold your laundry the right way? Did I not clean up after you fast enough? Was paying all of your living expenses not enough for you? Was giving you seven years of my life not a big enough sacrifice for you?"

Hailey's sadness often turned to anger really fast. Whenever we argued, her tears would turn into hurtful words within a matter of minutes. This night was no different.

"Hailey, please," I begged. "I just want to end on good terms."

"I'm sorry, but that's not possible," she began. "You broke my heart."

"Do you think I wanted this to happen?" I yelled. I was growing increasingly frustrated as my words were also turning hateful.

"I wanted to spend the rest of my life with you. I thought you were the one," I relayed in a calmer tone after I realized that I was starting to scare her with my raised voice. "Things just didn't work out."

Hailey fell to the floor and began crying into her hands. I didn't stop myself from running toward her and wrapping her in my arms. I felt her pain. The situation was hard for both of us.

"Please don't leave me," Hailey pleaded through sobs. "Please don't leave me, Logan."

I didn't want to let her go. I was actually so close to just taking everything back, but I knew we would end up right back in the same situation. There was nothing I could say to fix everything, so I just continued to hold her in my arms while we cried on the bathroom floor.

"We were supposed to be together forever," Hailey mumbled quietly, but loud enough for me to hear.

I still wasn't confident that there were any words in the universe that would make any of us feel better, so I continued to opt for silence. She just needed me to be there for her.

Hailey eventually wiped her tears and got up from the floor. She resumed her actions from before and proceeded to gather some of her stuff. The cluttered bathroom counter that I used to complain about was left bare. She was still in the same room as me, but the sight of the naked counters made me instantaneously miss her.

"I'm going to sleep in the office tonight," Hailey remarked. "I already spend most of my days there, anyway. It will just be easier."

I simply just nodded my head, watching her remove her pillow from the bed and disappear into the hallway.

For the first time in seven years, I was truly alone. I didn't have my partner by my side. I couldn't even remember life before Hailey, but I was about to feel what it would be like without her. I started reflecting on all the complaints I had about her, and suddenly they all seemed so petty. It was easy to point out all of her flaws when we were together, but it was hard to remember them when we were apart. I couldn't remember a single time when Hailey and I were happy a few moments ago, but her absence made all the positive memories flow back into my brain. For both our sakes, I wanted the breakup to be the right decision. I was really hoping that it was in the best interest for both of us, because if not ... I may have just made the biggest mistake of my life.

21

Logan

I woke up the next morning wishing the events of last night were just a crazy nightmare. There was no way I had actually followed through with breaking up with my long-term girlfriend. Our anniversary probably went extremely well, and all the bad memories that were flooding my brain surely couldn't have really happened. The stress of my job must have gotten to me and it was making me hallucinate insane scenarios. I actually almost believed that the breakup was simply my imagination until I rolled over and saw that Hailey was not next to me. Her side of the bed was undisturbed, and her pillow was missing—that's when I realized the previous night wasn't just a nightmare, it was my new reality.

The thing about life is that the world doesn't stop just because yours is falling apart. Everyone continues on as normal, and you either move on or fall behind. I had no choice but to try and go on with my life as if nothing had happened. I wanted nothing more than to just spend my Sunday curled up in my sheets, mourning the loss of Hailey, but work didn't stop just because my relationship did. One of the couples that visited the open house I held with Skylar but didn't end up buying because of the lack of a pool reached out to me when I sent them an alternative property. We scheduled a tour of the new home today, and I couldn't reschedule and miss out on an opportunity to sell my first house. I still was motivated to afford myself a place of my own, even if it wasn't with Hailey.

When I found the strength to roll out of bed, I got up and headed toward the bathroom to take a shower. The counter that was once covered with Hailey's hair products was completely bare. My toothbrush and toothpaste were the only occupants of the space. It was just another reminder that Hailey was no longer my girlfriend. We would eventually have to discuss our living situation, but I was hoping she would let me stay a little longer.

I wouldn't blame her if she kicked me out, but a part of me wished that she would give me a few more weeks, just until I completed a sale.

I knew breakups were tough, but I didn't know that they affected every part of your life. My shower wasn't as enjoyable as it once was, my clothes didn't look as sharp, and my cologne didn't smell as good. The bedroom that we used to share felt more like a dungeon, and I swore that the sun didn't even shine as bright. I passed the office where Hailey was sleeping on my way to my car. I debated checking on her, but I was probably the last person she wanted to see. Last night was rough for both of us, and I wanted to give her the space she needed. Hopefully, the awkwardness of living together would eventually subside because I did not want to move out of the apartment. We were living in a prime real estate area. It was next to parks and numerous restaurants. Most of my open houses were in the area, and I didn't even want to consider the alternative of living with my overbearing mom—that would be the ultimate nightmare. Nobody was going to hire a real estate agent who was living in the spare bedroom of his mommy's house.

The drive over to the house I was showing even felt strange. Granted, Hailey and I never spoke much in the car anyway, but I quickly realized there were multiple kinds of silence. The quiet that Hailey and I had endured was purposeful and sometimes comforting. Just knowing that she was there, feeling her presence, was enough for me. The silence that resulted from her not being there felt more eerie. It was just a constant reminder that I was alone. It was uncomfortable, and I immediately wanted to fill the void. Needless to say, I was relieved when the drive was over, and I finally made it to my destination.

I pulled into the driveway at the exact time that I told my clients to meet. However, on time was late in their book because the couple was already waiting on the front porch when I arrived. The wife was pregnant, so she was seated on one of the patio chairs. It wasn't a good look to have the potential buyers waiting on the real estate agent, especially an expecting mother, but I had a lot going on in my life. Besides, I wasn't technically late.

"Mr. and Mrs. Johnson, great to see you," I greeted as I shook both of their hands. "Sorry to keep you waiting."

"No worries, Logan," Mr. Johnson returned. "And, please, call us Nick and Lauren."

The couple smiled as I removed the house keys from the lock box. I wasn't surprised that they wanted to be called by their first names, considering they were only in their late twenties. They reminded me of Hailey and I; a young couple ready to purchase their first home. Well, I guess, they reminded me of what Hailey and I used to be.

I let Nick and Lauren Johnson into the front door of their future home. It was a property that needed some work, but it at least had a pool. I could tell the couple was underwhelmed with the interior since their smiles faded as soon as they stepped inside. I should've arrived a little earlier to remove some of the debris and scattered garbage, but usually Hailey helped me out with all that.

"So, what do you think of the living room?" I asked as I showed them around. "It flows seamlessly into the kitchen."

I led the couple into the kitchen, which was also a major disappointment. The appliances were outdated and covered in a thick layer of dust. There was a hole in one of the cabinets, and the size of the space was incredibly small. It barely fit the dining table that clearly was about to fall apart. The color of the wood didn't even match the color of the chairs. It was hard to even look at. In hindsight, I should've visited the property before showing it to the Johnsons, but I wasn't in the right headspace, and I was still new to the industry. I didn't have time to check out every single property before showing it.

"You can cook for your family in this beautiful kitchen," I pitched, trying to still find a way to sell the house.

Even though the room was ugly, I still had a job to do. I did feel bad about dragging a pregnant woman through such a dusty property, but I was on a mission to finally complete my first sale.

"It's ... umm ... interesting," Lauren commented.

"Definitely could use some work, but I see the potential," Nick added.

The first floor of the house also consisted of a half bathroom, small bedroom, and a random space that I assumed was a dining room, even though it was too tiny for any furniture. It was an odd layout, and as much as I tried to stay positive, I was even losing all faith in the home. The pictures online did not depict the true state of the house.

"Why don't we head to the backyard and check out the real selling point," I announced in an effort to escape the awful property, "the pool."

I quickly led Nick and Lauren to the backyard to show them the main reason why I wanted them to see the house, but I immediately wanted to go back inside as soon as I shut the sliding glass door behind us.

"Where's the pool?" Nick questioned as he stared at the yard that only contained overgrown weeds.

"Um, hold on, one second," I stammered.

I began to panic. I clearly remembered reading that the property had a pool. I pulled out my phone and scrambled to the listing of the home. I scrolled through the details until I found a sentence that read, *backyard big enough for a pool.* I guess that meant that there actually wasn't a pool, just an area big enough for one. The listing was definitely misleading, but it was my job to know the amenities that came with the house.

"I'm sorry, there must have been some sort of misunderstanding," I apologized.

"It's fine," Lauren answered with a smile, even though it was obvious that she was frustrated.

Nick Johnson wasn't as understanding about the situation though.

"So you're telling me you showed us a home without a pool?" he questioned. "All we wanted was a pool, and you couldn't even give us that?"

"I'm sorry," I pleaded, "I got confused."

"Did you not visit the house beforehand?" Nick griped.

"Relax, Nick," Lauren exclaimed. "It was an honest mistake."

"The mistake was trusting this guy," Nick blurted.

I could feel my career tanking with every second that passed by. I lost my girlfriend, and I was about to lose my dream job all within a couple of days.

"I can show you the rest of the house," I offered. "The upstairs has two bedrooms. It's the perfect home for you to start a family."

Lauren and Nick Johnson looked at me quizzically.

"Start a family?" Lauren questioned. "What do you mean by that?"

This was my opportunity to save myself. All I had to do was pitch how great this home would be for children. I should've known an expecting mother would thrive in the details of how kid-friendly the place was.

"The smaller bedroom on the second level could easily be turned into a nursery. It's far enough from the master bedroom that you have your privacy, but it's close enough that you don't have to walk too far to check on your baby. Even if you two decide to have more kids, this home would be perfect for that."

I smiled at the couple and leaped for joy internally. I could tell a flip switched in their mind when I mentioned the potential the home had for suiting a family. I was so close to having my career blow up in my face, but my quick thinking was turning things around. Maybe I actually was suited for the real estate industry.

"Um, we are siblings," Lauren affirmed.

"Yeah, Lauren is my sister, not my wife," Nick relayed.

Crap. I needed to pivot quickly.

"My apologies," I expressed, pointing to her stomach. "I just assumed that you were the father of her baby."

"What baby?" Lauren roared. "I'm not pregnant ..."

In that moment, I knew my time in real estate was over before it had even started.

"Thank you for your time, Logan, but I think we are going to head out now," Nick announced.

He took his sister back through the house and exited out the front the door. I chased after them frantically apologizing, but it was useless. I had already messed up beyond repair.

"Nick and Lauren, I swear I can find you the home of your dreams," I begged while I followed them to their car. "Just give me one more chance to show you another property."

"I think you've done enough," Nick warned as he slammed his car door in my face.

I watched them drive off and disappear down the street. My future was over, my relationship was over, and my career was over. At that point, my life was just a series of unfortunate events. I wanted to call Hailey and tell her everything that had happened. She was always the first person I wanted to tell everything to, good or bad. I didn't have my person there to comfort me and tell me everything would be okay. I didn't know what else to do, but I knew I needed to keep my mind busy or else I would absolutely lose it. I texted Dalton to meet me at the golf course, in which he agreed to before I even put my phone back in my pocket. He was always looking for a chance to golf. Thankfully, I kept my clubs in the trunk of my car because I didn't feel comfortable going back to the apartment. I didn't want to disturb Hailey, and it definitely didn't feel like home anymore. It was simply just a place to lay my head at night while I avoided my ex-girlfriend during the day—that was my new reality that I would have to live with.

She was no longer the person that I could go to. I was prepared to lose my girlfriend, but I wasn't prepared to lose one of my best friends, too.

22

Hailey

When I woke up that Sunday morning, I had a brief moment of panic because I wasn't used to waking up in the office. I thought I had sleepwalked into the room last night, or fallen asleep while working on something. There were numerous occasions where I found myself dozing off while working, and drooling all over my papers, but I knew it was a weekend, and I definitely never woke up on the air mattress. That thing was tucked so far in the closet, it was a mission just to find it. For a split second, I was confused about how it found itself blown up and in the middle of the office, but it didn't take that long for all the painful memories to swarm back into my head and remind me that I had chosen to sleep in there or, better yet, was basically forced to sleep there.

I offered to let Logan take the master bedroom while I slept in the spare bedroom that I had turned into an office. Since my family and most of my friends lived in Colorado, I never actually had a reason to convert the office back into a bedroom. I had a few people crash on my couch for the night, but never actually made use of the air mattress. I bought it for the rare case that I might need it, but it never made its way out of the box. I was pretty sure the receipt was still taped to it. Thankfully, it hadn't developed any holes while it was collecting dust in the back of the closet. I never thought I'd have to use it, but I also never envisioned Logan and I ever breaking up. I was surprised when he agreed that we should sleep in separate beds, but I was even more surprised that he didn't offer to sleep in the office. Since I was the one who paid the bills and it was technically my apartment, I figured he would be a gentleman and decide to give me the master bedroom—I guess not.

When I initially suggested sleeping elsewhere, I was basically just giving him the opportunity to fight for me. It would've meant a lot if he had insisted that we stay in the same bed, or at least insisted that I should get the bigger room. Either way, the decision had already been made. I would be sleeping in my office for who knows how long. It was probably in both of our best interests to discuss our living situation soon. I was more than okay with him still staying at my apartment. It would've felt too real that we were no longer together if he moved out. Deep down, I knew I was just delaying the inevitable pain, but I wasn't ready to let him go. I wanted him to stay as long as he wanted. Rather yet, I wanted him to stay forever.

I didn't want to face the reality that I was single, but out of anger, I deleted all the photos with Logan off my social media when we got home last night. It was hard to stare at pictures of us happy, whether they were fake smiles or not. I figured it was best to just remove those memories from the internet, but it caused more of a frenzy than I would've thought. It didn't take long before my inbox was flooded with messages asking if Logan and I had broken up. Megan lived on social media, so she texted me not even five minutes after I removed the pictures. She suffered a concussion due to her car accident so she shouldn't have been on her phone, anyway. I ignored her messages initially, but she followed up in the morning asking if I wanted to come over and hang out with her. At first, I refused. I just wanted to soak in my sorrows in the comfort of my air mattress on the office floor. I had no intention of leaving my apartment until the loneliness eventually ate me alive, however, I spent so much time in that room during the work week that it was actually making me more depressed by spending my weekend there. The place where I worked and banged my head against the walls because of all the stress was also the place where I slept now, so I didn't want to be in there longer than I had to. I finally decided that crying in my sister's arms would be less painful than crying on a dirty air mattress in a tiny room. I wanted to see her after her accident anyway, even though she wasn't seriously injured. I knew it had scared her, and I wanted to be there for her.

It wasn't ideal living off the few clothes and toiletries that I had managed to grab the night prior, but I heard Logan leave earlier in the morning, so I knew it was safe to go back into my actual bedroom. Eventually, I would probably have to invite Megan over to help move all my stuff into the office. I didn't want to constantly go back and forth between rooms. The office had a bathroom next door, but it didn't have the convenience of having it located in the same room, like the master. It was only a few steps away, but I already missed having an attached bathroom.

Everything about the breakup was hard. Living in separate rooms was difficult, knowing that we weren't together anymore was painful, and even getting ready for the day was an ordeal. I cried in the shower. I cried getting dressed. When I caught a glimpse of my heartbroken reflection in the mirror, I cried again. My eyes stayed in a puffy state, and I began to question how much water was left in my tear ducts. I surely had used all my tear supply already.

I tried to hide my face on my walk to my car, in case any neighbors saw a hysterical girl leaving an apartment in the morning. That definitely would not have been a good look. Fortunately, nobody noticed me, but honestly I wouldn't have been too mad if someone had. Living in grief and feeling the most alone I had ever felt in my entire life, someone actually seeing me and recognizing the sadness on my face would've made me feel less lonely. It would've made me feel loved and cared about, which was something I hadn't felt from someone outside of my family in a long time.

My mind was still trying to process the events from last night. It was hard for me to focus on anything other than Logan, so I wasn't surprised that my driving was more chaotic than usual. I already wasn't a great driver to begin with, but I was even worse that morning. In all honesty, I probably wasn't in the right headspace to drive over to my parents' house, but it was only fifteen minutes away. I had run a light that was more red than yellow, and I cut a few people off, but other than that, everything went pretty smoothly until I hit a curb about halfway into the drive—at least I thought it was a curb. For all I knew, it could've been a boulder by the way my car violently jerked when I hit it. I wasn't really paying attention to what I was doing until that moment because my car made a loud noise, and my low tire pressure light came on shortly after.

I groaned in annoyance as I pulled over into a nearby parking lot of a dentist office. I didn't think my day could get any worse, but of course during one of the hardest times of my life, I was having car problems. When my car was safely parked in the lot, I got out of my vehicle and saw that I had completely busted my front right tire. It was so flat that I couldn't even make it the rest of the way to my parents' house. There was a spare tire in my trunk, so I considered calling my dad, but he was almost as clueless about cars as I was. He would probably do more harm than good. I usually called Logan in a situation like this. He was really good with cars, and even if he didn't know how to change a tire, he would at least know who to ask for help. I even debated notifying the police because I was desperate to just have my car fixed, but I knew they would just laugh in my face. I didn't think a flat tire necessarily constituted an emergency in their book. Instead, I called the only other person who I thought would be able to help me.

***

Dalton arrived roughly fifteen minutes later. I was always happy when I was around him, but that day, it was the most excited I had ever been to see him. I probably caught him off guard with how hard I hugged him when he got out of his car, but I figured he could tell I was desperate for his help.

"I see you've got a flat tire there, Ms. Ross," Dalton commented while staring at the obliterated tire.

I didn't know why he always insisted on calling me by my last name. Sometimes it annoyed me, but there was nothing Dalton could do to annoy me in that moment. He could've called me his dog's name and I wouldn't have cared. I was just so relieved to have him there.

"Can you fix it?" I desperately asked.

"Well, I can't fix the tire," Dalton affirmed, "but I can put a new one on for you."

I didn't remember going in for a hug again, but my arms were wrapped around him just as tightly as they were when he first arrived.

"Thank you so much, Dalton," I muttered against his shirt. "You don't know how much I have been through."

"Well, it can't be any worse than what your tire has been through." Dalton chuckled.

"Ha, you have no idea," I exclaimed, as I let go of him so that he could fix my car.

I didn't know what he was doing or how he was doing it, but after about a half an hour, the damaged tire was being placed in my trunk while the new one took its place.

"You're still going to have to take it to a shop," he disclosed, "but this should hold you up until you're able to get to one."

"Thank you again, Dalton," I pleaded. "You are truly my hero."

He flashed his usual gorgeous smile. "Can't let a pretty girl like you drive on three wheels."

I blushed at his comment, but I was in no mood to flirt back. We both knew we had a relationship that went a little beyond just being friends.

There had always been some type of innocent banter when we talked to each other. We never actually came out and addressed it, but it was pretty obvious that there was some underlying flirting when we were together. I wasn't sure if it was because he was engaged or if it was because my heart was broken, but I just wasn't willing to flirt back at that time.

"Sorry you had to spend part of your Sunday changing a tire," I apologized. "I just didn't know who else to call."

"Is Logan working or something?" he questioned.

I stared at Dalton a little confused.

"He didn't tell you?" I asked.

"Tell me what?" Dalton responded.

I guess I didn't blame Logan for not wanting to tell people that we had broken up. I mean, it had only been less than twenty-four hours, and I hadn't told that very many people, either. I just assumed he would've told his best friend.

"Logan and I broke up," I managed to say before bursting into tears.

"Oh, Hailey," Dalton comforted as he pulled me toward him. "I'm so sorry."

I was crying into my ex-boyfriend's best friend's chest. It was more like his stomach because of how tall he was, but either way, it was the first time I had been comforted since the breakup.

"You're going to find your person," Dalton assured me while stroking my hair. "Everything will work out how it's supposed to. You're going to be okay."

I continued to soak his shirt with my tears, but he didn't seem to mind. I wanted to continue to be comforted by him, but I eventually released my arms from around him.

"I should probably let you go home now," I mumbled. "Don't want to waste any more of your weekend. Please don't tell Logan I told you about our breakup. I want him to tell you when he's ready." I wiped away the tears that were still streaming down my face.

"You're not wasting my weekend," Dalton asserted. "I'd spend all my weekends with you if I could. And don't worry, I'll make sure I act surprised."

I smiled a tiny grin. It wasn't much, but it was the first time I had shown any sign of happiness that day.

"Do you want to come with me to my parents' house, then?" I offered. "I'm sure they'd love to see you. My mom is making tacos."

I didn't know why I invited Dalton over, but he made me feel really safe and seen. I wasn't ready to go on with the rest of my day without his comforting presence.

"I wish I could, but Logan just invited me to go golfing with him," Dalton explained.

"Well, maybe next time." I smiled, but it was forced that time.

Dalton was always going to be Logan's best friend, therefore, he would always come before me. Sometimes, I would get lost in Dalton's sweet words and believe that I meant more to him than I actually did. A small part of me hoped he was going to immediately call off his engagement when I told him that I was single, but I figured that was just the pain talking. I already lost Logan, and firmly believed I was about to lose Dalton, too.

23

Logan

"Dude, you suck," Dalton commented as I hit another ball into the water. "Get your head out of your butt."

I dropped my head in shame and retrieved the last extra golf ball I had from my pocket. We were only on hole seven, and I had already lost five balls. Three of them splashed into the surrounding ponds, one landed in someone's backyard, and I had no idea where the other one went. It disappeared into a bunch of trees, and after ten minutes of trying to find it, I just gave up. At the rate I was going, I wouldn't be able to finish the entire eighteen holes without borrowing more balls from Dalton. The game was supposed to distract my mind from the disaster my life was becoming, but it only added to the chaos.

"Sorry, D. I'm just distracted," I noted as I lined up for another shot.

"I can see that," Dalton replied.

I placed my ball on the tee and used the last ounce of focus I had on making contact with it. Golfing wasn't my strongest sport, but the game usually came pretty easy to me. I tried to channel my natural skillset and golfing instincts, but so far, they hadn't worked out for me since I had already lost five balls. It was my mission to not make it six. Those little spheres were causing me a great deal of stress, and I was determined to finally aim one in the direction I actually wanted it to go. All of my concentration was focused on the ball. The sky could've turned purple, and I wouldn't have noticed.

"Any day now," Dalton chimed in.

"Just give me a second," I fired back.

I closed my eyes and gave myself a brief pep talk. I needed all the hype I could get.

"Why don't you give the ball a little kiss while you're at it," Dalton teased. "I'm sure it will listen if you give it a little love." Dalton chuckled at his own joke.

I rolled my eyes, but even his annoying comment wasn't going to distract me. The ball had gotten the best of me so far, but things were about to change. I pulled my club back without losing any focus, and kept my eyes fixated on my target. I swung my driver with all of my strength and the force almost made me lose my balance. I completed the entire motion without removing my eyes from the ball, which was disappointing when I saw it hadn't even left the tee after I had already swung. An object flew in the air, but it wasn't the golf ball—it was my club. My grip must've loosened under the force of my swing. I was so focused on the ball, I wasn't really paying attention to anything else, including how tight I was holding on.

"A swing and a miss!" Dalton cried out in laughter.

In a moment of frustration, I grabbed the ball off the tee and threw it toward the hole. I didn't care for the game anymore. My life was falling apart, and golf was just adding to it. Hailey and I were over, I probably wouldn't be able to work in real estate again, and it was a possibility that I would have to move in with my mom. Everything hit me all at once, and I just fell to the ground in complete frustration. I just sat on the course and let my face rest in my hands. The day couldn't have gotten any worse.

"Hey, man," Dalton muttered with sincerity. "Are you okay?"

When I first met Dalton, I had broken down a few times in front of him when I started really feeling the absence of my dad. Usually around the holidays, it would hit me the hardest. I would shut down and cry next to him, but that was years ago, and he hadn't seen me cry since. Dalton was my best friend, and I felt comfortable around him, but I was a grown man, and I didn't want to show any sign of weakness. My eyes were definitely starting to well up, but I kept my face buried in my hands until I was certain that I wasn't going to shed a tear.

"Hailey and I broke up," I managed to blurt out. Saying it out loud made it feel even more real.

"Oh, dude, I'm so sorry," Dalton responded as he took a seat on the grass next to me. "What happened?"

I was still on the brink of tears, so I kept my face hidden.

"I just couldn't take it anymore," I mumbled.

I didn't explain myself any further. Dalton knew how I had been feeling recently, so there was no need to elaborate.

"Well, I'm sure there's better for you out there," Dalton assured.

"I don't even want to think about that right now," I relayed.

I wasn't in the mood to envision my life without Hailey, let alone picture myself with another girl.

"I understand," Dalton assured, "but hopefully your next girl is better than you at golf so I can have some real competition." His side comments were always so unnecessary, but at least he got me to smile.

"You're so annoying," I jokingly let out. I finally removed my face from my hands and playfully punched him in the arm a few times.

"Hopefully she hits harder than you, too," Dalton uttered.

"Shut up, D," I exclaimed. "You know I'm stronger than you."

"Dude, you haven't even been to the gym in weeks," Dalton pointed out. "You're weak, bro."

"Who are you calling weak?" I taunted.

Dalton was a big guy, but his muscles were all for show. He didn't possess any kind of real strength.

"I could beat you in an arm-wrestling contest easily," I boasted.

"That's a long shot," Dalton returned.

"Bet," I noted.

Instead of sitting on the grass, I laid flat on my stomach with my elbow on the ground. There was only one way to settle this.

"Okay," Dalton began, "but just remember that you asked for it."

He mimicked my position, and we began arm wrestling on the grass of hole seven. He was stronger than I had remembered, but I was still confident that I was going to beat him.

"Um, excuse me?" an older lady standing over us exclaimed. "I'm trying to golf."

The strange woman couldn't have been any younger than sixty. Her wrinkly knees were staring back at Dalton and I, who were still on the ground arm wrestling. I felt bad that we were interrupting her golf game, and I debated getting out of her way, but Dalton wasn't going to stop until there was a clear winner.

"Just one second, ma'am," he announced. "We will be finished here shortly."

A second burst of strength forced my arm toward the direction of the ground, but I quickly recovered and regained my composure until we were back at a neutral position.

"Excuse me, I said I am trying to golf," the woman repeated with a little more anger.

"One more minute, ma'am, I promise," Dalton asserted as he tried to wrestle my arm to the ground.

The struggle continued as neither Dalton nor I had won yet. The lady grew increasingly frustrated with every second that passed by.

"If you don't move," she started, "I'll call the cops."

Her comment startled me, and I almost retracted my arm, but Dalton didn't seem alarmed at all.

"That's okay," Dalton answered. "I'm not afraid of a badge."

He may not have been scared of the cops, but I, on the other hand, was not trying to ruin my reputation. In the slim chance that I would be able to save my real estate career, I couldn't have an arrest record on file—that would certainly ruin me.

The lady returned to her golf cart while Dalton and I went back and forth. I debated giving up, considering we were in the middle of a golf course, but I was so close to winning. It would be the only victory I'd have all day.

I felt Dalton slightly weaken and figured that would be my chance to finally win. I used my last ounce of energy to forcibly push his hand closer and closer to the ground. There were only a few inches of space between his arm and the grass. I was on the brink of victory until suddenly a random puff of misty air was sprayed in my face. I assumed the sprinklers had probably gone off, until Dalton and I started choking. We both let go of each other's hand and started coughing hysterically.

"Next time, you boys should move the first time I ask so that I won't have to pepper spray you," the lady warned.

Half of me was disoriented, and the other half was trying to process the fact that an elderly woman just pepper sprayed us. I tried to see if Dalton was as confused as I was, but my eyes couldn't stop watering long enough to see. I tried to reach my arms out to feel for him, but I needed to constantly rub my eyes. I continued to walk in circles until I eventually ran into him.

"D," I called out in between choking fits, "we just got pepper sprayed."

"I know," Dalton hollered back, "that old hag got us!"

We continued to cough, trying to rid our systems of the toxicity.

"Old hag?" the lady repeated.

The next thing I heard was the sound of her pepper spray going off again.

"D, run!" I shouted. "She's gone rogue!"

I grabbed Dalton's arm, and we ran as fast as we could through the course. Neither of us had any concern for the golf clubs that we had left at the hole. Our first thought was just to get as far away from that lady as possible. We could go back for our stuff later, but in that moment, we just wanted to escape. Dalton and I continued to run frantically in random directions, not really sure of where we were going. My vision was slowly starting to return, but I still had no idea where I was running. We eventually stopped and took shelter behind some bushes. Our lungs were on fire from the cardio, and from the pepper spray. My eyes were burning, my legs were cramping, and I still had a nasty cough.

"You just had to call her an old hag, huh?" I mentioned while gasping for air.

"She deserved it," Dalton relayed. "She ruined our arm wrestling competition. I was about to beat you."

I laughed out loud at his delusional thinking.

"I almost had you pinned, D. You wouldn't have lasted a single second longer," I assured.

"Dude, I was literally about to end you," Dalton responded.

"You're insane," I answered back.

I leaned against the bush and continued to recover from our run. Dalton was also leaning against his own bush, but he suddenly switched positions and started lying flat on the ground.

"Round two?" Dalton proposed.

"You are not serious," I stated.

We had just escaped the wrath of an angry old woman, and all he wanted to do was arm wrestle again.

"I'm so serious," he disclosed. "Unless you're too scared because you know that I will beat you."

Dalton even finished his statement before I was also lying on the ground and grabbing his arm.

It was hard to focus. My eyes were still stinging from the pepper spray, so I couldn't see as clearly. I was really out of shape, so running only caused my lungs to beg for air. I had been sitting for a few minutes, yet I still hadn't fully recovered from running. My throat was on fire from coughing so much, and my arm was starting to catch a cramp. I could've easily just gone home, or at least returned to the hole to get my clubs, but instead I was arm wrestling my best friend behind the bushes of a golf course after getting chased with pepper spray by an elderly woman— it was the highlight of my entire weekend.

24

Hailey

"Hailey, can you pass the butter, please?" Megan asked, but I was so zoned out that I almost didn't even hear her.

My mind was focused on other things, so handing my sister something to top her potato with was the least of my concerns. I felt bad that I wasn't fully present during our family dinner, especially since Megan had just gone through a traumatic accident, but I just couldn't seem to get out of my depressed mood. My family knew the reasoning behind my absent-mindedness, considering I had to tell them we broke up when they asked why Logan hadn't come to the dinner. Megan already figured it out when I removed the photos of him off my social media, but she left it to me to break the news to our parents. My dad made Megan's favorite meal—steak with creamy peppercorn sauce, which was a dish I also enjoyed. Megan and I loved whenever our dad prepared it, but he usually reserved the delectable meat for special occasions. My sister going through a rough car accident was definitely reason enough for a steak dinner.

"Hailey!" Megan shouted.

She broke my trance. I left my thoughts and returned to the real world.

"The butter," Megan continued when I finally looked at her. "Can you give it to me, please?"

"Right," I stammered. "Of course."

The last thing I wanted was to draw any further attention to myself. I wanted all the attention to go to Megan and for everyone to ignore my sulky mood, but my sister shouting my name at the dinner table didn't leave me any room to hide—all eyes were on me.

"Thinking about how good the steak is?" my dad chimed in, trying to lighten the mood. "I sometimes just want to sit back and admire it too, but make sure you eat it before your sister steals it off your plate."

I looked at my dad and tried to force a smile in return, but even he knew my sadness wasn't going to be cured with a few jokes. I used to devour the steak he made within minutes, basically drinking the leftover peppercorn sauce after. Instead, it was staring back at me without one bite being taken out of it. It was a clear indication that I was in no mood for humor.

"So, Megan," my mom began in order to divert the attention away from me. "How does it feel to have completed your college applications?"

My parents redirected their focus to my little sister, which was a relief. I didn't feel like engaging in any more conversation. Honestly, I wouldn't have been mad if no one said another word to me the rest of the time I was there.

"It's definitely a relief," Megan answered, "but now all I can do is wait. I just really want to get into Princeton."

The thought of going to college was so thrilling to Megan. She lit up every time she talked about Princeton. I had never seen someone so ready to go to school and attend classes. It was unusual, but also refreshing at the same time. I remembered when I was that happy about life. Everything was just so great and wonderful. The world was mine. I just hoped Megan would never meet someone who would take that joy out of her like someone did to me.

"Well, I'm sure you will have fun and make lots of friends wherever you go," my mom assured.

She smiled at Megan with the utmost care in her eyes. Her youngest daughter was about to leave the house, and my parents would soon become empty nesters. I didn't think they were actually ready to not have any kids living at home.

"No boys allowed in your dorm, though," my dad advised in a typical fatherly manner.

"Oh my gosh, Dad," Megan groaned as she rolled her eyes. "Nobody said anything about boys."

Megan continued to roll her eyes while she took a few more bites of her potatoes. She had already scarfed down her steak a while ago.

"I know, I know. I'm just letting you know," my dad acknowledged. "Boys are just a distraction at that age. They don't know what they want."

"They never know what they want at any age," I grumbled under my breath.

It was only supposed to be for my ears, but by the way everyone looked at me, I had said it loud enough for the entire table to hear. I had done the very thing I didn't want to do the rest of the night, which was draw attention back on myself.

"Sometimes we grow up," my dad mentioned.

He grinned and tried to keep the conversation light, but we all knew there was nothing positive I had to say about men.

"Sometimes you grow up, and sometimes you waste seven years of a girl's life just to break up with her because you didn't feel like a priority in her life, when arguably she did ten times more for you than you ever did for her. And sometimes, you complain that your girlfriend doesn't support you, even though she basically let you live at her apartment for free while she cleaned up after you and you never even thanked her for it, but still found the time to switch careers. Oh, and sometimes, you leave the girl who was the best thing that ever happened to you, but you won't realize it until she's already gone."

I was met with silence and blank stares. Maybe I had gone a little too far and probably should've just kept my mouth shut, but it felt good to vent about it.

"So yes, Dad. Sometimes you do grow up," I added, "but sometimes you stay immature forever and decide it's easier to just break up with someone rather than actually nurture the relationship you're currently in."

When I finished my rant, I excused myself from the dinner table and went to my old bedroom. My mother had turned it into a place for storage, so there was random stuff everywhere, but it still had my bed. I jumped into it and buried my face into one of the pillows. I soaked one side of it before I finished crying, so I had to flip it over to the other side. Before I could drench the entire pillowcase in tears, I heard a knock at the door.

"Can I come in?" my mom uttered in a soft tone.

I didn't even have a chance to accept or deny her request before she let herself in. I was kind of glad she decided to take it upon herself and enter the room because I definitely would've told her no, but secretly would have wanted the comfort.

My face was still buried in the pillow, but I felt my mom sit on the bed. We sat in silence for a little bit while she stroked my hair. Even though she hadn't said anything yet, her presence made the emptiness inside me not feel as lonely. My mom was giving me a safe space to cry, so I took advantage of the moment and soaked two more pillows before any words were even exchanged.

"I can't believe this is my life," I cried out. "I didn't think we would ever break up."

I shifted positions and decided to weep in my mom's lap instead of a pillow.

"Oh, honey," my mom whispered. "I know it hurts now, but I promise you it will get better."

She continued to stroke my hair, which was comforting even though her words weren't. She could promise me anything she wanted, but she couldn't guarantee that things would get better. It felt more likely that I would feel that way forever than for things to magically change. They say time heals all, but time had never been screwed over by its boyfriend of seven years.

"This can't be life," I wailed. "We were supposed to be together forever."

"Sometimes life doesn't work out in the way we had planned," my mom relayed.

"That's not very encouraging," I responded in frustration. "What kind of advice is that?"

I was crying my eyes out over my failed relationship and all she could do was tell me that life wasn't fair. I liked it better when we weren't talking.

"Well, it's true," my mom insisted. "We often have this plan for our life, and it usually doesn't happen in the way that we had imagined, but sometimes it turns out even better."

"I don't know what could have been better than marrying the love of my life," I noted. "Relationships, love, dating, it is all so stupid. I don't even get the point of finding someone when all they will do is blindside you and break your heart in the end. I'm just going to be single forever."

Another stream fell from my eyes as even my anger came out in the form of tears. Every emotion that I was feeling didn't know how to behave except to show itself in the form crying.

"Honey, don't get so down," my mom remarked. "Take all the time you need to grieve, but you're not going to be single forever. You don't know what the future holds."

"Do you think we will get back together?" I blurted out. "Maybe if I continue to support his new career, then he will want me back."

I had a random burst of energy that I used to start brainstorming ideas on how I could win Logan back. If his biggest complaint was that I didn't make him feel important, I could dedicate my life to showing him how much he really did mean to me.

"Hailey, is that really what you want?" my mom asked.

"Of course it is!" I shouted without even giving it a second thought. "Are you and dad thinking of selling the house in the near future? We could give Logan his first sale!"

I had it all planned out. My parents would decide that they want to downsize since they won't have any more kids living there, and therefore, they would need to sell the house. Logan would be the real estate agent, and we would make sure that we gave him his first sale. He would have no other choice than to fall back in love with me and want to be with me forever.

"I'm sure the idea of being with Logan again sounds nice right now, but weren't there a lot of aspects of the relationship that bothered you?" my mom recollected.

"What are you talking about?" I responded.

Of course, Logan and I had our problems, but so did every relationship. I was sure there were things about my dad that she didn't like. I had told her about some recurring issues that we were experiencing, but nothing that justified me not wanting to get back with him.

"I know you haven't been very happy in the relationship recently," my mom reasoned. "I can recall a few times where you mentioned to me that you weren't sure if he was truly the one for you because you guys were starting to act more like roommates than a couple."

She had a point, but I still would've jumped at the opportunity to get back with Logan.

"And didn't you just admit at the table that you were paying all the bills and doing all the chores?" she added.

I knew my mom was right, but all those complaints I had about Logan seemed petty once we had broken up. I felt like I could've gone the rest of my life dealing with those issues if it meant I got to spend it with Logan.

"Yeah, but I could look past all that. I just want Logan ..." I remarked before tapping into my endless supply of tears for what seemed like the millionth time.

"Do you want Logan or do you just want to feel loved?" my mom questioned. "I think you are confusing comfort with love."

"What do you mean?" I answered back.

I didn't know where she was going with her line of questioning, but I thought she was drifting in the wrong direction.

"Well, it sounds like you weren't really in love with Logan anymore. He was just your comfort zone," my mom began. "You knew you deserved more than a guy who didn't recognize how much you did for him, but you stayed because it was easier to do that than to leave him. You were settling."

"Maybe, but it still doesn't excuse the fact that he just broke up with me out of nowhere," I griped.

"I know you hate Logan for breaking your heart, but I think you both were in the relationship a little longer than you should've been," she preached. "He just hit his breaking point before you did."

My mom continued to comfort me while I imagined what it would've been like if I had reached my breaking point before Logan had. Would I have actually broken up with him? If he had truly pushed me beyond my boundaries, would I have had the guts to end the relationship? It didn't take long for me to conclude that the answer would be, no. My limits were reached, my breaking point was hit, and I did nothing. I stayed in a relationship that wasn't serving me because I was afraid of being alone. Turns out, our fate was probably already set in stone from the beginning, and it would've hurt much less if I had just been honest with myself and left the relationship once it wasn't working out anymore. It probably would've been a lot less painful.

As much as I was absolutely dying inside, Logan did us both a favor. He had the confidence to break up with me while I was hiding behind my fears of loneliness. One day, I would thank him for having the guts to do something that I could never do. I would've let myself completely lose it before even considering breaking up, yet he was able to actually follow through with it. I truly believed that someday I would look back and be grateful that I wasn't with him anymore, however, that day was not coming anytime soon. For now, I would just continue to cry and hope that he would come running back to me. We all had our limits; he was just pushed to his before I was.

25

Logan

Word traveled fast, so I wasn't surprised when Skylar called me that following morning, asking about the disastrous showing I had. I didn't enjoy starting my Monday off having to relive all the mistakes I had made, but Skylar was surprisingly super patient and understanding when I told her what had happened. Apparently, what I did was a common mistake among new agents. She advised me to always visit the properties myself before I showed them, in which I agreed, but she didn't have much advice for confusing siblings as a couple and accusing one of them of being pregnant when she surely was not. We both just agreed not to comment on those types of things in the future. I'd never make that mistake again.

Skylar saw a lot of potential in me and wanted to help save my career. We both decided that I would have to start working with her more closely until I gained a better understanding of the business and developed more confidence. Our plan would entail me having to spend a lot more time learning from her, but it wasn't the worst thing in the world. Working kept my mind off Hailey, so I didn't mind having to throw myself further into my career. I was determined to make it in the real estate industry, and Skylar was super supportive. She was the only reason why I was able to show another home.

We had joined forces again at an open house. It was part of Skylar's master plan to get my career back on track. She wanted to take me under her wing and have me work alongside her. It was nice to get back in front of buyers again and have them see me in a more positive light.

"And over here you have the kitchen," I explained as we guided a few buyers throughout the home. "It has such great appliances."

I smiled as I gestured toward the kitchen. Skylar gave me a sly wink and gently squeezed my arm, so I figured I was doing a pretty good job.

"Yes, the kitchen is just under two hundred square feet with ten-foot ceilings," Skylar added. "It is super spacious and perfect for those who like open concepts, however, I'd argue that the best part of the kitchen is the self-cleaning, stainless steel, freestanding double oven."

The group huddled around the oven as if they hadn't seen one before in their lives. It was definitely an attractive appliance, but Skylar's introduction of it made it sound a lot cooler than it actually was. She truly had a gift of selling things and making them sound a lot more appealing.

"I'm not sure how often you all cook, but doesn't this oven just make you want to whip up a nice dinner?" Skylar remarked. "Imagine cooking a Thanksgiving meal in this kitchen and with this oven. You would be the envy of all your family members."

The group of potential buyers continued to gawk at the kitchen that Skylar was successfully hyping up. To be honest, it was an average kitchen at best, but even I would've bought it because of her incredible pitch. Needless to say, the guests were definitely more impressed with her level of detail in explaining the features of the house than mine, but working alongside her helped boost my confidence. It allowed me the chance to understand what facts I needed to learn about the homes and what questions buyers frequently asked. She also displayed poise and composure when honestly explaining when she didn't know an answer, which was rare.

I was in complete awe of her. Not only were her selling skills impressive, but her people skills were, too. Everyone that walked through the doors gave Skylar their contact information after the tour, whether they had intentions of buying the home or not. She was super likable and just an overall fun person to be around. It honestly had me wondering what Skylar would be like as a friend outside of work, or even a potential partner. I didn't plan on my brain going in that direction. I had no intentions of asking her out, especially after just getting out of a relationship, but I couldn't help my attraction toward her. We just vibed so well together. Her age didn't bother me at all because her face still looked young, and her body hadn't missed a beat. She was a catch.

"Thank you all for attending the open house," Skylar chirped to the group. "Feel free to continue to look around. Logan and I are here to answer any of the questions you might still have."

She ended her speech with a smile and dismissed the buyers to venture through the home on their own. The few people that did have questions made sure that they directed them to Skylar instead of me. A little line even formed in front of her, but everyone decided to wait for her rather than head over to me. I was a little disappointed, but I didn't blame them. I'd ask Skylar all my questions, too.

After a few more hours of touring groups around the home, the event started to wind down. It was crazy to think how little I knew about the house when I first started the day, because by the end, I could've repeated back every detail in a similar manner as Skylar. I had heard the same facts over and over again that I had them memorized. Being a real estate agent would be easy if I could continuously just show the same property, but unfortunately, it didn't work that way. That home was going to be sold, and I would have to remember a whole new set of facts for the next one, but it was still exciting. I was determined to learn as much as I could about the next one so that I could try to compete with Skylar's expertise.

"So what did you think of the event?" she asked when the last guest finally left.

We had been on our feet for almost five hours, so it was nice to take a seat on the couch and debrief on the day.

"Well, I'd say ending an open house with three offers would be considered a success," I answered.

I was jealous of how easy it was for her to receive a bunch of interested buyers, but one day that was going to be me.

"I definitely would call it a success," Skylar agreed as she raised her water bottle. "Cheers!"

I met her water bottle with mine. "What are we celebrating?" I inquired. "Getting offers is a normal occurrence for you." I chuckled as we drank our waters in a celebratory manner.

"To a successful event and a successful relationship," Skylar indicated.

"Successful relationship?" I repeated.

"A successful working relationship, I mean," she clarified. She blushed as she took another sip of her water to hide her emerging smile.

I didn't understand women that well, but if I wasn't mistaken, I would've assumed that Skylar was developing a little bit of a crush on me. She was always smiling at me, and often found small ways to touch me. Even seated on the couch, she had her hand on my thigh. The only reason I noticed all of that from her was because I was also developing a little crush on her. In the same way she found excuses to get close to me, I also did the same thing to her. I knew she was nine years older than me, but that didn't stop my feelings that were slowly growing for her.

"I love our working relationship, too," I noted. "I'm excited to see where it goes ... to see what it develops into." I threw some bait out there to see if Skylar would catch it. If my assumption was right and she was feeling me in the same way I was feeling her, she would react positively to my last comment.

"Me, too," Skylar agreed with a flirtatious grin. "I'm looking forward to spending more time together."

At that point, I was almost certain she saw me as more than just a coworker, but I needed to test her one more time. We were already sitting pretty close together on the couch, but I scooted even closer to her and invaded all of her personal space. There was nothing left between us but air and opportunity.

As expected, Skylar didn't move away from me at all. She seemed to enjoy my close proximity to her, and it appeared as though she was looking for a way to get even closer, but it wasn't possible without being completely on top of each other. Her body leaned into me slightly, giving me the final answer I needed to confirm my suspicions—she was into me.

Skylar didn't say anything, and she didn't have to. I saw the way her eyes were staring at my lips. She wanted me to kiss her ... badly. I found joy in tempting her by bringing my mouth even closer to hers without actually touching it. The way she groaned for me let me know that it was torturous for her. I kept teasing her. I was having fun with it, but at some point, it also became a form of torture for me, too. It was becoming increasingly harder to resist her lips. They were plump and pink, but more importantly, the way she bit the corners of them made it seem as though they were just begging for me. It was so hot. I eventually put an end to both of our misery and kissed her with so much force that she ended up on her back. I was on top of her, kissing her, continuously invading all areas of her mouth. The couch started as our makeout spot until we somehow ended up on the floor.

I didn't think we had plans of ever stopping, but of course the sound of my phone ringing abruptly ended our makeout session. It pained me to have to remove my mouth from hers, but my phone was blaring the special ringtone that I had especially reserved for my mom. If I didn't answer, she would've probably showed up to the house and found a more disruptive way to interrupt my time with Skylar.

"Hey, Mom, what's up?" I answered, slightly out of breath from giving Skylar all of my energy.

"What are you doing?" she asked forcefully. "The open house was over thirty minutes ago."

"I'm just finishing up a few things," I answered. "Something in the house caught my attention, so I got a little distracted." I gave Skylar a little wink which turned her face bright red.

"Are you still coming over for dinner?" she interrogated. "I already finished cooking because you said your event was over half an hour ago."

"Yes, Mom," I answered. "I'm on my way."

I looked over at Skylar. Her hair was a little messed up and her lips had gone from pink to red, but she was looking as beautiful as ever. I never thought I would ever feel sparks again, but Skylar showed me that there was a whole other level of love, care, and concern that I was missing out on. She was bringing out a side of me that I hadn't seen in a long time. In only a short amount of time, Skylar had proved to me that she was going to support me and be there for me no matter what. She met me when I was at a low point in my life, yet she still stuck around. I didn't know what I did to deserve her, but she was truly a blessing.

"Okay, I'll see you when you get here!" my mom exclaimed.

"Sounds good," I answered back.

I was about to hang up, but I needed to add one more thing before heading over to her house.

"And by the way, Mom," I continued on, "I'll be bringing a friend."

26

Hailey

The breakup turned me into a robot. I got so good at suppressing my emotions that I was starting to not be able to feel anything at all. I was becoming numb to life. It was either feel everything or feel nothing, and I decided that my emotions were overrated. I'd rather just go through life without having feelings there to cloud my judgment. Fortunately, being an accountant didn't require a hefty amount of sentiment. I used to dread Mondays, but now it meant that my job would provide a guaranteed time slot where my brain did not even have time to think about Logan because it was solely focused on numbers. The long hours and demanding schedule didn't seem so bad anymore, and I was actually kind of disappointed when it was time to log off. I usually counted down the seconds until I could close my laptop for the day, but I was at the apartment alone and didn't have anyone to share the night with. Logan had an open house, followed by a dinner at his mom's that I wasn't the least bit sad that I wasn't invited to. I used to find any excuse to not have to go, but since I was no longer his girlfriend and there was no reason for me to go, I didn't have to find a way out of it this time. I guess the breakup did have a silver lining. I definitely wasn't going to miss Ms. Tate at all.

Despite it still being early in the evening, as soon as I finished work I completed my nighttime routine and took my place in the comfort of my air mattress, which still remained in the office. I didn't have the energy to do anything else, and I was confident I wasn't going to have to get up unless it was to use the bathroom. My appetite still hadn't returned, so it took a lot of convincing just to get myself to consume some snacks. It made sense for me to get everything done that I needed in the bathroom before Logan returned home, so I wouldn't have to run into him. I wanted my presence to be felt as little as possible so that maybe he would miss me. I told myself that when Logan eventually returned home from dinner with his mom, I would stay tucked away in my room and not show my face unless he actually wanted to see me. However, I did purposely skip flossing for the night, just in case I needed to give myself an excuse to go back into the master bathroom and see him. I shouldn't have been giving myself reasons to see my ex-boyfriend, but it was really hard to let him go. It was probably time to have a discussion about our living situation, but I wasn't ready to have that conversation. I still wanted to see him every day, even if it was just for a few seconds in passing. I guess I wasn't as strong as I thought I was.

On the other hand, Logan seemed to be handling the breakup a lot better than I was. I didn't get the sense at all that he was devastated by our recent split. In fact, he seemed to be doing better than he was before. Maybe all these years I had been holding him back from the life he really wanted to live. He seemed happy, even relieved, that he was single and not having to constantly think about me and my feelings anymore. His work definitely kept him busy, so he probably didn't even have time to grieve. Logan was out there following his dreams while I was mourning the end of our relationship.

I stayed wrapped up in my blankets, like a depressed cocoon, waiting to fall asleep so that I could just get on with the next day and start another work shift. I tried to close my eyes and hope that when I opened them it would be Tuesday, but it was still light outside and my body knew that it was far from its usual bedtime. I tried counting the cracks in the ceiling and watching videos on my phone, but nothing seemed to work. I was still fully awake, and the pain in my heart was continuously nagging at me. I was able to push down some of my emotions, but the hurt never went away. Crying was the only thing that made me feel a little bit better, so I tried to let myself shed a few tears. My eyes remained dry though, as it was hard for me to turn off the numbness that I had already trained my mind to stay accustomed to. I would just have to stay a robot for the rest of the night.

There were still plenty of hours remaining in the day, and I was still wallowing in my heartache, so I tried to shift my mindset and think about the positives. I tried to imagine the happiness I would feel when I would finally find the person I was meant to be with, but it was hard to get myself to think about letting anyone close to me again. It would take a lot of time and trust to let a guy know me as well as Logan had. I didn't have the energy to date again and explain to someone what my favorite color was or how many siblings I had, let alone give my heart to someone or share an apartment with.

I'd been spared from entering the dating pool for seven years, and although I wasn't single during that time, I saw what the dating world was like and I wasn't excited for that to be my new reality. Hopefully, I would get lucky and my next boyfriend would just fall into my lap. Maybe I wouldn't have to go out with a single guy and my soulmate would just show up at my door. That would be the greatest gift of all because I've seen how modern dating works, and it was one of my biggest nightmares. Nobody was looking for anything serious, and standards were at rock bottom. Worst of all, it seemed that all the good guys were already taken. At my age, it felt as though everyone was either in a long-term relationship, married, or engaged. Girls were smart and snatched up all the good guys before anyone else had a chance to experience them. There are plenty of fish in the sea, but I was just a bottom-feeder in an ocean full of coupled-up sea creatures, hoping that someone's leftovers would seemingly fall through the cracks and end up in my presence. I didn't want to settle, but I wanted to be realistic about my expectations.

Thinking about dating again overwhelmed me and I quickly ruled out the chance of ever finding love again, concluding that there was nobody left in the world for me. I decided to try and refocus my thoughts on how I would accept my fate of being single forever. I didn't want to come to terms with the fact that I wouldn't have a wedding day or have someone to start a family with, but not everyone was lucky enough to find their person. There were plenty of people that never got to grow old with someone or meet their match. I just needed to realize that I was one of those people. Maybe I'd write a book one day or be a famous speaker spreading the word on how to be alone. I'd imagine it would be quite popular. Or, I could spend my days traveling around the world and claiming that settling down with a man would ruin my constant adventures. After my lease, I could rent a place in a different country each month. I would surely have to downsize and get rid of most of my stuff, but at least I would be on an endless vacation.

If I didn't find love again and if I got tired of traveling, my third option could be getting back together with Logan. Although a long shot, I couldn't rule it out. He certainly wouldn't find anyone as good as me, and it wouldn't be that hard to believe that he would eventually come crawling back to me. It may take a few years, but I had heard plenty of stories of couples reuniting after some time apart and making it work. Since option three was definitely a high probability, I could not ignore it.

After successfully only passing by an hour of time thinking about my future and not getting anywhere closer toward exhaustion, I decided to turn to the one thing that had all the answers to every problem—the internet. I did a quick search for ways on how to get over a heartbreak; the results were disappointing to say the least. The answer that popped up the most was encouraging the brokenhearted to get with someone else, but after dismissing that terrible advice, the answers didn't get much better. Most involved picking up a hobby such as cooking, hiking, or reading, but whoever came up with those ideas must not have had my demanding work schedule. Other responses included partaking in relaxing activities such as spending the day at the beach, taking a vacation, or going to a spa. Clearly, those suggestions were merely just attempts to get me to spend my hard-earned money on temporary happiness. I was looking for an immediate solution with long-term results.

I scrolled through several more websites, coming up empty with no real resolutions. I was desperate to at least try something, so I opted for the recommendation that almost every article proclaimed to work—journaling. It sounded ridiculous in my head. I couldn't envision how putting my depressing feelings into words on a piece of paper would help, but I figured it must have some benefit as it was constantly listed. Since my new bedroom also doubled as my office, it didn't take me long to find a blank notebook and writing utensil. I flipped to the first available page and put my pen to the paper. I waited for any type of thought or feeling to transfer from my brain to my hand, but I came up with nothing. I stared at the empty page a little bit longer, hoping that words would magically appear, but unfortunately, the paper stayed empty.

Journaling proved to be a lot harder than the internet had made it out to be. Writing my thoughts and feelings down in a tiny notebook sounded a lot easier than it actually was. I didn't know where to start or what to write, so I just jotted down the first thing that came to mind:

Dear Journal,

Logan and I broke up ...

I reread my first note and stared back at it, disappointed that I hadn't been able to come up with some elaborate sentence. I wasn't sure if I was doing the whole journaling thing correctly, but it was the first thing that I could think of. Well, it was the only thing I thought of. My total being was still consumed by the fact that I was no longer with Logan. I felt stupid that I tried to make myself feel better by using a sheet of paper and a cheap pen. Surely, it would take a lot more than writing to heal the pain I was feeling. A simple internet search was not going to solve my problems, but I decided to keep writing anyway. It may not make things better, but it certainly couldn't damage me any further. I was already at one of the lowest points in my life, therefore, I picked the pen back up and finished my initial entry:

Dear Journal,
Logan and I broke up ... and I want him back.

27

Logan

"What if she doesn't like me?" Skylar whispered on the walk up to my mom's front door. "What if she thinks I'm weird?"

She continued to think of every worst-case scenario as we made our way closer to the house.

"Don't worry," I muttered, comforting Skylar, "she'll love you."

I grabbed her hand and gave her a quick peck on the cheek before coming into view of my mom, who was standing on the porch waiting for me as usual.

Skylar and I drove separately to the open house, so we took our own cars to my mom's. It would've been better if we drove together so that I could've given Skylar the rundown of my mom before having to meet her, but we didn't want to leave her car stranded at the house, even though I would've been more than willing to drive her back afterward. Instead, she was going in blind to meet my mom for the first time. However, I wasn't worried at all. If anyone could make a great first impression, it was Skylar.

"Hey, Mom," I greeted as I gave her a hug. I could tell by her expression that she was a little irritated with my tardiness, but the sight of Skylar seemed to erase all her concerns.

"Hello, son," she returned, quickly releasing me from the hug in order to get a better look at my guest, "and who is this?" My mom smiled as she shook hands with my newest love interest.

"I'm Skylar Williams. I work with Logan," Skylar answered. "It's a pleasure to meet you. I've heard such great things about you."

My mom seemed pleased with her introduction, but appeared to be more thrilled at the idea that I had spoken to Skylar about her.

"Oh, and what have you heard?" my mom gushed at the potential of hearing a compliment.

"Just that you are the greatest mom in the world," Skylar said with a smile. "You raised a great son, Ms. Tate."

I definitely didn't remember bragging about my mom's parenting skills, but I was happy that she had said exactly what my mom wanted to hear.

"Oh, please," my mom uttered, "call me Alice."

I almost gasped at her response. I couldn't remember the last time my mom had let someone call her by her first name. She definitely had never let Hailey do that. Everyone knew to call her by her last name, even though it technically was my father's last name. My mom never went back to her maiden name, although she'd been divorced for years. I believed it was her final way of holding on to that relationship. Surprisingly enough, she allowed Skylar to call her Alice. It probably had something to do with her age. Skylar was in between my age and my mom's, so she could relate to us both pretty easily. She carried herself maturely, but still gave off a young presence. Her brain acted in its thirties, but her body still presented as if it were in its twenties.

"Well, Alice," Skylar continued on, "I can't wait to indulge in the delightful dinner that you prepared. Logan says you are quite the chef."

The three of us walked into the kitchen where we were met with the delicious smell of lasagna. Skylar continued to boost my mom's ego while my mom served us each a plate. I got to enjoy the majority of my dinner in peace while the women talked amongst themselves. It mostly consisted of Skylar handing out compliments, but my mom was loving every second of it.

"So how did the open house go, Logan?" Mom directed at me once she was finally ready to take a break from the endless praises.

"It was great," I answered. "Skylar got three offers."

"We got three offers," she corrected. "I couldn't have done it without you."

I slightly smiled at her comment. It was definitely all of Skylar's hard work that got her the offers, but I was happy that she was passing along some of the credit.

"My son is amazing, isn't he?" my mom chimed in.

"He's the best," Skylar agreed.

My mom continued to revel in the recognition of my real estate skills.

"Alice, do you mind pointing me to the nearest restroom?" Skylar asked.

"First door on your left," my mom directed, pointing in the vicinity of the closest bathroom.

She removed herself from the kitchen table. "I'll just be a moment," Skylar noted, dismissing herself down the hall.

Once she disappeared out of sight, my mom wasted no time in blurting out the question that had been on her mind all evening. "So, is she your new girlfriend?" she asked.

"Mom, relax," I returned, collecting the dirty plates from the table and placing them in the sink. I wanted to be a good son and do the dishes after she had just cooked an elaborate meal, but I also knew this conversation was coming and wanted to have it while my back was facing her. I didn't want her to see how bright my face would get at the mention of our developing relationship, or how sad my expression would be at the sound of my ex's name.

"What about Hailey?" she added. "Did you guys break up?"

I wasn't sure if I would be able to answer her without choking up, so I just nodded my head slightly and continued to scrub the leftover lasagna off the plates.

"Oh, honey, I'm so sorry," my mom muttered. "I know you really liked her, but I think it was for the best. She was holding you back."

Hailey definitely had her unsupportive moments, but I wouldn't go as far as to say that she was holding back my life. My mom didn't know what she was talking about. She didn't know Hailey like I did, but I didn't have the energy to defend her. I would've probably ended up breaking down if I began to talk about her, anyway. It was hard enough to try and get the thought of her out of my mind. Work and Skylar were a great distraction. As long as my head was focused on something other than my failed relationship, then I was fine. I just needed to stay busy.

"I'll be fine," I responded, hoping Skylar wouldn't return from the bathroom in the middle of a conversation about my previous girlfriend.

"You will be more than fine, son," my mom affirmed. "Skylar is quite the beauty, and she has the brains to back it up, too."

"Yeah, she's pretty great," I added, the happiness slowly starting to return now that the conversation was about Skylar. "She's going to help me sell my first house."

"How old is she?" my mom boldly returned.

"Only thirty-two," I replied as nonchalantly as I could. I was hoping that if I sounded chill about her age, then my mom would, too. Nine years was a pretty significant gap, but it didn't bother me, and I didn't want it to be the only thing my mom focused on.

"Well, she seems lovely," my mom relayed. "As long as you're happy, then I'm happy."

I smiled, as that was her way of giving her blessing.

"Thanks, Mom," I exclaimed just as Skylar returned from the bathroom.

"What did I miss?" Skylar said as she took her seat back at the kitchen table.

"Nothing," I explained with a smile. "Nothing at all."

I rejoined my mom and Skylar at the kitchen table after completing the dishes. They were already in the middle of their own conversation once I sat back down, so I just pulled out my phone and started checking my work emails until they began talking about something that was worth eavesdropping on.

"So, do you want children one day?" my mom asked without any boundaries of knowing what questions were too personal to ask the first time a girl comes over.

"Yes, hopefully soon," Skylar replied honestly. "That's actually one of the reasons why my ex-husband and I divorced, well, other than the constant cheating. He didn't want kids, but I did. I thought marriage would've changed his mind, but it didn't."

"You've been married before?" my mom uttered while she shot me a look out of the side of her eye. I was able to get my mom to look past her age, but I wasn't sure I would be able to get her to overlook Skylar's previous relationship.

"It only lasted a year," Skylar mentioned. "It was an ugly divorce. He had multiple girlfriends while being married to me, but of course the media only focused on our financial issues."

"Financial issues?" my mom repeated back.

Usually my mom's nosiness was extremely annoying, but I was also curious about the details of Skylar's marriage. The press definitely didn't paint a pretty picture of it.

"Well, once I found out our commitment to each other meant nothing to him, I drained our bank accounts so that he was left with nothing."

"Nothing?" my mom and I said at the same time.

"Absolutely nothing," Skylar reiterated with a sly smirk. "I had some houses that I knew I was about to sell though. The commission was enough to get me back on my feet. I just had to wait until the divorce was final so that I wouldn't have to split the profits with him."

Skylar seemed pleased with her actions, but it definitely rubbed my mom and I the wrong way. I never knew she was capable of such crazy actions, but I quickly brushed it to the side. I couldn't lose one of the only things in my life that was bringing me happiness.

"That's so cool that you are able to sell houses that fast," I interjected, diverting the conversation away from her previous marriage.

"Just trying to be able to provide for my future kids," she affirmed.

I was hoping my mom would see that everything Skylar did had good intentions behind it. She just wanted to create a better life for her future family.

"And how quickly, exactly, do you want kids?" my mom asked, clearly indicating that she knew Skylar was older than me and most likely on a different timeline than I was. I wanted children of my own one day, but wanted to be financially stable first. Ideally, I'd like to wait at least five or six years.

"Hmm ..." Skylar took a moment to think about her answer. I didn't blame her. I'd want a few minutes to think over my answer if my future partner's mom was asking intrusive questions about kids. "Probably within the next year or two."

Skylar smiled at me, and I tried to return one back to her, but the panic in my face prevented me from showing any hint of a smile.

"Wow, that's really fast," my mom commented, reading the horror all over my face.

"I know what I want," Skylar relayed proudly.

"Well we probably should head out now," I quickly inserted. "Skylar and I have a lot of work to do tomorrow."

I got up from the table and Skylar followed suit. It was an abrupt ending to the night, but my mom had learned enough about her for the time being.

"Thank you again, Alice, for the lovely dinner," Skylar said, hugging my mom and then accompanying me on the walk to the front door. "I hope to see you again soon."

"It was great meeting you, Skylar," my mom exclaimed. "Have a great day of work tomorrow."

I kissed my mom on the cheek goodbye. She smiled, but behind her eyes I could tell that she just wanted to make sure that I knew what I was getting myself into. Skylar had some flaws, but she saved me from heartache, and that meant more than a rocky past and a rushed timeline.

"I'll come by again soon," I told my mom. "Love you."

"I love you, too, sweetie."

I closed the front door behind Skylar and I, and walked her back to her car.

"Your mom is wonderful," Skylar began. "I think she likes me."

"She definitely likes you," I assured.

I grabbed her hand and held it the rest of the way to her car. There may have been a few things that Skylar and I would disagree on, but it felt nice being with her. She made me feel important, which was something I had been craving from Hailey for a while.

When we finally reached her car, I slowly removed my hand from her grip and opened her car door for her.

"Thank you for coming over," I stated. "I'm glad you got to meet my mom."

"It was such a pleasure," Skylar voiced. She threw her purse into the car before turning to face me. "Meet me at my house tomorrow?" she offered. "I can text you the address. I figured it would be better to work from my place instead of a loud coffee shop."

"Works for me," I noted.

"Great." Skylar smirked. "I'll see you tomorrow."

I stared into her eyes a few more seconds before eventually pulling her in for a goodnight kiss. Her lips fit perfectly against mine.

Skylar came into my life at the perfect time. The kiss was only a small act of gratitude for standing by my side. I didn't know how I would ever make it up to her for distracting me from the breakup with Hailey. I truly could not have gotten through it without her.

28

Hailey

Logan came home pretty late from his mom's house, but I was still awake when I heard the front door close and his footsteps walk past the office door to head straight to the main bedroom. I used to hate how thin the walls were, but that night I was grateful to hear every sound coming from the other side. Our lives used to be so intertwined, and I wasn't prepared to be so separated from him, but listening to Logan turn on the shower made it feel as though we were somewhat close again. I could hear the water so clearly that it felt like I was in the same room as him. I closed my eyes and tried to imagine myself waiting for him to come to bed, like old times. I reminisced on the nights where we would lay awake and just spend hours talking about our day. We used to be so infatuated with each other that a discussion about mundane tasks would keep us up all night. Laughter always filled the room, and I never wanted to put an end to the fun by falling asleep. Logan knew this and would sometimes rub my back until exhaustion eventually caught up to me. He was truly a nice guy and a great boyfriend.

I figured part of my heart withered away and died when we broke up. The amount of happiness that I felt during our relationship didn't seem possible again. Logan gave me some of the best moments of my life, and I wouldn't be able to replicate that feeling on my own. I wasn't sure how I was going to move on from the relationship, but I knew I wouldn't be able to forget all the memories we had made. It would take a long time for me to get over the fact that the love of my life was gone. I was going to be experiencing an unbearable amount of pain for an amount of time that nobody knew the answer to. I loved timelines because it gave an approximate end date to something. For example, I knew Logan's showers usually lasted ten minutes, which was how long I had left to continue to imagine that everything was normal. I knew the commercials that interrupted my shows continued for about three minutes before the regular program re-turned. It was enough time to get a quick snack and run to the re-stroom before I missed anything. Approximate timelines were essen-tial, and all I wanted was for someone to tell me how long the healing process would take. If I knew how long I would have to endure the pain, maybe it would make it easier because at least I would know that the feeling wouldn't last forever because it felt like my heart was incapable of being fully fixed.

I laid still on the mattress, until just as expected, in roughly ten minutes, the water ceased and I heard the shower curtains pull back. Logan had finished in the bathroom, which meant my blissful fantasy did, too. I wanted nothing more than to feel even a fraction of the happiness that I had when everything between Logan and I was great, so I decided it would be a good time to suddenly remember to floss.

The air mattress flopped as I got up and headed for the door. I entered the dark hallway, following the light seeping under the master bedroom door. Even though it was my apartment, I gently knocked. I still wanted Logan to have his right to privacy. He must've still been in the bathroom though because he didn't answer. Therefore, I carefully creaked open the door and tiptoed into the room.

"Hailey?" Logan exclaimed when he saw me enter the bathroom. "Did you forget something?" He was putting on lotion when he no-ticed me, briefly stopping when I appeared into sight.

"Yeah, just forgot to floss," I muttered quietly, hoping that it would sound like a legitimate excuse.

Logan opened one of the drawers and grabbed the floss. He broke off a piece and handed it to me.

"Thanks," I whispered as I found some mirror space and began the final step of my dental routine.

I would only be able to floss for a few minutes before it would've been too obvious that I was only in the bathroom so that I could be in his presence. I had to come up with a longer reason to be there

"How was your mom's?" I asked, reaching for the lotion. Colorado was unusually dry, so I figured hydrating my skin was also a legitimate reason to stay in the bathroom for a little while longer.

"Good," Logan answered nonchalantly. "She made lasagna."

"Oh, I always hated her lasagna," I commented, quickly pausing after realizing I just insulted his mother's cooking. I covered my mouth in embarrassment, and there was a moment of silence as the words I just muttered were registering in Logan's brain.

"It's okay," he finally responded, "so do I."

We both started laughing. Her cooking was never that good, but I never felt like I could say anything because it was my boyfriend's mom. Since we were no longer dating, I figured I could actually say the truth. It felt good to admit that her skills in the kitchen needed work, but it felt even better that Logan agreed and we could laugh about it.

"I better get used to it though," Logan began. "I'll probably move in with her soon so that you can have your space back."

My stomach dropped at the idea of him moving out. I never thought I'd be the girl who still lived with her ex, but because of our busy schedules, sometimes these late nights were the only times I got to see him. If he moved out, I didn't know when our paths would cross again, and I still wasn't ready to completely let him go. Breaking up was enough, not seeing each other anymore was too much to handle on top of that.

"Why don't you just get your own place?" I suggested, knowing Logan couldn't afford it. I just wanted him to review all his options before ultimately deciding that nothing would be better than just staying at my apartment.

"I need to get on track with my real estate career before doing that," Logan admitted. "Staying at my mom's will allow me to save money until I am ready to get a place of my own, even if it means having to buy all of my meals because my mom can't cook."

I chuckled again at Logan's openness about his mom's poor cooking abilities.

"Why don't you just stay here until you sell your first house, then?" I offered. On the outside I was calm, but on the inside, I was screaming in my head for him to not move out yet.

"Are you sure?" Logan questioned. "I'm not sure how long that will take."

"Well, are you still working with that agent that's supposed to be mentoring you?" I inquired. "What was her name again? Taylor?"

"Skylar," Logan returned.

"Right, Skylar," I noted. "Isn't she going to help?'

On one hand, I was hopeful that the Skylar girl would help Logan complete his first sale. It'd been on his mind for a while, and he's been working hard toward it. He deserved it, and she seemed to be very experienced.

However, another part of me was hoping that his streak of not being able to sell anything would last a little longer so that he wouldn't have a reason to leave.

"Yeah, she's helping," Logan stated, "but I'm still not sure how long it will take me to sell a home. I just don't want to crowd your space for too long."

"You're not crowding my space," I replied. "I don't mind having you here."

"Oh my gosh. Thank you so much, Hailey." Logan breathed a huge sigh of relief. It seemed as though his living situation was a stressor that was finally alleviated by the conversation. He was unaware of the fact that I wanted him at the apartment probably more than he wanted to remain there. Logan would get to continue to live at an apartment rent-free, and I would get to still be around him for a little while longer. It was a win-win situation.

"Take all the time you need," I added politely.

Logan pulled me in for a hug, thanking me for allowing him to live with me. At first, it was a gentle squeeze and felt super friendly, but after some time, it crossed my mind that it might mean a little more. It appeared that neither of us wanted to let go. We just stood in the middle of the bathroom, hugging each other.

"Hailey ..." he eventually whispered. "Thank you so much."

I finally released him from the hug and saw the genuine expression on his face. "No matter what, dating or not, I'm still going to be there for you," I calmly said. "I still have a lot of love for you, and I always will."

"I'll always have love for you, too," Logan answered back.

We stared into each other's eyes, and it was obvious that there still were a lot of feelings between us. Just because our title had changed, didn't mean that our love for each other had. Logan wasn't my boyfriend anymore, but he was still my person.

"I hate breakups," I whispered to him.

"Me, too," Logan agreed.

My heart was starting to ache even more.

"Can we just have one night of normalcy?" I pleaded. "One night where it doesn't feel like we are broken up?"

Logan studied my face, contemplating my question until finally pulling me in for a kiss. His lips felt like home. We kissed with more passion than we had in years, and in that moment, I knew Logan was mine. He would always be mine.

He slowly pulled away, smiling before eventually leaving the bathroom. I stood there, alone, until he turned around when he noticed I hadn't followed him. "Coming to bed?" he cheerfully asked.

The pieces of my heart that had been shattered and broken magically came together. The pain that had been weighing me down was suddenly lifted. I felt like an even better version of myself than I was before we broke up.

"I'm right behind you," I chanted, smiling from ear to ear.

All the hurt that was building inside me would have to wait, because for the night, Logan and I were not broken up. For just the night, we were together again.

29

Logan

"Ready to get to work?" Skylar playfully greeted me when she let me into her home. "We've got a lot of properties to scour through."

Skylar lived in a beautiful neighborhood on the more affluent side of town. It had modern finishes and windows that started from the floor and reached the ceiling. The wooden floorboards looked like they were imported from a foreign country and installed with the utmost precision. All the appliances appeared to be brand new, and the furniture seemed as if it hadn't been touched. The couch that she led me to didn't even look like it had been sat on before. The flat screen television that was mounted on the wall was almost too large for the living room space, and the kitchen that the open concept seamlessly transitioned into was straight out of a magazine.

"Do you like my place?" Skylar asked. "My ex-husband let me have it in the divorce. He claimed that he couldn't bear to live in the house that we created memories in, but I think there's plenty of room for more memories to be made."

She gave me a sly wink and a quick peck on the lips.

"It's beautiful." I smiled, returning the favor by planting a few of my own kisses onto her soft mouth.

I didn't know why, but I felt guilty kissing Skylar after having just made out with Hailey the other night. I didn't owe anyone anything, as I was a single man, but it didn't feel good knowing that the taste of two girls was on my tongue.

Hailey definitely caught me at a weak moment. Last night was just a sign that I still had love for her, but it did not mean that I wanted to get back together. I hoped she understood that. We were just in the moment and she was throwing herself at me. There was no way she actually expected me to resist her. Hailey knew what she was doing. I'd been constantly asking for intimacy throughout our entire relationship, and once we had broken up, she decided to actually give it to me. It was too late now, but I was just a man. If a beautiful girl, ex-girlfriend or not, wanted to come to bed with me, I wasn't going to say no. I just really hoped Hailey understood that and didn't get her hopes up or anything. Skylar was my focus now. Hailey and I were done.

"I was thinking we could start by finding a home for the Martins," Skylar began.

"Is that the family that came through the last open house?" I confirmed. "With the twin boys?"

Skylar smiled at my recollection. "That's exactly them," she praised. "They are looking for a three-bedroom home, or four, if we can squeeze it into their budget."

I opened my laptop and navigated to a site that was specifically reserved for agents. It listed every home for sale. I began to filter the list for the parameters of the Martins' request. "And what's their budget?" I asked.

"Unlimited," Skylar stated.

"Unlimited?" I shouted. I started salivating over the potential sale. The commission on that type of transaction could allow me to get a place of my own if the price of the home was high enough.

"Well, they said five hundred thousand," Skylar corrected, "but in this business, you need to know that every client is going tell you a lower amount than they can actually afford. I bet that if we show them a house that they absolutely love, even if it is out of their price range, they will still buy it."

I questioned her tactic for a minute before eventually speaking up. "But what if half a million dollars is truly what the Martins are able to spend?" I countered.

Skylar had definitely been in the real estate industry longer than I had been, but something didn't seem right about disregarding the client's budget. I didn't think showing a property slightly outside of their price limit was all that bad, but viewing their budget as unlimited rubbed me the wrong way.

"Logan, you have so much to learn," Skylar pointed out. "You know more than the client. They don't truly know what they want. It's our job to show them what they actually need."

"I'm not following," I relayed. "So, you are going to convince the Martins to buy a house outside of their budget?"

Skylar shook her head frantically. "No, Logan. I am going to give the Martin family the home that they actually need but didn't realize they needed," she answered.

I didn't really understand how pushing them to purchase a property that they couldn't afford was in their best interest, but I trusted Skylar. She obviously knew what she was doing. I quickly let go of my apprehensions, and removed any price filter from the website. I began to look for homes that fit the Martins' description, leaning toward listings with an extra bedroom. Despite Skylar's explanation of her tactic, I still stayed around five hundred thousand dollars. There were plenty of properties even below their budget that were worth showing them.

"What about this one?" I offered my laptop to Skylar so that she could see the home I had selected.

"Looks good, Logan," Skylar commented, "but what do you think about this one?"

She handed me her laptop which pictured a property that looked almost identical to the one I had shown her, but with a heftier price tag.

"Seems like I'm on the right track," I said. "We chose similar houses."

Both listings would be a good option for the family, but considering the one I landed on was under budget, I figured mine was worth showing more than Skylar's.

"Should I save the home I found for the Martins?" I retorted.

Skylar let out a tiny giggle. "You mean the home I found?" she noted. "You are definitely starting to get it, Logan, but the house I showed you has a fence around the backyard. Perfect for the twins."

"True," I agreed, "but the one I showed you is pretty similar for almost two hundred thousand dollars less. The Martins can put in their own fence, and it would still cost less than the other home."

Skylar and I exchanged laptops. Once she was in possession of her own again, I saw her write down the address of the home she chose. She didn't even consider the other option. My face formed a confused expression as she finished writing down the details of the more expensive choice.

"I may have failed to mention that I am willing to give you twenty percent of the commission that I earn from each sale," she casually stated.

I still felt bad that we had passed up a perfectly good listing in order to propose a home that was out of budget to the Martins, but I didn't feel as bad when I learned that I would be receiving a payout, even though it was Skylar's client. It was important to keep the client's best interest at heart, but I also had my own interests, and getting a place of my own was my main motivation.

"On second thought, I think they would like the property you chose better," I relayed.

"I thought so." Skylar smirked. "And with how good you look in a suit, anyone would want to buy a home from you."

She put her laptop on the coffee table and snatched mine out of my hands, placing it next to hers. I was confused as to what she was doing until she climbed on top of me, straddling my lap. Work time was over. Skylar pulled my face toward hers and started running her warm tongue around the inside of my mouth. The way she took control was so hot. I should've gone for older women from the start.

"Have I ever told you that you are the sexiest real estate agent in the entire business?" she mumbled as she began unbuttoning my shirt.

I happily watched her work her way down my chest, each button coming off with more and more eagerness.

"In the entire business?" I repeated. "I think that deserves more than twenty percent of your earnings, then." I smiled and brought her mouth back onto mine.

My chest was exposed—something that Hailey had conditioned me to be ashamed of—but Skylar made me feel proud of it. Ever since I had stopped going to the gym, my body wasn't the same as it used to be. I knew it made Hailey less attracted to me which was why she probably stopped wanting to be intimate with me. She had a thing for abs, and I hadn't had those in a long time. Too bad Hailey couldn't get past my body because now it was being kissed on by a new girl.

"Maybe I'll give you thirty percent," she teased.

"Maybe?" I grinned. "What does the sexiest real estate agent in the business have to do for the extra ten percent?"

Skylar thought about it a little bit before finally answering. "Stay the night," she encouraged.

She kissed my neck a few times, urging me to choose to stay over. I thought about how Hailey would feel if I didn't come home that night, but quickly remembered that I was single and didn't have to think about her feelings anymore. I didn't know what explanation I would give her when I would return the following morning, but that was something I could think about at a later point in time.

"I guess we are having a sleep over then," I noted.

I picked Skylar up and carried her up the stairs while she guided me to her bedroom. She squealed in excitement the entire time. Once in her room, I threw her onto the bed and removed the rest of my shirt that she had already unbuttoned. She looked at me in awe, admiring my body. I brought myself closer to the bed, hovering over her and kissing her. Skylar continued to giggle from underneath me. Each kiss was more passionate than the last, and I was super excited to see how the night with her would go. From the way our time together was going so far, I knew I was going to get that extra ten percent.

30

Hailey

Logan never came home last night. I knew it was none of my business, but when he walked through the front door the next morning, I wanted to grill him about his whereabouts. He didn't even have the courtesy to let me know what he was doing. Just because he wasn't my boyfriend anymore didn't mean I didn't want to know where he was at. He was still living in my apartment and sleeping in my bed, so I felt like the least he could do was let me know that he wasn't going to be home. We were at the very least still friends, so I thought the friendly thing to do was to have some respect and keep me updated on what was going on. I didn't need detailed texts every hour telling me about his day, though I wouldn't have minded that. All I wanted was to at least be aware if he was planning on sleeping elsewhere, so that I could have a night that didn't consist of sleeping on an air mattress.

My laptop was set on the kitchen counter, facing the front door. I usually worked from the office, but I relocated to the kitchen after I went into Logan's room that morning and noticed he still wasn't there. His toothbrush was still dry, which meant he hadn't come home after I had fallen asleep, and then somehow managed to quietly leave this morning. Although, I had witnessed several occasions where he skipped dental hygiene in his daily routine. I debated blowing up his phone even more than I already had the night before but figured his mom would have reached out if something was really wrong. She never liked me and probably never planned on actually building a real relationship with me, but I believed she would have at least notified me in the case of an emergency.

It was a tough situation, navigating being Logan's new ex-girlfriend. I was stuck between caring about where he was because I still had a lot of love for him, and trying to convince myself that whatever he did with his life was none of my business. In all honesty, I didn't think I was that good at being an ex. I cared too much and loved too hard to just be single. I liked sharing my life with someone and having a person to give all the affection that I carried in my heart. Being in a relationship was when I felt the happiest. I wasn't meant to be alone. Life was too complicated to endure on my own. I needed a partner to help me navigate the lows and celebrate the highs with.

I needed Logan.

Fortunately, the front door led right into the kitchen, so when he finally did return to the apartment, I was sitting there waiting for him. I tried not to appear as though I had been anticipating his arrival for hours, and that my decision to work from the kitchen was purely for the change in scenery. I tried to only just briefly glance at him when he walked through the kitchen, and pretend that my main focus was on my work. It was hard to ignore him because part of me wanted to run into his arms, and the other half of me was angry that he didn't even have the decency to text or call me back. I felt relieved seeing Logan walk through the door after not knowing if he was even okay, but my anger was slowly starting to take over. I thought about berating him about his blatant disregard for my feelings and not thinking about how his actions would affect me. However, when he got closer, I decided against yelling at him when I saw the heavy bags under his eyes and his constant yawning. He looked tired, as if he hadn't gotten a lot of sleep the night prior. His curly hair was a matted mess, and his shirt wasn't even buttoned up all the way. I was too far away to confirm for certain, but it appeared as though his pants weren't even zipped up all the way, either.

"Hey," Logan greeted nonchalantly as if he hadn't totally ignored my calls or failed to come home last night.

"Good morning," I answered back in a similar tone.

I didn't want to seem too eager to see him when he returned, so I opted for mimicking his casual tone. It would've been pathetic to admit that I stayed up until midnight waiting for the sound of the front door to open, or that I got up extra early to see right when he came back, but I was really hoping that we would be able to have another night where we pretended that we were back together; maybe even pretend for an entire day.

While I was waiting for him last night, I passed the time by conjuring up another excuse to use the master bathroom again. I was actually really excited to see him, but when I never heard him come home, I got worried. My mind went into panic mode, and I quickly listed off every worst-case scenario. I even debated calling Dalton, but I didn't want to be known as the crazy ex-girlfriend. I eventually just settled on the idea that he must have been busy or fallen asleep at Dalton's house. I tried calling and texting Logan multiple times, yet he never answered. He probably just needed some space to process his emotions. Even I needed a minute to fully understand our relationship and the events that unfolded the night prior. We were supposed to be broken up, but we decided to ignore that fact for the night. It ended up working out in our favor because we got to leave all the pain and hurt behind. For a brief moment in time, we just got to be a happy couple again. It felt so right to sleep in the same bed, and we wasted no time in sharing how much we truly still loved each other. It was such a great night that Logan was most likely regretting the whole breakup. I wasn't even the one who ended it, but I would have definitely wanted to date again after the night we had shared. Everything was just perfect.

"There was some mail for you," I notified him, gesturing toward the pile of envelopes on the counter. They were mostly just annoying advertisements, but I figured he'd at least want the option to look through it all. Neither of us had gotten into the habit of checking our mailbox, but it was one of things I decided to do while waiting for him.

"Thanks," he mumbled.

He shuffled through the pile rather quickly before discarding it all. I didn't think he even fully read any of the mail he received before considering it junk.

"How was your night?" I casually asked him, trying not to sound too nosy, but wanting to continue the conversation. It had been a while since we had last talked, and I was dying to hear his voice again.

Logan grabbed an apple out of the refrigerator, and took a bite. He never really liked fruit, so I was surprised to see him eating one. Wherever he had been, there must not have been a full fridge.

"Good, nothing special," he insisted between chews. "You?"

"Same. Nothing special," I relayed.

I watched him continue to take bites out of the apple, though he did not seem like he was enjoying it.

"Cool, I'm going to take a shower now," Logan noted, throwing away the barely eaten fruit.

When I spent my night worrying about where Logan was, I came up with crazy answers. I assumed he could have been in a car accident, that he was gravely sick in the hospital, or even worse, that he just decided that he didn't want to stay at my apartment anymore. Seeing that Logan returned hungry, tired, and dirty, it was obvious that he had definitely crashed on Dalton and Piper's couch last night. He was never able to get solid rest while sleeping on a couch, and he probably snuck out of their place before raiding their pantry or using their shower. The night with me must have really had him in his feelings.

"Okay, sounds good," I returned. "Have a good shower."

Logan started heading up the stairs toward the bedroom. He was lugging his backpack by his side as if it had weighed a hundred pounds, and his eyes could barely stay open.

"Did you have a long night?" I questioned, examining his sluggish demeanor.

"Why?" Logan snapped back. "Why would you ask that? Why would you just assume I had a long night?"

Logan was always irritable when he didn't get enough sleep. He must've been up all night thinking about the future of our relationship, or maybe Dalton's couch was really that uncomfortable.

"Chill out," I calmly countered. "You just look tired."

Logan seemed to realize his tone had come across super aggressive as he quickly retracted his statement and apologized. "Right, sorry," he explained. "I've just been up all night."

His level of exhaustion put him in a vulnerable state. I took advantage of his tiredness and saw it as an opportunity to get more information out of him.

"Where were you?" I inquired, finally asking the question that had been on my mind all night and all morning. "You never came home last night."

Logan hesitated before giving his answer. I was starting to believe that he didn't even know where he was last night.

"Work stuff," he responded. "I've got to get my first sale. I don't want to have to invade your space for too much longer. I know living together as exes isn't ideal for either of us."

I felt bad for him. He was working so hard at trying to make it in his career that he was starting to neglect his health. He wasn't sleeping right, he barely visited the gym, and from the amount of fast-food bags that were piling up in the trash, he wasn't eating great, either. Logan was stressing himself out just so that he could give me my apartment back.

"You're right. It's not an ideal situation," I agreed, "but you are not bothering me at all. You can stay as long as you need." I offered him a kind smile, indicating that his presence was actually more welcome than he had initially thought.

"Thanks, Hailey," Logan muttered, returning his climb back up the stairs.

"I just want you to know that I'm super proud of you," I exclaimed, pausing his journey to the shower. "I know you are going through a lot right now, both personally and professionally, but you are handling it so well. I truly am proud of you."

I felt as though I was pouring my heart out to him, but he simply returned my compliment with a slight grin before heading back up the stairs.

"Um, Logan," I called after him, still not ready for him to be out of my sight again.

"What's up?" he responded, stopping in the middle of the staircase.

"Did you want to do dinner tonight?" I shakily asked. "I bought some steaks. I figured we could grill them."

I've asked Logan to eat dinner with me on numerous occasions, but never as exes. My nerves were starting to intensify as every second that ticked by while I awaited his response felt like an eternity.

"Uh, sure," Logan casually noted.

"Okay, great," I stated, nodding my head in the direction of the top of the stairs to show that he could continue his climb without any more interruptions.

My insides fluttered at the idea of eating with Logan. When he was finally out of sight, I let out a little happy dance. I was craving some quality time with him, and I was excited to be able to get that again. He and I just fit so well together. The breakup was probably just a tiny hiccup in our love story because there was no way we were going to be able to completely leave one another alone. Logan and I just always wanted to be around each other, which explained why he was so happy to still be able to live with me. I didn't want to tell him that it was obvious how much he regretted ending things between us, but his actions made it very apparent. First, we slept in the same bed, and then he agreed to have dinner with me. With the way things were going, I was strongly considering the idea that we would probably end up back together sooner than I had originally thought. I assumed we would probably go on to live our single lives for at least a month or two before being apart became too unbearable, but now it was seeming like it was going to happen a lot faster than that. I wasn't opposed to being his girlfriend again. The thought actually excited me. We had our issues in the past, but I figured we both realized that the love we had shared for seven years was worth more than a few petty arguments.

"Hailey," Logan called out, racing down the stairs in just a towel while carrying an overflowing laundry basket.

"Do you think you could do a load for me?" he asked, presenting the dirty laundry to me.

I rolled my eyes but accepted the basket of clothes. "What would you do without me?" I asked, smirking behind a pile of soiled garments.

"Probably die alone surrounded by a pile of dirty laundry," he answered sarcastically.

A giant smile painted itself across my face as Logan dismissed himself back upstairs to shower, leaving me with the full basket of clothes. He may not have given his comment a second thought, but I was left blushing—not at the thought of Logan dying of course, but at his admission that he couldn't live without me.

31

Logan

Skylar's bed became our permanent workspace. I came over with the intent of studying every detail of the property for our next open house, but ended up studying every detail of Skylar's body. My laptop didn't even make it out of my backpack before she started kissing me. At first it was just a few pecks, but it didn't take long for it to intensify. Once we ended up in her bed, we just never left it, and I ended up spending my entire Thursday afternoon cuddling my mentor.

It had only been a day since the last time I saw her, but Skylar evidently missed me a lot. She couldn't stop smiling at me, and she never passed on an opportunity to kiss me. She was clinging onto me, but I didn't mind because I missed her, too. Sleeping alone wasn't as fun as sleeping next to her, and I couldn't remember the last time I had been desired that much by a woman. Hailey surely was annoyed by my presence for the past couple of years. She would've never given me the affection that Skylar did as soon as I walked through the door. Affection was a missing piece to my relationship with Hailey, but Skylar gave me an endless supply of it.

"We probably should get some actual work done," Skylar said after we had been lying in her bed for a while.

The sun was pouring into her bedroom, reminding me that it was not even close to nighttime, and I still had a full day of work ahead of me. Although, I still probably could've fallen asleep until the next day if I had closed my eyes for long enough.

"Can we just lay here forever?" I protested, continuing to wrap my arms around her and refusing to let her leave the bed. "I'm not ready to work."

Skylar giggled against my chest, trying to wiggle her way out of my cuddle. "We have to prepare for the open house this weekend," she reasoned. "Don't you want to show off how much you know?"

She tickled my sides, which made my grip around her loosen, but I still maintained to hold her close to me. I didn't want to let her go. Cuddling Skylar made me forget about all my worries. When I was around her, everything seemed right. She made work more fun, and she was always able to put me in a good mood. I was able to be myself around her and not have to think about all the things that were going on in my life. Skylar was able to restore all the joy in the world, and she never failed to put a smile on my face. I loved being in her presence. She made me forget about the pain. She made me forget about Hailey.

"I guess we can get to work," I complained. I released her from my arms, but she didn't leave my side.

"Is everything okay?" Skylar questioned.

"Yeah, I'm fine," I lied. "Let's just start working."

I removed myself from the covers and rolled to the edge of the bed, preparing to head downstairs and start learning the details of the home we were showing on Sunday. It was a listing that Skylar was super excited about because it came with a nice price tag. She loved the expensive properties, or rather, she loved the commission that came with it. I had done some research on it during my own time, but I was ready to learn from Skylar. I wanted to see firsthand how she was able to memorize so many facts about a house.

As I was about to leave the bed, I turned to face Skylar who hadn't even moved an inch. She was still lying comfortably in the same spot. "What are you doing?" I asked. "Aren't we going to get started?"

Skylar eyed me up and down. "Tell me what's on your mind," she insisted. "I can tell something is bothering you."

I wasn't the best at expressing my feelings. I was usually reluctant to say what was on my mind, but Skylar was just so easy to talk to. "I'm just stressed," I admitted.

"Stressed about what?" she asked.

I left the edge of the bed and rejoined Skylar in our original spot.

"It's just been difficult living with Hailey," I confessed.

I didn't want to talk about my ex with a new girl I was getting to know. I was pretty sure that was like rule number one when dating, but it was the honest truth. I thought living with Hailey as exes would be a seamless transition from living together as a couple, but I was wrong. It was hard to ignore the pain of the breakup and get her out of my mind when I would have to come home to her every day.

"Difficult how?" Skylar inquired.

"It feels like I'm living with my mom," I explained. "Hailey wants to know where I've been, what I've been doing, where I'm sleeping, and when I'm coming home. It's just so annoying."

"Oh my gosh, that is so weird," she agreed.

"Tell me about it," I exclaimed.

When I walked into the apartment yesterday, Hailey was waiting for me in the kitchen. She never worked from there, so I knew she was just doing it to see me when I got home. We weren't even dating anymore, but she still felt entitled to know where I was at every moment of the day. It was none of her business where I was sleeping or who I was sleeping with. What I did with my life shouldn't affect her anymore. I never asked her to tell me when she wouldn't be at the apartment, so she shouldn't expect me to tell her, either. I thought one of the benefits of being single was not having to answer to anyone, but Hailey was still in my business.

"She's acting like you guys are still dating when, in reality, you don't even like her anymore," Skylar expressed, becoming more infuriated.

"Well, I didn't say all that ..." I answered.

"She thinks you are still in a relationship," she argued. "Little does she know, you have clearly moved on."

"I mean, I still care about her ..." I interjected, but Skylar seemed to continue to ignore me.

"Your ex is crazy. She needs to be in an insane asylum. Questioning where you've been is so weird, and is such an invasion of privacy," she proclaimed.

Skylar was out of line with some of her comments, but I liked that I had someone in my corner.

"Speaking of invasion of privacy," I added, "she went through my mail."

"Now that is illegal," Skylar commented.

I didn't think reading the advertisements addressed to me was against the law. It's not like she opened any envelopes. She just sifted through the mail and separated out the ones that weren't for her. I wanted to tell Skylar that I was more upset with the fact that my life was still intertwined with Hailey's and mail was just another reminder of that. I wasn't upset at the fact that she touched my mail, just at the idea that she had access to it. I tried to explain that to Skylar, but she was already too worked up about it to hear me out.

"One of my neighbors is a cop," Skylar ranted. "I can have him set up surveillance or something. We can catch her on camera going through your mail."

"I appreciate your help, Sky, but it's not that big of a deal," I clarified. "It's not about the mail. I just feel like I don't have any space. She is always breathing down my neck."

It was already hard enough still living with the girl that I thought I was going to spend the rest of my life with. Every day was a reminder that we weren't together anymore. If I had any chance of moving on, I would have to get my own place. I just needed to get the funds to be able to do that.

"Yeah, the last thing you want after a long workday is to be interrogated," Skylar acknowledged. "I would never do that to my man after a stressful day."

"Exactly," I agreed. "She always wants to ask me a million questions. I just wanted to be alone so that I could focus on my work, but she just kept talking to me. I even had to have dinner with her."

Skylar's eyes widened and her face became red. "You had dinner with her?" Skylar asked, sounding somewhat offended.

"She asked me to have dinner with her, and I didn't have the heart to say no," I explained.

Skylar went quiet. She seemed super upset that I shared a meal with Hailey.

"Did I do something wrong?" I asked.

"No ..." Skylar responded. "I'm just confused."

"What are you confused about?" I answered. "We just ate together, that's it."

I wasn't sure why Skylar was so distressed. She seemed to be making a big deal about something that wasn't even that serious.

"Like, you went on a date?" she interrogated.

"No, I just grilled some steaks at the apartment," I explained.

Skylar contemplated my answer. She still appeared to be annoyed that I had eaten with my ex-girlfriend.

"I just don't understand why she thinks she can just have dinner with you as if you were still her boyfriend," she exclaimed.

I moved closer to Skylar and wrapped her in my arms, kissing her forehead.

"It wasn't anything serious," I said, comforting her. "It was just two people having dinner. I promise as soon as I am able to save up enough money, I will move out. Once I have a place of my own, Hailey and I won't have dinner ever again."

Skylar was jealous of my night with Hailey, and although she completely overreacted, it was kind of hot to see her so possessive of me. I couldn't remember the last time Hailey expressed that feeling toward me.

"Why don't you just move in with me?" Skylar offered. "Then you can start not having dinner with her now."

"You'd really let me stay here?" I exclaimed.

"Of course," Skylar noted. "You are over here all the time, anyway. It will be easier to work together, too, if you stay here."

I couldn't believe it. Moving out of Hailey's apartment was the key to getting over her and Skylar was my golden ticket.

"That's so generous of you," I exclaimed.

"Unlike her, I won't ask you a million questions or go through your mail. I actually understand common courtesy and can respect others' privacy," she added.

I brought my lips to Skylar's, putting a halt to any further explanation of why living with her would be beneficial. I was already convinced.

"Is that a yes?" she giggled against my mouth.

I continued to kiss her amazingly soft lips. "That is definitely a yes," I answered.

32

Hailey

The call with my sister was lasting almost as long as my entire work shift had. After I clocked out for the day, Megan called me to catch up. It was nice to know what was going on in her life, though she spent most of the time saying how excited she was to go to college. She was ready to finally move out of our parents' home and meet friends who had similar interests as her. Her excitement didn't bother me, though, because it was the one day a month where I actually had to go into the office, so the conversation with her made the drive home go by a lot faster. With all the curveballs that life had been throwing at me lately, it was nice to just talk with Megan. I was enjoying our conversation until the clock that originally read five o'clock at the beginning of our call quickly turned into ten o'clock. We had been on the phone for five hours, and she showed no signs of hanging up anytime soon.

"So what's going on with you and Logan?" Megan asked after she finished ranting about college. "What's it like living with your ex-boyfriend?"

I was glad she couldn't see my face because the sound of him being referred to as my ex-boyfriend made me roll my eyes.

"Um, I guess it's not as weird as it sounds," I replied.

To an outsider, the idea of exes living together might sound awkward, but Logan and I made it work. We had been together so long that I didn't believe it was that strange that we continued to live under the same roof. It probably would have been weirder if he had actually left as soon as we broke up.

"Is he going to move out, though?" Megan questioned.

"I don't know," I answered honestly. "He doesn't have the money to get a place of his own right now."

"I can't believe you let him live there for free," Megan announced. "I would never do that."

I didn't think I would ever financially support a guy, either, but love made me do a lot of crazy things.

"He helps when he can," I explained. "I said he could stay with me until he sells a home."

Megan chuckled through the phone. "Well, that's never going to happen," she stated.

"Megan!" I yelled back at her. "That is so rude."

My sister had little faith in Logan's real estate agent capabilities. She thought his career change was stupid and he should've stuck to being a customer service rep. Deep down, I didn't think I was ever fully convinced he would sell a home, either, which was why I was confident we would continue to live together for a long time. In all honesty, we would probably end up dating again before it even got to the point of him completing a sale.

"What?" Megan returned innocently. "It's not like he's any closer to selling a home than he was a few months ago."

"Actually," I interjected, "he is getting mentored by a successful agent. She is going to help him make a lot of money."

I was probably trying to convince myself more than Megan. If Logan got to a place in life where he was financially stable, I believed it would take away a lot of his stress. He would actually be able to pitch in for the bills and finally get us our dream house.

"She?" Megan repeated.

"Yeah," I confirmed. "She's a woman."

"Are you okay with him spending a lot of time with a girl that isn't you?" Megan questioned. "That would make me very uncomfortable."

"It's not like that," I explained. "I looked her up before. She's like forty."

"Well, why doesn't he just go back home and live with his mom then?" Megan argued. "He would be able to live there rent-free."

"You've met his mother," I countered. "Would you want to live with her?"

It didn't take long for Megan to understand my point. "Not at all," she answered, "but living with your mom sounds better than living with your ex. I mean, what if you guys start dating other people? That would get really awkward."

The thought of Logan being with someone else made me sick to my stomach. I knew I would have to cross that bridge eventually, but we both literally just got out of a seven-year relationship. I didn't think either of us had any intention of dating someone else anytime soon.

"We actually might be getting back together," I said.

"No way!" Megan exclaimed through the speaker.

"Yeah, we just have been hanging out a lot and we haven't had a single argument. I think we just needed a break for a second," I disclosed.

Saying the possibility of Logan and I dating again out loud made it feel even more real. I got butterflies in my stomach just thinking about the idea of being his girlfriend again.

"Wow," Megan began. "Mom is going to owe me ten bucks."

"Excuse me!" I shrieked. "You bet on my relationship?"

"On your ex-relationship," Megan corrected.

"Oh my gosh, you are so annoying," I affirmed. "Just wait until you fall in love one day. You will see how complicated things can get."

"Can't be that complicated," Megan responded, "I obviously knew that you guys would get back together. I'm the one who is going to win the bet."

Megan had a point. She should've bet more than ten dollars.

"Dinner is on you then," I noted sarcastically. "You can take me out to eat for once."

"Yeah, right," Megan protested. "This ten dollars is going straight toward my college fund."

"You're going to need a lot more than ten dollars to pay for college," I remarked.

The front door creaked open and then abruptly closed with a loud thud—Logan was home. I didn't pay him any attention though as I figured he would probably just go straight to his room. Instead, I continued ranting to my sister about how crazy love was until I heard a gentle tap on my bedroom door.

"Hailey, can we talk?" Logan whispered, slowly peeking his head through the door.

I learned from my past mistake of taking a phone call when Logan wanted to discuss something serious, so I wasted no time in hanging up on my sister. I hoped this would show Logan that I truly was changing and finally making him a priority in my life.

"I'll call you back, Megan," I explained before ending the call with her. I put my phone away and turned my attention back toward Logan. "Come in," I muttered.

I gestured toward Logan to enter my bedroom. He inched his way slowly around the door. His only options were to either join me on the air mattress or take a seat in the office chair, so when he fully made his way into the room, he opted to stand. I noticed that he was carrying a backpack that appeared to be overly stuffed. Logan always carried it with him to hold his laptop and anything else he needed for work, but it was never that full. His demeanor was timid as if he had something serious on his mind. The last time I witnessed such behavior was when he ended the relationship. I couldn't imagine what he had to say this time.

"There's no easy way to put this, Hailey," he began, breathing heavily, "but I want to start by thanking you for letting me live with you in the first place. I know I haven't been able to contribute in the way I wanted to, but I appreciate you picking up the slack while I've been trying to get back on my feet."

"You're welcome ..." I hesitantly responded, hoping the conversation wasn't going in the direction that I thought it was headed. I guess the relationship with his mentor worked out and she was able to help him sell a house sooner than I had anticipated.

"I truly appreciate how much you have done for me. Please never forget that," Logan encouraged.

"I won't ..." I said, waiting for the point of the conversation.

"Like you are really such a great girl," he insisted.

"What are you trying to say, Logan?" I blurted out impatiently. "Just say it already."

He took a deep breath and a big gulp. I knew what he was about to say before he even admitted it, but I wanted him to have the courage to tell me to my face that he had sold a house and was leaving. Deep down, I was super excited that he had accomplished a goal that he had been working so hard for, but at the same time, I was upset that I wasn't going to be able to live with my best friend anymore.

"I'm moving out," he expressed calmly.

"When?" I responded, trying to hide my sadness.

Logan looked at the heavy backpack on his shoulders. "Right now," he whispered.

"Right now?" I shouted. "Like in this exact moment?"

Logan didn't answer. He simply nodded his head.

"Did you sell a home?" I questioned.

"No," Logan admitted.

"Then why are you moving out?" I shouted. "Where are you going?"

I couldn't think of any other reason why he would just pack up his stuff and go. I completely understood that our living situation wasn't ordinary, but I had no problem with him staying at my apartment. I thought I had made it a comfortable place for him to stay, but I guess not.

"I'm going to stay with a friend for a while," he admitted.

"A friend?" I repeated. "Who? Dalton?"

"No, a different friend," Logan stated.

"What friend then?" I exclaimed.

Logan hesitated. He seemed to not want to tell me the name of the person he was staying with. I pretty much knew everyone that Logan hung out with, so I wasn't sure why he was making such a big deal out of it.

"Her name is Skylar," he eventually confessed.

"Your mentor?" I questioned. "Why are you staying with your mentor?"

"She just offered," Logan affirmed.

"So?" I fired back.

"So, I said yes," Logan responded.

Logan was out of his mind. He was giving up a perfectly good living situation to stay with a coworker. Logan was literally ruining a friendship with me just so he could further his career.

"You are not serious," I stammered.

"I am," Logan relayed. "It's probably best we give each other some space, anyway."

"No, Logan!" I shouted. "I don't want space. I want you to stay here."

I started crying in the middle of the air mattress. Logan tried to join and comfort me, but I quickly pushed him away. I needed to get used to not having him there to make me feel better.

"Why would you do this to me?" I cried. "Please stay."

"I'm sorry, Hailey. I can't," Logan assured.

I didn't know what I did wrong to make living with me such a terrible experience, but Logan obviously did not enjoy my presence. He wanted to get away from me so badly that he decided to go live with his mentor. She probably had a big house and lots of money, which was most likely why he decided to switch living situations so quickly. I wasn't sure if she had kids or not, but hopefully she asked them if it was okay before inviting a man she barely knew into her home.

"I don't want you to go," I disclosed. "Don't leave me here alone."

"You will be fine," he affirmed. "It's for the best."

"How do you know what's best for me, Logan?" I questioned through tears.

"I guess I don't ..." he admitted.

"Clearly you don't because the last few decisions you have made have completely broken me," I explained.

He didn't say anything. He just stood there in silence as if the right words were eventually just going to pop in his head.

"Well, are you going to say something or just stand there?" I shouted, my sadness turning into anger. By now, I was an expert in the stages of grief.

"I'll be back tomorrow to get the rest of my stuff," Logan quietly shared.

And with that, he took his backpack and left the apartment.

33

Logan

"It was awkward moving my stuff out," I explained. "Hailey cried the entire time."

Skylar was in the passenger seat, listening to me detail the events of the prior night. We were headed to Dalton's house for his birthday party, so I took the drive over there as an opportunity to fill Skylar in on how things went down when I told Hailey that I was moving out. I knew it was going to be a hard conversation, but nothing ever prepared me for seeing her cry. I hated hurting her, but it had to be done. It was too painful to live in the same apartment as her. Just seeing her pretty smile every day made me want to instantly take her back, but I knew our relationship was causing more harm than good. We just weren't meant to be together. It took a year of me trying to emotionally detach myself from her and mentally check out of the relationship before I even had the courage to end things between us. It was one of the toughest decisions I ever had to make, but I couldn't let either one of us continue on in a relationship that wasn't serving us. I had to get out of that apartment before I eventually caved in to the heartbreak and asked her to be my girlfriend again.

"She is so emotional," Skylar began. "I don't understand why she takes everything to heart."

"She was just upset that I wasn't going to be living with her anymore," I said, defending Hailey's reaction.

"I don't know why," she remarked. "You guys have been broken up for a while now. She needs to move on."

"We were together for a long time, Sky," I reminded her. "Seven years."

"Yeah, but you even said that you had been checked out for a while, so some of that time doesn't even count," she pointed out.

"I mean, I guess," I relayed.

Although I was still pretty shaken up from how things went down, I was still excited to finally introduce Skylar to Dalton. I was ready to put everything behind me and enjoy a wild Friday night with my best friend. He loved to party, especially when the event was about him. I wouldn't have been surprised if he was already dancing on top of a table by now. That man knew how to entertain a crowd. Piper would probably spend most of the night simply keeping an eye on him and making sure he didn't get himself in too much trouble. He didn't have very many limits when it came to partying.

"You guys weren't even married," Skylar continued. "I was able to move on faster from my ex-husband than she's able to move on from you."

"That is not fair to say," I casually stated, trying to get my point across without escalating the situation. "Everyone handles things differently."

"Trust me," she began. "It is not normal to act how she's acting."

I understood where Skylar was coming from. I wasn't expecting Hailey to react how she did, either. The tears were expected, but I didn't think she would beg me to stay. I figured that me living there was as painful for her as it was for me and that I was doing us both a favor. However, I didn't think it was Skylar's job to judge how Hailey handled her grief.

"Can we just talk about something else?" I urged.

"Fine," Skylar muttered. "As long as you agree that she's overreacting."

I fell silent, not wanting to continue to talk about Hailey. I was just ready to leave the entire situation in the past.

"Well, are you going to say it?" Skylar continued. "Admit that your ex is crazy, and that she is completely overreacting."

"I am not going to do that," I protested.

"Why not?" Skylar questioned.

"Can we please just not talk about this?" I pleaded.

I found some street parking near Dalton's house. His neighborhood was already filled with the cars of the people attending his party, but I was still able to find an empty space not too far away.

"I'm not getting out of this car until you tell me what I want to hear," Skylar affirmed. "Your ex is ridiculous, and you know it. Just say it."

"Sky, let's not do this right now, please," I begged, hoping we could just drop the argument and head to the party.

"I'm waiting ..." Skylar remarked.

"I really don't think Hailey acted that crazy," I finally disclosed. "She can be emotional sometimes, but it's been a tough time for both of us."

"Oh, don't tell me you're defending her now?" Skylar stammered. "All those times you complained about her to me and now you want to have her back?"

"Skylar ... stop," I insisted.

"She completely freaked out about you deciding to live with me," Skylar reasoned. "That's literally the definition of overreacting."

I stared out the window, wishing I was anywhere but my car. The conversation was completely unnecessary, and I forgot how it even started. I didn't even really know what we were arguing about.

"You did tell her that you're talking to me now, right?" Skylar asked.

"Not necessarily," I answered.

"Are you kidding me?" Skylar shouted. "Are you trying to hide me or something? Do you even care about me?"

"Of course I care about you," I uttered. "I just didn't think it was the right moment. I'll tell her tomorrow when I get the rest of my stuff."

"Okay, fine," Skylar agreed, seeming to finally calm down.

I was glad she was starting to let everything go, but thinking about having to see Hailey again and mention Skylar to her was making my stomach sick. I had already put her through enough, and now I was going to deliver another blow to her heart. I wasn't sure how she would survive that conversation. I didn't know if I was even going to be able to survive that conversation.

"Can we just go to the party now?" I urged.

"Yes, just one more thing," Skylar started. She leaned over to the driver's seat and pressed her glossy lips onto mine. "You made the right decision by leaving her," Skylar assured. "I know it was hard, but you made the right choice."

She finished off her statement with one more kiss before exiting the car. I wasn't sure what just happened. I didn't know how Skylar could chew me out in one breath, and then just switch up and kiss me in another. It all happened so fast. I didn't have time to process it all. However, in that moment, I was just happy to finally move on and start celebrating with Dalton. My mind couldn't handle anything else.

When I got out of the car, Skylar grabbed my hand as if nothing had happened. I assumed that was her way of saying she was sorry and that she wanted to put our argument in the past. We walked hand-in-hand all the way to Dalton's house. Although her outburst had almost completely ruined my mood for the night, I knew it was something I was just going to have to accept and move on from. I didn't believe I would have been able to handle losing two girls.

"Look who it is!" Dalton shouted from across the room when Skylar and I finally made it into the house. "Now the party can really start." Dalton met us in the middle of the living room and greeted me with an enthusiastic hug.

"Happy birthday, D," I announced.

"Thanks!" Dalton said with a smile. "And who do we have here?" He turned toward Skylar, who was still holding on to my hand.

"This is Skylar," I introduced. "Skylar, this is my best friend, Dalton."

He was clearly enjoying his birthday. He was smiling from ear to ear, and from the armpit stains that were seeping through his shirt, I could tell he had already taken a few trips to the dance floor.

"Nice to meet you, pretty lady," he exclaimed. "You must be a very patient person to be able to put up with this guy." He lightly punched me in the arm, thinking his joke was funnier than it actually was.

"Speaking of pretty ladies, where is my beautiful fiancée?" he inquired, searching for Piper in the crowd of people that were packed inside his house.

"She just walked out of the kitchen," I stated, pointing to Piper carrying a tray of snacks.

"Piper!" Dalton shouted, gesturing for her to come over to us.

Piper smiled at the sight of him. She quickly set the tray down on the nearest coffee table, and made her way to his side.

"Piper, this is Skylar," Dalton announced, taking over the introductions.

"Nice to meet you," Piper greeted. "You are so pretty."

"Thank you, so are you," Skylar returned.

"I know, isn't she just the cutest?" Dalton agreed, kissing Piper on the forehead.

It was nice to see my friends getting along with Skylar. She seamlessly fit into my life.

"There are drinks and food in the kitchen if you guys want anything," Piper explained. "Help yourselves to as much as you want."

"We have plenty of everything," Dalton interjected.

"Alright, we will head that way then," I remarked before leading Skylar into the kitchen.

Dalton wasn't lying when he said they had plenty of stuff. There were pizza boxes piled to the ceiling, and drinks that lined the entire kitchen counter. The dessert section caught my eye the most as dozens of cookies surrounded a giant birthday cake.

"I can't wait to dive into this," I announced after examining the entire kitchen, salivating over the abundance of food.

"Mhm," Skylar mumbled.

"Are you good?" I asked, noticing her shift in mood. She was all happy a second ago, but now she seemed irritated. I didn't know what could have happened on the short stroll to the kitchen that upset her so much.

"Why didn't you introduce me as your girlfriend?" Skylar questioned. "Dalton was raving about his fiancée, but you didn't do that about me."

I wanted to roll my eyes at Skylar's comment, but I didn't want to anger her any further. We had just gotten over our first fight, and I was in no mood to start another.

"Well, I mean, you aren't technically my girlfriend yet," I shakily answered.

"I think we should change that," Skylar noted.

I didn't know how to respond. Of course becoming official was on my mind. I just didn't like that it felt like I was being forced into it.

"You are happy with me, aren't you?" Skylar asked.

"I'm really happy with you," I replied.

"So what are you waiting for?" she questioned.

I truly was enjoying my time with Skylar. I didn't know how I would have survived my breakup with Hailey without her. Skylar had been there for me the entire time and even let me live with her. I guess I didn't really have a reason to not make it official.

"Okay, so will you be my girlfriend?" I asked Skylar.

She paused for a little, appearing to contemplate my question as if she wasn't the one who prompted the entire conversation to begin with. "Can you ask me a little differently?" she asked. "Maybe with a little bit more enthusiasm? Like you actually mean it?"

I let out a heavy sigh. I thought I was doing what she wanted, but even that wasn't good enough for her.

"Skylar Williams," I began. "Will you make me the happiest guy in the world and be my girlfriend?" I exaggerated a little bit, but the last thing I wanted was for her to make me redo it.

"Oh, wow!" Dalton shouted, approaching us right as I popped the question to Skylar. He stared at her intently, waiting for her to respond.

"I'd love to," Skylar replied.

"She said yes!" Dalton yelled.

He began to cheer as if I had just asked her to marry me, wildly dancing around the kitchen. I think he had a few drinks in him.

"Kiss! Kiss! Kiss!" he chanted.

He was being absolutely ridiculous, but I loved his crazy energy. I obviously had to give the birthday boy what he wanted, so I pulled Skylar in for a kiss, which was met by Dalton's obnoxious hollers.

"Okay enough about me," I insisted, turning to Dalton. "Now it's time to celebrate you." I poured myself a drink and raised the cup in the air. "To many more years of life and friendship," I said. "Happy birthday, D."

Dalton met his drink with mine.

"Cheers to us," Dalton declared. "Life wouldn't be the same without you."

I took a sip of my drink, happy to be surrounded by my best friend, a giant birthday cake, and of course, my new girlfriend.

34

Hailey

The silence in my apartment was unsettling. I couldn't get the thought of Logan out of my head because the quietness that flooded the apartment was a constant reminder that he was no longer living there. I tried to keep my mind busy by finally packing up the air mattress and shoving it back into the closet in order to move back into the master bedroom. I was grateful that I was going to be able to sleep in my own bed again, but I would have rather continued to camp out in the office if it meant that Logan would come back.

He had only taken a backpack of his stuff, so most of his things were still in the apartment. Therefore, even for the split second that my brain was able to kick the thought of my ex-boyfriend out of my head, it wasn't long before something would remind me of him. Everywhere I looked, there were signs that Logan had once lived with me. His socks were still scattered around the bedroom, the nightstand still held his watches, and the laundry basket was still full of his clothes. I almost caved and threw the entire basket into the washing machine, but decided against it. Logan no longer lived with me, and that was the reality I had to face.

When I entered the bedroom, I moved some of his stuff out of the closet so I could replace it with mine. He had suits that I carefully placed outside the room, but everything else I just threw out into the hallway. I thought that removing some of his items would make the memory of him go away, but his smell still lingered. I took out his shoes, his ties, and every displaced sock, yet he still felt present in the room. It was one thing to remove all the physical reminders of him, but his aroma and the memories were forever embedded into the walls. I was tempted to just move back into the office and sleep on the air mattress again because being in the bedroom that we shared for so long was almost too painful. I was starting to think that I was never going to be able to escape the crippling feeling that came with Logan's absence. He could move to the other side of the country if he wanted to, and I'd probably still feel like he was close by. With all the years we had spent together, it was obvious that he would always have a permanent place in my heart.

I continued to replace his items in the closet with mine, creating mounds of clothes in the hallway as a result. I was proud of myself for not breaking down, but my quiet apartment made me increasingly uncomfortable until an even worse sound filled the air—the front door opening. Logan had finally come back to get the rest of his stuff. Fortunately for him, I had already given him a head start by moving his clothes out of the closet and into the hallway. Honestly, he's lucky I didn't burn them. It wouldn't have taken long for my nagging grief to turn into anger and easily create a nice bonfire with his stuff.

"Hey, Hailey," Logan hesitantly greeted, stepping over the piles in the hallway.

"Hi," I quietly murmured.

"I'm here to get the rest of my stuff," he explained.

He quizzically examined the mess in the hallway, and I didn't think it took him too long to realize that the toppling piles were made up of things that belonged to him.

"I know, you told me that yesterday," I answered, continuing to organize the closet.

The sight of him still made me feel at ease, even though I was crumbling on the inside.

"I put most of your stuff in the hall, but I haven't gone through the bathroom yet," I relayed.

Logan tiptoed his way further into the bedroom, grabbing his suitcase and extra backpacks that he had shoved under the bed. He used them to pack up the mounds of clothes. We spent our afternoon slowly dismantling the living situation that we had once been in. I was rearranging the closet that was now only filled with my stuff, and Logan was wrangling the items in the hall. It was an awkward arrangement that continued in silence until he moved on to the bathroom.

"Is this mine or yours?" he asked, holding up a blue razor.

"It's mine," I answered nonchalantly.

I was trying to hide the fact that watching him move out was probably the second hardest thing I had to endure. I didn't think anything could have topped the actual breakup, which hopefully meant things could only go up from here.

"Oh, I've definitely used this multiple times," Logan claimed.

"I mean, you can take it if you want it," I responded.

Without hesitation, Logan threw the razor into a bag and continued to raid the bathroom for anything else that he wanted to bring along with him.

"What about the body wash?" he questioned.

I didn't know why he wanted to bring soap to Skylar's house. She probably had plenty, but I had no energy left to fight him on it.

"Just take whatever you want," I calmly relayed.

Logan continued to shove items into the bag that he had brought into the bathroom.

"I just want to make sure I don't forget anything," he explained.

"You know you can always come back," I answered. "You don't have to grab everything at once."

Of course I would have loved another opportunity to see him again, but I was serious about him not having to take everything in one visit. It's not like I was going to lock him out of the apartment. He had a lot of stuff, and I didn't want him to feel pressured to grab it all. There was no harm in coming back another time.

"It's probably for the best that I just get everything now," he insisted.

"Best for who?" I questioned. "I don't mind if you have to come back, unless you have a problem with it."

He hesitated before answering. "It's not us that I'm worried about," he explained. "I don't think Skylar would be too happy about it."

"Who cares what she thinks? She's just your mentor," I fired back. "I don't understand why you coming back would bother her anyway. It's not like she's your girlfriend." I let out an uncomfortable laugh.

"Um, about that ..." he slowly began.

"It's not like she's your girlfriend," I repeated with a little more force. "Right, Logan?"

He immediately stopped what he was doing. A look of guilt flooded his face as he carefully put down the overfilled bag. I had a bad feeling about what he was going to say next, but I couldn't bring myself to believe that he would already be in another relationship. Skylar was way older than he was, and she was his superior. They wouldn't cross the lines of their working relationship. There was no way he would betray me like that. I really believed that I had nothing to worry about, but I wasn't liking the look of Logan hesitantly walking over to me.

"Hailey, I don't want to hurt you," Logan stammered, his eyes filling with tears.

"Then don't," I responded.

When he reached me, he grabbed my hand. The simple touch sent chills throughout my body.

"Is she really your girlfriend?" I managed to croak through the lump in my throat.

I demanded an answer from him. However, I really just wanted him to let me go back to the time where I didn't suspect him of moving on already.

"Please don't make me say it," Logan pleaded.

"Are you dating your mentor or not?" I shakily asked again.

Logan appeared to grow increasingly uncomfortable. His movements were twitchy, and beads of sweat started to form on his forehead. "Yes ..." Logan eventually whispered.

I quickly removed my hand from Logan's grip. His answer crushed me. My heart and all my sanity were completely obliterated from one simple word. I would've rather had him just lie to me. I liked it better when my heart had only been pummeled once.

"Get your stuff," I started, "and get out."

My mind and body went into complete shock. I couldn't react. I couldn't even cry. Seven years down the drain so that Logan could get with someone not even two weeks later. I didn't believe our relationship ever even mattered to him. I questioned whether he even loved me, because if he truly had, he wouldn't have moved on so quickly.

"Hailey, I can explain," Logan stammered.

"Please get out," I reiterated.

Luckily, he had already packed up all of the clothes that I'd thrown into the hallway, and he made significant progress in the bathroom. There were probably things that he would have to leave behind, but that wasn't my problem anymore. He could bother his new girlfriend for some body wash. Clearly, she meant more to him than I ever did.

"Just hear me out," Logan asserted.

He complied by taking all of his backpacks and suitcases out of the room, but he insisted on getting the last word. Apparently, he had some prolific explanation as to how he ended up in another relationship so quickly, but I was in no mood to hear it. Once his stuff was finally out of the room, I thought that he would stop, but Logan continued to plea for me to listen. He stood in the doorway, begging me to let him explain.

"It's really not what it looks like," Logan argued. "I can explain everything."

"Did you sleep with her?" I interjected.

"What?" Logan bellowed. "Why does that matter?"

"Tell me the truth," I pleaded calmly so that my anger wouldn't scare him away from answering.

I didn't want to hear what Logan had to say, but I needed to know the answer. I didn't care for the story of how they magically fell in love so abruptly. The details of their connection were not important to me. I just had one question, and the answer to that was all I was willing to hear. I figured his sudden pause and pale face were all I needed to know, but I wanted verbal confirmation.

After a few moments of silence, Logan finally gave me what I wanted. He hesitantly nodded his head once. I wanted to scream. On the second slow nod, I wanted to cry. When he was in the process of nodding a third time, I slammed the door in his face. Logan really had some nerve to break up with me, and then get with another girl shortly after. All the crying I had done over him had made me feel like the weak one between us. I thought I was the only one dying inside. This whole time, I believed Logan was unaffected by our breakup and was doing just fine without me. In all actuality, he was the broken one; he was the one falling apart. I thought all the crying I had done was an indication of weakness. However, it was actually a sign of strength because I was able to move on from our relationship on my own ... he needed someone else to help him do that.

35

Logan

I didn't know what was worse; ending a seven-year relationship, moving out of my ex-girlfriend's apartment, or telling Hailey that I was dating Skylar. Just when I thought I was done hurting her, I went right back and did it again. I was hoping that would be the last time I would have to deliver news that would break her precious heart, but I wasn't going to hold my breath. With the way life was going, I wasn't convinced that more bad news wasn't on the horizon. Sometimes I wished I could go back in time, before Hailey and I had even broken things off. Life was simpler back then. We had our disagreements, but tolerating our differences was way easier than facing our feelings. Maybe I should have just ended things before it got too bad—before we invested seven years of our life together. We could've gone our separate ways years ago. It would have saved both of us years in an unhealthy relationship, and probably wouldn't have hurt as much, either.

"You're quiet," Skylar noted, setting a plate of roasted chicken and vegetables in front of me. She had just finished cooking a nice meal for us in honor of our first dinner officially living together. I really wanted to enjoy the moment with her, but my thoughts were preoccupied. I wasn't really in a celebratory mood.

"I just have a lot on my mind," I answered, moving the peas around my plate with a fork. "Thank you for cooking dinner, though."

I gave her a soft kiss on the cheek before returning back to my seat at the table, but there was no feeling behind it. I just wanted to put her mind at ease. The whole situation was hard for me, but I couldn't ignore the fact that it was affecting Skylar, too. I had dragged her into a messy breakup, and she didn't deserve any of the baggage that came with dating me.

"Let me guess," Skylar began as she took a seat next to me, "you are thinking about Hailey." She rolled her eyes and angrily started cutting her chicken.

I gently placed my hand on her arm, and in turn, she set the knife down. "It's not just Hailey," I relayed, assuring Skylar that I wasn't always thinking about my ex. "I just moved out of the apartment I had been living in for a while, and I just got out of a relationship. Now, I am starting a new career. These are big life changes for me."

"Do you miss her?" Skylar asked bluntly. "Be honest, because you can move out just as fast as you moved in if you want to be with her."

Skylar's anger was starting to increase with each second that ticked by. She usually kept a calm and professional manner, but any mention of Hailey seemed to set her off.

"No," I responded firmly. "It's just an overall stressful time for me. I am going through a lot of change right now."

"When are you going to get over her?" Skylar questioned. "It's been forever since you guys broke up. It's time to move on, Logan."

"I am over her," I explained sharply. "I told you, life is just stressful right now."

The way Skylar refused to make eye contact made me feel as though she didn't believe me. I didn't know why she insisted that I still had feelings for Hailey. The whole reason I moved out was to get over my feelings for her. Evidently, seven years of love didn't just go down the drain the minute we broke up, but I was actively trying to move on from her. I didn't understand why Skylar couldn't see that.

"Trust me, Skylar," I muttered. "You are the only girl I want."

"Promise?" Skylar asked.

"I promise," I answered, leaning toward her and sealing it with an affirmative kiss.

I turned my attention back to my plate once I was certain that Skylar's mood was finally back to normal. I hated when she got upset.

"Prove it," Skylar continued on.

"What?" I exclaimed.

"Prove to me that I am the only girl that you want," Skylar encouraged.

My mind raced as I tried to think of something I could do or say to show her that I was serious about her. I couldn't come up with anything, so I just gave her another kiss.

"Does that work?" I nervously asked.

"I guess," she sluggishly answered.

Skylar's eyes were fixated on her plate, but she hadn't even taken a bite of her food yet. Her shoulders were slumped forward, and her mouth drooped into a frown.

"Are you okay?" I asked, observing her defeated body language.

"Sorry, it's just been a long day," Skylar apologized. "I lost a client today, and it's all I have been able to think about."

"It's okay," I noted, comforting her. "We all have our moments. Anything I can do to help?"

"No, this is above your head. You haven't even sold a house yet, so there's no way you could help with this."

Ouch, attacking my personal life and my professional life. Skylar was on a roll tonight.

"Well, okay then," I uttered.

"I shouldn't have lashed out at you like that or accused you of still having feelings for your ex. I know you aren't stupid enough to go back to her," she remarked.

"Excuse me?" I let out, almost choking on a carrot. "Did you just call me stupid?"

"No, silly," Skylar asserted, "I said going back to your ex would be stupid."

Skylar had a tendency to not have a filter. She was a super headstrong woman who always said what was on her mind, but I noticed that it sometimes made her come off as an inconsiderate person. At times, I would question if she was even capable of empathy when she would go on her rants. Hailey was often the source of her complaints, which I quickly noticed. I didn't want to lose Skylar. She was one of the only people in my life really there for me after the breakup. I just wished she would keep some things to herself.

"Why would going back to Hailey be stupid?" It apparently was the wrong question to ask because Skylar's calm demeanor quickly turned into rage.

"See, I knew it!" she shouted in my face. "I knew you weren't over her."

"Skylar, what are you talking about?" I defended. "I don't want to date Hailey again."

"Ugh! Why do you even say her name?" Skylar yelled. She threw her hands in the air in defeat and stood up from the table.

"Am I not allowed to say her name?" I questioned.

"You don't get it, do you?" she exclaimed. "I don't want to feel like I am in a competition with your ex. Out of the kindness of my heart, I let you move in with me, yet all you can do is talk about her."

This was not how I envisioned living with Skylar. Every little thing set her off, and we somehow always found ourselves in another argument.

"Skylar, please listen to me," I stated in a low voice, hoping it would also calm her down. I encouraged her to sit back down, in which she reluctantly did. She was still angry, but my calm demeanor put her at least a little bit at ease. "I am so happy with you. I do not want anyone else."

"Do you mean it?" she asked. "Like, do you actually mean it?"

"Absolutely," I insisted.

"So do you love me?" Skylar asked.

"Uh ... well ..." I began, her question catching me off guard. "I mean, we just started dating, Skylar."

I wasn't sure what she wanted me to say. I didn't want to lie to her, but at the same time I didn't want to hurt her feelings, either. There was no right answer.

"Do you love me or do you love your ex?" Skylar rephrased.

"Skylar, that is not a fair question," I argued. "I was with her for seven years. I still have love for her, but I am not in love with her anymore."

"Well, are you in love with me?" she questioned. "I'm your girlfriend now."

I started sweating, trying to think of an appropriate response. Obviously, I cared for Skylar deeply, but not enough to say that I loved her. Maybe one day it could develop into that, but in that moment, I didn't have those feelings for her.

"I think we should just slow down," I eventually responded. "I don't want to move too fast."

"Excuses," Skylar hissed. "All men are the same. They just want to lie through their teeth and then cover it up with excuses."

"That's not what I'm doing," I explained to her.

"Maybe we shouldn't actually be together," Skylar suggested. "Maybe this was all just a big mistake."

The conversation was taking a sharp turn for the worst. I had only moved my stuff in a couple hours ago, yet it had already turned into a disaster. We were a new couple, but we spent more of our time arguing than anything else.

"What are you talking about?" I stammered.

"I want to sleep alone tonight to think about everything," Skylar admitted.

"I just moved in ..." I reminded her.

"Okay, and?" she fired back.

"Skylar, please," I insisted. "You are the one that I want."

"Just get out," Skylar remarked. "I need some space. I'll call you tomorrow."

This was definitely not how I planned the evening to go. Getting kicked out by two girls in one night had to be some sort of record. Skylar didn't appear as though she was going to change her mind anytime soon, so I slowly stood up from the table and grabbed my backpack.

"The rest of my stuff is in your room," I relayed. I hadn't fully unpacked, but I had brought all my suitcases into Skylar's house and put them in her bedroom.

"You can get it tomorrow," she stated.

With that half-hearted response, I left her house with only a backpack that contained a few items. I was too embarrassed to go back to Hailey's, and I didn't want to explain to my mom or Dalton that my new relationship was already falling apart, so I got into my car and drove to an empty parking lot.

I had never slept in my car before, but there was a first time for everything. It wasn't the most comfortable, but it was at least peaceful. As I reclined my seat all the way back, I thought about how a month ago I was cuddled up with Hailey in a comfortable bed, and now I was alone in a parking lot—life sure changes fast.

It's crazy how the year started with an overwhelming sense of courage. I took the leap of faith and left my old job behind to follow my passion in real estate. It was a scary jump, but I followed my heart. I found the guts to end a relationship that wasn't serving me anymore—a decision that I didn't take lightly at all but was brave enough to follow through with. I was fearless and took a chance by dating a new girl who helped me through a time of grief. I was the definition of a strong soldier, battling everything that was thrown at me. I made a lot of courageous decisions that altered my future, but if I would've settled, my life would've been average. If I would've continued on as a customer service representative, my life would've been boring. If I would've stayed with Hailey, my life would've been stagnant. If I would've kept my relationship with Skylar strictly professional ... well ... maybe I wouldn't have ended up sleeping in my car.

36

Hailey

I didn't think it was possible for a broken heart to break again, but mine definitely did just that. I thought once was enough, but apparently hearts can shatter twice. The space where my beating heart once lived was now replaced by millions of broken pieces. It was nothing but a pile of jagged fragments. I thought about trying to put the brokenness back together, but there was no point. Why would I rebuild something that could be potentially crushed again? I'd rather just stay damaged because at least I couldn't be destroyed any further.

My heart didn't need a mechanic; it needed a replacement. I couldn't be fixed. I needed a fresh start. It took all the energy I had to get out of bed that Saturday morning and put myself together enough to meet Piper for coffee, but I figured it was my first step toward moving on. It would take a while to part ways with my old life, but Piper was a compromise. Hanging out with her allowed me to make my own friends and have a social life outside of Logan. However, she still felt comfortable because she was tied to the memories that I had created in my past relationship.

It felt freeing to leave my apartment, a place where my fondest memories had turned into some of my worst nightmares. I thought the escape would clear my mind and relieve my thoughts from the consumption of Logan, but everything reminded me of him. Every song that played on the radio prompted a flashback to when I was happily in a relationship with him. Each car that passed by that was the same model as Logan's made me feel a tiny sense of excitement—only for that excitement to be crushed when I would notice that driver was far from being my ex. Unfortunately, that didn't stop me from pulling into the lot of the coffee shop and parking right next to a vehicle that looked exactly like his. I was still committed to the idea of moving on from him, but any sign of him seemed to put my hurting heart at ease, even if it was only for a few seconds.

I got out of my car and headed to the coffee shop, mentally preparing myself to be social. The introvert inside me wanted to head straight home, but starting over meant I needed to actually talk to people. I couldn't rebuild my life from the inside of my apartment.

The door that led into the cafe was unusually heavy. I managed to make my way inside without showing too many signs of struggle, but I swore that the door had been filled with bricks. Maybe I was becoming weaker, as it had been a while since I'd been to the gym. I spent so much time crying that working out was the last thing on my mind. I thought about reaching out to Dalton and scheduling a gym session with him, but he was probably busy planning a wedding. He most likely would have declined my invite, anyway. Dalton was Logan's best friend, which meant his loyalty was with him. I knew it wasn't his place, but I was kind of shocked that he hadn't reached out to check on me. The last time I saw him was when he changed my tire, and he seemed pretty open to seeing me again. I figured he would have at least texted me, but it was evident that his friendship with Logan came before ours. For both of our sakes, it was probably best that we went our separate ways. Our flirty friendship was fun, but now I didn't have a boyfriend holding me back. I didn't trust myself around him, especially in a grieving state. The last thing I would ever want to do would be to put him in a situation that would harm his relationship with Piper in any way. They were getting married, Logan had a new girlfriend, and I was the single outcast.

Piper was already seated when I walked inside the café, but she didn't notice me. She was too busy taking pictures of her coffee and of herself. I managed to order my own drink, wait for the barista to make it for me, and then bring it back to her table before she even finished her mini photoshoot.

"Hi, Hailey!" Piper exclaimed when she finally saw me. I thought I was interrupting her photos, but she continued to take pictures even after I had already sat down.

"Hey, Piper," I returned awkwardly, trying to pretend that she wasn't creating social media content right in front of me.

"Sorry, I can't miss out on an opportunity to take a picture with my ring. I still haven't gotten used to having such a big diamond on my finger," she explained. "It's so sparkly, especially in this lighting."

She continued to try and capture the perfect photo that encompassed her beautifully crafted drink and the shimmering rock on her finger. I scooted my chair slightly to the side to get out of the background. I enviously watched her gush over her own ring. By now, I thought I would've been engaged already, too. I wanted to gloat over an expensive diamond and stress over wedding plans. Logan and I could've had that, but he wanted to throw that away in order to be with someone else. As much as I would've loved to be in a pretty white dress and parade around in front of all my friends and family, I really just wanted to be married because it meant that someone had actually chosen me. Getting engaged would have meant that a man was declaring his love for me and saying to the world that he wanted nobody else. I just wanted someone to want me, to choose me. Obviously, Logan wasn't the guy for me because I wasn't enough for him. He found better in someone else.

"So what's new with you?" Piper asked enthusiastically, finally putting her phone down. "How's work? How's life? Tell me everything."

She took a sip of her coffee, awaiting my answer. Her positive energy was usually refreshing, but it came off as though she didn't care or realize that this was a very hurtful time for me. I didn't expect her to be as down as I was, but she could've at least toned down her happiness a little bit.

"Well, work is fine, I guess. I am working a lot of hours and don't feel like I am being fairly rewarded for all my time," I began, "but at least it is distracting me from everything else going on." I figured that hinting about my life being so chaotic that I needed work to distract me would spark a lightbulb in Piper's mind that something was wrong, but she continued on in her blissful happiness.

"Oh my, why don't you just quit then?" she asked.

"It's more complicated than that," I shared. "I've been looking, but I just haven't found something else that I like."

"You like coffee, right?" she offered. "You could be a barista!"

Piper had no idea what it meant to try and find a job that had a salary that someone could live off of. She was set in life because she was marrying a man who had a good-paying job. Dalton was making enough for the both of them, which allowed Piper to be able to do her photography. It didn't bring her much income, but she was insanely passionate about it. She was lucky to be able to have a guy that allowed her the chance to do that.

"I don't think I'd be a good barista," I admitted. "I was thinking something that had to do with fitness, since I love working out."

"Oh, you could be a personal trainer!" Piper suggested.

"Yeah, maybe," I responded, "What about you? What is going on in your life?"

"Everything is great!" Piper exclaimed. "I can finally focus on wedding planning now that Dalton's birthday party is over."

"Dalton had a birthday party?" I asked. I was sort of hurt that I hadn't been invited, even though I guess he was technically Logan's friend and not mine.

"Yes, it was insane. He had a blast though," Piper relayed.

"Was Logan there?" I inquired, finally cutting to the chase and bringing him up. I wanted an opportunity to talk about him and how the breakup was affecting me. I thought she would have eventually asked, but she seemed too caught up in her own world.

"Yes, he was there," she confirmed, her enthusiasm starting to fade.

"That's good," I stated. "I hope he had fun, too."

"He ... umm ..." Piper began. "He actually brought someone."

I could have assumed that Logan had invited Skylar, but hearing it confirmed by Piper made it hurt all over again. It was hard to face the reality that he was already bringing her around our friends. Everything that Logan and I had done together, she was now experiencing. He was replacing me.

"It's okay, Piper," I started. "I already know he's with someone else."

"Okay, good," Piper uttered in relief, "I thought I had said something I wasn't supposed to."

Her smile returned, and she took another sip of her drink. She was pleased with herself that she hadn't been the one to reveal Logan's new girl to me, but her being reluctant to tell me said a lot—I was alone in this break up. Dalton and Piper were loyal to my ex. I thought Piper was my friend, but she was engaged to Logan's best friend, which meant she was on Logan's side. Had she not accidentally told me about Skylar, she was fully prepared to just let me find out on my own. I had no one on my team.

"Are you excited to get married?" I asked, switching the subject. Honestly, I wanted to just go home and cry, but I needed to push through the time with Piper. Hopefully, it wouldn't last much longer because my attempt at having a fresh start was failing miserably. I couldn't escape Logan. He was everywhere.

"I'm so excited!" Piper shouted. "We are getting married next summer. I've been planning my wedding since I was like ten, so I already know what I want. It's just a matter of bringing it to life now."

"Congratulations," I remarked as happily as I could. "Happy for you both."

"Are you going to come?" Piper asked, "We haven't sent out wedding invitations yet, but you are totally invited!"

I didn't know if Piper had discussed the guest list with Dalton yet, because I wasn't sure if I would be on it. However, it was her wedding as much as it was Dalton's, and if she wanted me there, then she was more than capable of inviting me. I wanted to support her, but I also knew it would be harder to move on from Logan knowing that I would see him again in a year. I could already imagine myself holding on to the hope of him falling in love with me all over again at their wedding, and ultimately getting back together. It was a hard decision, but my emotions were still raw—my heart was still longing for Logan. I couldn't pass up a chance to see him again.

"I'd love to come," I said to Piper. "Count me in."

"Perfect! I can't wait. It's going to be such a fun time," Piper expressed. "And don't worry, you can bring a guest."

"Ha, you won't have to worry about that," I answered with a chuckle. "I don't plan on dating anyone for a long time."

Unlike Logan, I was actually capable of being single.

37

Logan

I woke up to the sound of a car horn, beeping at the customer in front of them in the drive-thru lane. My back was stiff, and the sun was beaming through the windshield, almost blinding me. Sleeping in my car was not worth it. I should've gone crawling back to Hailey, or at least just gotten over my mom's judgment and slept at her house. Either way, my sore joints were paying the price of my stubbornness. I needed to make sure that Skylar was willing to let me move back into her house because I could not survive another night in my car. I decided to jump into the crazy drive-thru line and grab Skylar some breakfast before heading back to her place. I didn't want to risk angering her any further, so I ordered doughnuts, a breakfast sandwich, cinnamon rolls, avocado toast, and a cup of coffee. Surely, she would like at least one of the items. Next time, I would make sure I took note of what she actually enjoyed eating in the morning because my wallet wouldn't be able to handle the continuous guessing game of what Skylar actually liked.

Long-term relationships were way easier than new ones. I knew Hailey's order at every restaurant like the back of my hand. If this breakfast was for her, I would have had no problem ordering her a bacon, egg, and American cheese breakfast sandwich—on a biscuit instead of a bagel. I wouldn't have forgotten to order two doughnuts and claim they were for me because she thought the food tasted better if it was actually mine. I'd easily remember to order her an iced caramel latte with extra caramel drizzle. She wouldn't even have to remind me to substitute the side of hash browns for a fruit cup. If this order was for Hailey, I could have recited it in my sleep. Instead, I had to order almost one of everything off the menu because I didn't even know Skylar's eating habits.

I probably looked like a delivery driver when I made it back to Skylar's house because I exited my car with multiple bags of food and a wobbly drink carrier. The coffee almost toppled over on me multiple times. I was fully preparing myself to be covered in a burning liquid. Thankfully, I was able to make it to the front door without spilling anything, but I had to knock with my foot in order to avoid dropping everything.

"I brought breakfast," I announced with a smile when Skylar eventually opened the door. She didn't look as angry as she did last night, which was a relief, but she didn't look the happiest, either.

"Come in," she directed, further opening the door so that I could enter her house.

When I made it inside, I immediately relieved my hands by placing the breakfast items on the kitchen counter. I was grateful that I didn't spill the cup of coffee on me because that was the only thing that Skylar took. She grabbed a seat at the kitchen table, where her laptop was already sitting open. I assumed she must have gotten a head start on the day. We had an important open house to prepare for tomorrow, which I figured she was working on.

Since I had an abundance of breakfast choices, I grabbed a doughnut out of one of the bags and took a seat next to her. I wasn't sure if she wanted to focus on real estate or our argument from yesterday, so I just followed her lead. I pulled my laptop out of my backpack and began working.

"So how was your night?" Skylar asked, still clicking away on her computer.

"Been better, you?" I returned the question.

"Fine," Skylar answered.

I didn't know what to say next, so I just sat there quietly. I didn't want to do anything that would make her mad.

"Well, don't you have something to say?" Skylar encouraged. "Like, maybe an apology?"

I hated when she talked to me like I was a child, but at least I knew what she wanted. Hopefully a simple apology would fix everything. I couldn't risk another restless night in my car.

"Skylar, I am so sorry," I responded sincerely, hoping that would solve our issues.

"And what are you sorry for?" she urged. "Explain what you did wrong."

"I'm sorry that you felt like I still had feelings for my ex-girlfriend?" I guessed.

"Are you questioning your apology?" she replied.

To be honest, I didn't really remember what I did wrong. All I knew was that Skylar became enraged at any slight hint of Hailey, so I figured that was the apology she wanted to hear.

"No," I answered. "I am certain about it."

"Fine, I'll accept it," she muttered. "But I'm not always going to be this forgiving."

I got up from my chair and stood behind Skylar. She was still seated at the table, but I wrapped my arms around her and started kissing her cheek.

"So, you like me again?" I playfully asked her, reveling in the sound of her giggles as I kissed her.

"Yes, Logan, I like you again," she affirmed. She tried to uphold her angry front, but I could tell she was as relieved to be done fighting as I was.

"And I can sleep here tonight?" I asked, which was really the question I wanted an answer to.

"Yes, you can," Skylar stated.

I started kissing her more passionately, shifting from her cheeks to her lips. She laughed against my mouth. I was happy to have my girlfriend back, but I was more excited to actually have a place to stay.

"Okay, stop messing around," Skylar insisted. "We have to prepare for the event tomorrow."

"Yes, ma'am," I agreed, returning to my seat. "Anything for my wonderful girlfriend."

I could tell Skylar was trying not to smile. She liked to put on an intimidating exterior, but I could tell that my compliment got to her because her cheeks started turning bright pink. Skylar was happy, so everything was right in the world.

"What's the commission on this home?" I asked, pulling up the listing.

"Thirteen thousand," Skylar answered. "You should know this."

I pulled out my phone to quickly calculate thirty percent of thirteen thousand.

"Wow, almost four thousand dollars," I exclaimed, shocked at how fast my finances could turn around after one sale.

"You mean twenty-six hundred," Skylar corrected. "I agreed to twenty percent, remember?"

"I thought you said I could have thirty percent of what you earn," I proposed.

"I considered it," Skylar noted, "but decided against it. You are not ready for thirty percent."

"Skylar, come on," I pleaded. Even though I had successfully made it out of Hailey's apartment, I still wanted to be able to afford a place of my own one day. It was still a goal of mine.

"I'm letting you stay at my house for free," Skylar argued. "You should be grateful for any cut that I give you."

I didn't like that my finances were in her hands, but she had a point. I was glad that she had agreed to let me move in with her, but I didn't know there were strings attached to our arrangement. When I lived with Hailey, she didn't make me forfeit some of my salary in order to stay there.

"Don't seem so depressed," Skylar added. "Now you have something to work toward."

I quickly dismissed her comment and focused on our upcoming open house. Skylar and I had just gotten back on good terms, and I didn't want to ruin that. Maybe I would bring it up again when we were in a better place, but for now I just decided to push it out of my mind.

"Should we pick up a few appetizers and desserts on our way to the event tomorrow?" I offered.

"Yes, that would be perfect," Skylar confirmed.

I felt proud of myself for suggesting an idea that my girlfriend actually agreed with. She was hard to impress.

"My mom actually makes really good brownies," I noted. "I could have her bake some and then drop them off."

"Hm, I don't think that's the best idea," Skylar declared. "This is an important event. We will want to ensure that the food we provide accurately represents the house. It would be safer to just get the desserts from a real bakery."

"I hear where you're coming from," I countered, "but I think home-made brownies would make the property feel more comforting. We could even have her bake them at the open house, so that the kitchen even smells like chocolate."

"Sorry, not happening," Skylar stated.

"But, Skylar," I began.

"End of discussion," she interjected.

I respected Skylar's expertise in the business. She had been doing this a lot longer than I had, but she didn't seem receptive at all to new ideas. I wasn't sure how this mentorship was going to work out if she didn't let me contribute.

"Skylar, I really think it would be a nice touch," I added. "Plus, my mom would love to feel involved."

"Your mom will be fine not being included in this open house," Skylar remarked.

"I know she will be fine," I began, "but it would make her really happy."

"You're obsessed with your mother," Skylar pointed out. "You are a grown man. It's time to act like a big boy now."

I wanted to snap at Skylar, but I bit my tongue. Her condescending tone would have to change because I was not willing to continue to deal with it. I figured it was best to play nice for now, until we got through this open house and I was able to make a solid amount in commission and not be financially tied to her. But after that, I'd make sure that my issues with her were known.

"Okay, we can just pick up some baked goods tomorrow then," I muttered.

"Logan, we would be able to avoid a lot more arguments if you just agreed with me from the start," she remarked.

She started chuckling at her own comment, but I didn't find it funny at all. Skylar was starting to push me to my breaking point.

"Love is all about compromise," she added.

"Right, compromise," I affirmed, fully aware that whatever we had going on was far from a compromise. I tried not to say too much because I was close to exploding with anger.

We worked for a couple more hours, studying every detail of the property we were going to show tomorrow. Most of our session was done in silence, but I preferred it that way—at least we weren't arguing.

Around noon, Skylar closed her laptop, signaling that it was time to take a break. I followed suit, hoping our next course of action was deciding what to eat for lunch, but Skylar didn't move. She just started batting her eyelashes at me. I was still pretty upset with how she had been treating me lately, but still managed to return a smile in her direction.

"You're so handsome when you're working," Skylar stated.

"Um, thank you?" I replied, accepting the random compliment.

"I know I have been putting a lot of pressure on you, but it's only because I want to see you do great things. You have a lot of potential, and I just want you to always be your best," she relayed.

"I appreciate that," I answered.

If Skylar knew how to do one thing, it was knowing what to say. She always found the right words to calm me down. There were still some things that I wanted her to adjust in order for our relationship to work, but I knew her intentions were pure. She just needed to work on her delivery.

"Can I treat you to lunch?" she politely offered.

"That would be great," I said. I closed my laptop and attempted to place it in my backpack but paused when Skylar gently rested her hand on my arm.

"Logan," she whispered, "you are seriously the best boyfriend ever. After my divorce, I never thought I would be able to find love again, but you are honestly the best thing to ever happen to me." She gave me a gentle kiss on the lips before grabbing her car keys.

Hearing Skylar say such nice things about me made me rethink my initial feelings about her. Maybe I had been a little too quick to pass judgement. Her arrogant demeanor and egotistical mindset got on my nerves sometimes, but I could tell she always meant well. She had her moments where she came off as rude and inconsiderate, but maybe she wasn't so bad after all.

"Hey, Skylar," I called after her, "you are the best thing to happen to me, too."

38

Hailey

I successfully suffered through the rest of the coffee date with Piper without succumbing to my urge to pretend that I had an emergency to tend to and darting out of the café like a madwoman. Listening to her describe how great her life was going, while mine was falling to shambles, was not how I thought my Saturday was going to go. I didn't think I could listen to her go on and on about her wedding plans any longer until Dalton eventually called her and needed her for something. She wasted no time in immediately ending our conversation in order to head back to him. Piper apologized profusely, but little did she know, I was more than relieved to finally end our chat.

The morning quickly turned into the afternoon, and I was no closer to healing from Logan than when I had first sat down with Piper. I thought meeting with her would have helped to give me some closure, or maybe just peace of mind. Selfishly, I was hoping that she would've told me how unhappy he seemed. Instead, she did quite the opposite. When we said our goodbyes and I returned to my car which was no longer comfortably parked next to the one that looked like Logan's but instead one that looked like it belonged to a soccer mom, I took several moments to empty the tank of tears that had been filling up. I couldn't wait for the day when crying wasn't part of my daily routine. Life was complicated, and I had definitely not figured it out yet. Dalton and Piper were moving on to the next step in their relationship, and Logan was happily in love with someone else. I was running out of time to find my person. It wouldn't be long before twenty-three turned into thirty-three, and I would be no closer to finding someone to settle down with. I guess not everyone was lucky enough to find their happily ever after at a young age. At least I got to be in love once. Maybe that was all that was in the cards for me.

Once I finally pulled myself together and finished feeling sorry for my-self, I backed out of the parking spot to head back home. It was crazy how the absence of one person could change my entire life. Even simple activities, such as driving, didn't feel the same. Everything just felt less purposeful. I just wanted to feel a sense of happiness again. I wanted to smile—and mean it.

The drive back to my apartment was taking longer than usual because of the traffic. I lived by a park that transformed into a farmer's market on the weekends, and it usually drew quite the crowd. I was always curious about it, but Logan and I had never been to it because he claimed that it was just a way for vendors to use sympathy as an excuse to charge people more money. He didn't really care to pay the premium price to support local growers. Logan was perfectly happy paying for processed produce at the grocery store because it was a few cents cheaper.

I quickly realized that his protest of farmer's markets was no longer a factor in my life. There was nothing holding me back from experiencing it this time. I was already sitting in the traffic lane that led to the parking lot anyway, so I just continued to follow the road until it led me to my destination. The lot was crowded, but I didn't have any trouble finding a spot. It was mostly just filled with mothers rummaging through their trunks to pull out strollers for their children.

I felt out of place going to the market by myself. Everywhere I turned there was either a couple or a family. I didn't know why Logan had never taken me here. We didn't necessarily have to buy anything, but it was surely a cute date idea. I would've loved to spend some time with him, browsing all of the stands. There was more than just fruits and vegetables to look at, too. There was homemade soap, handcrafted jewelry, and even a petting zoo. I assumed one of the goats had a crush on me because when I walked by his eyes followed me the entire time. Perhaps a pet goat was in my future.

"Hi, miss!" a man called out to me. "Would you like a free sample?"

I walked over to him, observing his little stand that was clearly selling cheese, a product that I could not resist.

"Thank you," I exclaimed as I accepted the tiny slice.

I moved on to the next vendor who was displaying a wide variety of candles. I thought they were normal handmade candles until I got a closer look at the scents. They weren't ones that I would usually find in a store. I was expecting smells that replicated fresh laundry or a newly baked pie. Instead, the candles were labeled, *It's Finally Friday*, *When Plants are on*

Sale, and *Booking a Tropical Vacation.* I spent a few more moments in the stand, getting a chuckle out of most of the names. They were all so creative that I couldn't resist buying at least a few. I checked out with the shop owner and gave her a ten dollar bill in exchange for *Independent Woman* and *Homebody.* Satisfied with my purchases, I planned to just take my candles back to my car and head home. The time by myself was actually more enjoyable than I had thought, and it gave me the confidence to try more things alone. However, after my coffee date with Piper and adding the farmer's market on top of that, my social battery was drained. I didn't think I could talk to another person without completely shutting down.

I was walking back to my car, candles in hand, when I passed the most irresistible stand in the entire market—puppies. I immediately darted toward the cute little animals playing in a makeshift pen. A flimsy fence enclosed the adorable creatures, and I was already planning on which five I was going to take home. The puppies' attention was already divided by the numerous children that had discovered them before I had, but a few hobbled over to me when I stepped inside their designated area. I wasted no time in crouching down to their level so that they could climb all over me. I tried to talk some sense into myself and remember that I lived in a small apartment and didn't have the space to house such adventurous animals, but their cute faces made me dismiss any argument I had.

"Interested in a puppy?" I heard someone call out. "They are free."

I looked up and saw a man staring at me.

"They are purebred black Labrador Retrievers," he added.

The man looked around my age but carried himself as though he was a lot older. His dark hair was long enough to touch the top of his eyebrows, but his kind brown eyes were still clearly visible. He had facial hair, a beard that looked like it was growing back in after having been shaved recently. Since I was crouched down, I couldn't tell his exact height, but he appeared to be tall. His white t-shirt, that was covered by blue overalls, and cowboy boots made it look like he wrangled horses rather than someone who raised puppies, but I was kind of liking his rugged look.

"I'm just looking," I answered, petting the two puppies that hadn't left my side since I had gotten there. They were two little black balls of fur with a wet nose and shining eyes. One was determined to rip apart my shoelace, and the other was trying to eat my sock. I thought their puppy teeth would hurt, but it was more ticklish than painful.

"Well, Peanut Butter and Jelly seem to really like you," he responded.

"Peanut Butter and Jelly?" I repeated with a chuckle. "What kind of names are those?"

"I named them myself," the man proudly answered. "Those two don't leave each other's side. They are always stuck together."

"Like peanut butter and jelly," we both said at the same time.

I smiled at how in sync the man and I were. He wasn't necessarily my physical type, but his sense of humor and love for animals made him more attractive.

"As much as I would love to take this pair home with me, I live in an apartment with a demanding job," I admitted. "I don't have the time or the space to properly care for them."

I reasoned with myself that bringing them home would not be in my best interest, although with some convincing and a little more puppy licks, I'd be open to changing my mind.

"Do you have a family member, or rather, a boyfriend, that could help you out?" he asked.

"Well, I just got out of a relationship," I shared, still hurting every time I admitted my new relationship status out loud, "and my sister is going away for college soon."

He seemed relieved at my answer, even though it was further proof on why I couldn't adopt Peanut Butter and Jelly. I figured he was more interested to see if I was dating anyone rather than genuinely interested if I had the proper means to care for the dogs.

"Sorry to hear about your breakup," he relayed.

"It's fine. It's in the past," I remarked solemnly.

"I just got out of a relationship about a year ago, so I totally understand how you feel," he relayed. "What was your name by the way?"

"Hailey," I replied.

"I'm Andrew," he introduced, leaning over and sticking out his hand.

I was reluctant to shake it, as I wanted to continue petting the dogs, but I reached for his hand and properly greeted him.

"Well, Hailey," he began, "I know you are recently single, but maybe we could grab dinner sometime? I know a place that serves really good meatballs."

I admired the courage Andrew had to ask me on a date. For a moment, I actually panicked, forgetting how to be single. It had been a while since the last time I went out with anyone other than Logan. Don't get me wrong, Andrew wasn't ugly. However, I knew that my heart was in a vulnerable place. Going out with him would just be a way to try and heal myself. If there was one thing I learned from my seven-year relationship, it was that settling was one of the worst things someone can do. It's the silent enemy. Logan was my first boyfriend, so I didn't have anyone else to compare him to, but I could tell something was off. I didn't expect it to be fireworks and butterflies all the time, but I did feel as though there should have been something more to the relationship than just simply tolerating each other. I promised myself that no matter where life took me, I would never lower my standards again, for anyone or anything, and that the next relationship I decided to get into would be one that I was fully confident in. I deserved better than the relationship I had with Logan.

"These puppies are free, right?" I asked, totally ignoring Andrew's initial question.

"Um, yeah they are," Andrew confirmed, probably questioning whether I had actually heard the part where he asked me on a date.

I grabbed my bag of candles and picked up Peanut Butter and Jelly from their playpen.

"Sorry, Andrew, I can't go out with you," I began with two squirming animals in my arms. "I've got some puppies to take care of."

I left Andrew and the farmer's market behind as I made the journey back to my car, finally ready to head back home. I was still dreading going back to the empty apartment that Logan no longer lived in, as I was still getting used to his absence. I knew it would be a while before things felt normal again, but at least I wasn't alone anymore. This time, I was going back home with two new roommates.

39

Logan

"Hi, welcome in!" Skylar greeted each person that walked through the doors of the open house.

She flashed her most charming smile, one that she had reserved for when she went into work mode. It was an emphatic facial expression, but it gave the impression that she was super excited to be in everyone's presence. The smile was also used during special occasions, like when she really wanted something. In this case, she turned on the charm in the hopes that it would make someone be more inclined to put in an offer on the house. However, I'd also seen that expression when she wanted me to give in to her relentless demands, for example, when I asked her to be my girlfriend. I was starting to think that her innocent outward appearance was all an act because the woman who I met in the beginning seemed like a whole different person than who she was now. The sweet girl who had agreed to mentor me was beginning to feel more like a manipulative tactic.

"Please feel free to pull me or my assistant aside if you have any questions," she informed the guests.

"Assistant?" I questioned.

"Relax, Logan," she whispered under her breath so as to not bring on any unwanted attention. "Don't be so uptight. It's just easier to call you that."

"You could refer to me as your colleague," I suggested.

"Just let me handle this," Skylar proposed. "I don't want any potential buyers getting confused on who the actual listing agent is."

I wanted to roll my eyes at her lousy explanation, but didn't want to appear unprofessional while at work.

"I think it's pretty clear that this is your listing," I countered. "Your face is literally on the sign out front."

I pointed in the direction of the front yard where a giant sign displayed Skylar's face along with the hours of the open house.

"Well, I just want it to be extra apparent," Skylar relayed, turning her attention back to the arriving guests.

I decided to ignore Skylar's dismissive attitude and see if anyone had any questions about the property. She was probably just stressed about selling the house. Ever since she had lost a client a few days ago, she'd been on edge. I assumed she was banking on their business to help further her career, but they ended up finding a different agent because they didn't think Skylar was a good fit. That was a huge failure in her eyes, and I believed she was using this open house as a way to prove to herself that she still was the best of the best. The completion of this sale would help her ego and her bank account.

There weren't any inquiring buyers who needed help yet, so I just watched Skylar from the kitchen. She happily greeted everyone that entered, trying to sell the house, and herself. Her outfit made her appear more like a lawyer than a real estate agent—a gray dress that went all the way down to her ankles. I thought she would've appeared more approachable and relatable if she wore something shorter with some color, a dress more youthful, but I was sure my wardrobe suggestion wouldn't have been taken too kindly. Skylar knew best, and I could not come across as if I knew more than she did.

I eventually got bored of just watching Skylar fraternize with potential buyers, so I started thinking about what I would do with the commission earned on the home. Hopefully, this sale would put Skylar in a good mood and possibly make her more willing to give me a higher percentage of the earnings. However, I was well aware of the fact that Skylar was no stranger to chasing money. She did everything she could in order to have a little more cash in her pocket. Her determination was something I had really admired about her at the start, but it also was a huge character flaw. It was hard to date a woman who didn't even think twice about putting the next sale over her relationship. I thought Hailey had put me on the back burner, but Skylar took it to a whole other level. Skylar fought hard for her career, but on the other hand, she also fought hard for me. She linked my future in real estate to hers, which meant that she was investing a lot of time into both of us. All the hard work she was putting into all the listings and open houses directly impacted me, as well. I could complain all day about how Skylar sometimes belittled me, but at the end of the day, she had my back, and I appreciated her for that. It's possible that I could have jumped into dating Skylar maybe a little too quickly, but she did also help me open my eyes to how bad Hailey had truly treated me. I made the right choice in dating Skylar. I'd be sad and lonely without her.

"Excuse me?" I heard a young voice ask. "My mom said I could have the bigger room and my brother has to have the smaller room. Which bedroom is bigger?"

I looked down and saw a little girl, around seven or eight years old, staring back at me. Her big brown eyes popped against her rosy cheeks. Her dark hair was tied into a ponytail, but it looked like it hadn't been out of that hairstyle in a while. She had strands flying in every direction, and her bangs were nowhere near straight. She must've been a feisty child that didn't like to be told what to do because her parents let her out of the house with two different shoes on and a shirt that was clearly on backwards—her unusual style matched her unkempt hair.

"You see those stairs over there?" I asked her, crouching down to her level and pointing to the stairs.

The little girl nodded.

"If you go up them and turn left," I began. "Do you know which way is left?"

She nodded her head again, holding up her hands and using her pointer fingers and thumbs to make the shape of an *L*.

"This way is left," she proudly answered, correctly shaking her left hand.

"That's right," I acknowledged. "So, if you go up the stairs and turn left, the first bedroom that you see is the bigger room."

"Thank you!" the girl shouted as she ran to find the bedroom.

I was proud of her sense of direction, but more impressed at her determination to secure the room she wanted.

"You should really talk to the parents about the details of the house rather than children."

I stood up and saw Skylar giving me a disappointed look.

"She just wanted to check out the bedrooms," I replied.

"Well, she will not be the one to put in an offer on the house," Skylar argued, "so don't waste your time. We need to focus on the real clients."

Skylar motioned for me to follow her, but I stood firm in the kitchen. There was nobody within earshot and I wanted some privacy to be able to have an actual conversation with her. It seemed as though she wanted to continue on with the open house and put the topic to rest, but she needed to hear me out. I wasn't ready to drop the conversation and act as if nothing had happened.

"She's just a kid," I rebutted. "What did you want me to say? Go away?"

Skylar didn't seem too amused that I refused to leave the kitchen, but it forced her to have to communicate with me. "You should have asked to talk to her parents," Skylar remarked. "Do you want this house sold or not?"

"I do," I insisted, "but think about it."

"Think about what?" Skylar asked, arms crossed across her chest. I could tell that the last thing she wanted to do was talk to me.

"If the kid likes the bedroom, then she will probably beg her parents to get it," I started. "Trust me, that little girl gets whatever she wants."

"You don't know her, and you don't know her parents," Skylar noted. "Just stick to talking to people who can actually afford to place an offer."

Skylar turned away from me before I could answer her. She started to head out of the kitchen but stopped when she realized I still hadn't followed her.

"Logan, don't get too flustered. You are still early in your career," Skylar pointed out, walking back over to me. Her heels were clicking against the tiled floor. "One piece of advice that I learned when I first started in this business was to keep my conversations limited to those who have a bank account that I would be jealous of."

"You talked to me, though," I pointed out.

"What do you mean?" Skylar asked.

"I don't have nearly the funds that would make anyone jealous, yet here you are, talking to me," I explained.

It was obvious that Skylar only interacted with people who could offer her something in return, but my wallet was a ghost town. I didn't know what she could possibly gain from being with me.

"Yeah, but you are my little project," Skylar started, gently petting my arm and looking at me as if I was a lost a puppy.

"Project?" I repeated. "I am no one's project."

"That's not what I meant," Skylar assured. "I just meant that our relationship isn't monetary. You give me things money could never buy."

She gently kissed me on the cheek before giving me a playful wink.

"With a young, handsome man like you by my side, we are guaranteed to sell any house on the market." She flashed her usual charming smile. "Besides, my ex-husband swore that I would never find another man like him. Now look at me, dating a guy that is half his age. He could cheat on me with as many women as he wanted, but I bet none of them were as young as you are. Who has the upper hand now?"

Skylar gave me another kiss before skipping out of the kitchen. This time, I decided to follow her as I had nothing else left to say. I felt used. I was just her little trophy to show to all her friends and her ex-husband. This was just a power move to Skylar, and I was merely a pawn to the bigger game that she was playing. I was the perfect target for her—a young man fresh out of a relationship simply looking for a way to get ahead in the real estate industry. She preyed upon my vulnerability and used me to feel better about herself. In hindsight, it was pretty obvious, but I still felt stupid. However, I guess that's why our relationship worked. We were both just using each other. She was using me to get back at her ex-husband, and I was using her to get over my ex-girlfriend. It wasn't the most ideal situation, but I couldn't get rid of Skylar until I was absolutely ready to. I wouldn't be able to face the long healing journey that I would have to endure if I had to be alone again. I needed to stay with Skylar until the part of my heart that still belonged to Hailey had fully moved on. It may take a while, but our arrangement wouldn't last forever. It was only a matter of time before one of us didn't need the other person anymore. Eventually, one of us would finally get what we were in search of. For my sake, I just hoped that person would be me.

40

Hailey

I couldn't remember the last time I had been in a pet store, but adopting two new puppies made it a necessity. I still couldn't believe that I had actually gone through with taking them home, but I couldn't resist their cute faces. Usually, every decision I made was carefully thought out, weighing every pro and con. However, it felt kind of good to step outside my comfort zone and just make a decision for myself. I didn't have a boyfriend that I had to run every idea by. It honestly felt liberating.

I thought owning two new dogs would be nothing but joy and cute puppy kisses, but I was wrong. Last night, they decided that my bed would also be their bed, so I spent most of my night being suffocated by fur. I would wake up in the middle of the night to aggressive licks and puppy breath. When I would remove Peanut Butter from my face, Jelly would climb right on top of me and replace her brother's spot. Additionally, each time I tried to get myself comfortable, one of them would switch positions, forcing me to also adjust. I believed most of the night was spent tending to dogs rather than sleeping. Needless to say, our current nightly arrangement was not going to work.

Thankfully, my parents let me drop off Peanut Butter and Jelly at their house while I went on my venture to find the perfect dog bed. I had originally reserved this Sunday to clean out the apartment and get rid of any of the items Logan had left behind, but my plans quickly changed. As cute as PB&J were, they consumed a lot of my time. I didn't expect two tiny animals to need so much attention, but now most of my day was consumed by them. At least my job allowed me to work from home, but I was nervous about how I would be able to juggle such a demanding job and rambunctious puppies at the same time. Maybe I would have to add dog cages and a puppy camera to my shopping list.

Logan would chuckle if he knew that I had recently impulsively brought home two dogs, and he would laugh even harder over their names. He knew that it was so unlike me to make a rash decision, but I enjoyed the idea of knowing that I was evolving as a person without him. It was evident he didn't necessarily like that I always wanted to stay home and not socialize. He had told me before that I had a tendency to be boring. I didn't think I was boring, though. I just didn't enjoy the same things as he did. If he had seen me walking around with two new puppies, maybe he would reconsider his perspective of me. It might make him realize that the girl he had broken up with was not the same person anymore. In the short time that we had been single, I figured that I had changed and grown enough that he might consider the idea of getting back together in the future. The old me definitely wouldn't have taken the puppies home. I thought about reaching out and sending him a picture of Peanut Butter and Jelly, but I figured the last thing he wanted was to hear from me. Knowing that Logan already had a new girlfriend deterred any urge I had to message him. He was happy with someone else and probably didn't want to be bothered by me. I decided against reaching out to him, but I wished I could move on as quickly as he did. It sure would've made life a lot easier.

I tried to refocus my thoughts away from my ex and shift them toward my original mission to find an alternative sleeping situation for Peanut Butter and Jelly. I took an indirect route to the aisle with all the dog beds as I realized there were a lot of pet supplies that I didn't have yet. After I got the dogs, I knew I had to buy them food, toys, and a collar, but there were so many other things that I didn't even think about getting. I added brushes, shampoo, conditioner, toothbrushes, toothpaste, nail clippers, and even more dog toys into my cart. By the time I actually reached the dog beds, I barely had any space left. I thought being single would save me more money since I didn't have to pay for dates anymore and the utilities would be lower with one less person living in the apartment, but now my money was going toward my new pets. At least they wouldn't constantly nag me about not making them a priority or drag me to boring social events.

The aisle contained every dog bed imaginable, so I took my time in examining each one. Some were quickly dismissed, as they were too small or too thin, but there were a lot of viable options. I also had to decide if I wanted to buy one small bed for each of them or a giant one for them to share. However, I didn't ponder on that decision for too long because there was no way Peanut Butter and Jelly would sleep separately. Like their name, they were always stuck together.

After a few more minutes of reviewing my choices, I picked the dog bed that was big enough to sleep both puppies comfortably. It was soft enough that hopefully it would be a more attractive place for them to sleep instead of my bed, but the thought did cross my mind that they would simply ignore it and continue to lay with me. Before heading to check out, I navigated to the aisle with all the dog treats. I needed to bribe the dogs to use the bed, and then reward them after.

Of course, there was an even greater variety of treats than beds. My indecisive mind was running crazy trying to take in all my options. Unlike the beds, I couldn't test them out before purchasing, so I was just basing my decision on the price and packaging. I scanned the shelves, hoping that there would be a brand that would jump out at me. I had no idea where to even begin. I was spending more time pondering that aisle than my entire duration in the store itself.

"Can't decide?" an older gentleman's voice uttered to me.

"I'm a first-time pet owner," I admitted, still staring at my options. "I'm not sure which treats to get."

I continued to browse the choices and decided that I might just close my eyes and pick one.

"I recommend these," he exclaimed as he handed me a style of dog treat that resembled bacon. It looked like real meat and even appeared appetizing to me, so I figured it would appease the dogs, as well.

"Thanks," I answered, taking the treats from him, relieved that I wouldn't have to spend another minute contemplating which snack to feed my dogs.

I had been staring at my choices for so long that I didn't even really look at the man until I took the bag from him. He was older, probably in his late fifties, with a touch of gray in his hair and beard. Although I could see the signs of aging in the wrinkles in his face, his body was in good shape. He had bigger biceps than most twenty-year old men I knew. He definitely wasn't a stranger to the gym. However, the thing that stood out most about him was the bright orange Princeton hoodie he was wearing.

"I like your sweatshirt, by the way," I noted, pointing to it. "My sister actually just applied there."

"It's an amazing university," he explained, his face apparently lighting up at the mention of his school. "I graduated almost thirty years ago, but it still feels like yesterday. It gave me some of the best memories of my life."

"That is great to hear," I remarked with a smile.

I thought the conversation with the stranger was going to end there, but he continued on. "Are you in school?" he inquired.

"I just graduated," I affirmed. "Not from Princeton, though."

I giggled to myself as I imagined what it would've been like if I had gone to an Ivy League school, but quickly dismissed the idea. I definitely wouldn't have survived the rigorous academics that Princeton would have to offer.

"What do you do now?" he asked.

"I'm an accountant," I answered, "for now."

"For now?" the man repeated.

"Don't get me wrong, I love working with numbers," I began, "but working fifty hours a week accounting for businesses that I don't have any interest in is not how I envisioned my life going."

I didn't know why I felt the need to explain my sentiments about my current job with a stranger in a pet store, but I didn't get out much these days. It felt good to talk to someone.

"What do you want to do with the rest of your life then?" he questioned.

"I'm interested in fitness," I admitted. "I wish I could combine my love for numbers and working out. That would be awesome."

"Well, if you're interested," he began, "I live on a property with a lot of land. It's where I host my boot camps. I could use some help with the finances."

"Really?" I exclaimed.

I wasn't surprised by his job. He definitely looked like a boot camp instructor, but I never imagined quitting my job anytime soon. I had been working so hard to prove myself to the company and my managers, that I never really entertained the idea of leaving. However, I also never thought that accounting for a boot camp even existed. A possible opportunity was knocking at my door, and I was thinking about answering it.

"Yes, and assuming you have dogs," he looked at the treats in my hand, "you could bring them over to the property and have them run around while you work if you want. I actually have a few pets of my own—three dogs, four cats, and a turtle."

"Wow, you have a lot of animals," I replied.

"I like the company," he answered, "and my clients love having them around."

Knowing that the guy had a whole zoo at his house made me even more intrigued. It sounded like Peanut Butter and Jelly would have a place to run free while also making new friends.

"I'd definitely be interested in hearing more about the role," I affirmed.

"That's great," he relayed. "Here, take my business card." The gentleman handed over a small piece of paper that read, *Bobby's Boot Camp*, along with an address and a phone number. "Feel free to call me anytime," he remarked.

"Thank you," I responded. "I'm Hailey Ross, by the way."

"Bobby Pierce," he said, shaking my hand. "I hope to hear from you soon, Hailey."

He smiled and took his cart, pushing it past me as he headed further down the aisle.

I went into the pet store with the intent of buying a dog bed, but was going to leave with a lot more than that. I was still greatly feeling the loss of Logan, but adopting PB&J and the possibility of landing a new job gave me hope—hope that there was more to life than just my relationship with Logan, and hope that my life wasn't ending, but that it was just beginning.

ONE YEAR LATER

41

Logan

"You may now kiss the bride."

Everyone cheered as Piper and Dalton kissed, signaling their lifelong commitment to each other. The joy on their faces shined as they walked back down the aisle, waving to all their guests. As his best man, I followed closely behind as the rest of the groomsmen and bridesmaids left the altar. After the ceremony, we all met up at a quiet location surrounded by the beautiful Rocky Mountains, away from the rest of the wedding guests in order to take pictures. Dalton and Piper chose a nice outdoor location for their wedding that displayed Colorado's stunning scenery. There wasn't a bad spot for a photo. I admitted I wasn't really into the whole wedding thing, and I was happy that I wasn't in Dalton's shoes when I saw all the planning that went into it. However, seeing my best friend get married changed my mindset. Secretly, I had hoped that it was my wedding that everyone had gathered for. Watching him and Piper express their love for each other in front of their closest friends and family was worth being envious of.

Dalton and Piper took a few photos of their own before the rest of the wedding party joined them. I knew they were in the middle of taking pictures, but even when the camera wasn't in their face, they were still smiling and laughing with each other. The love that they shared had always been apparent, but today it felt even more real.

"Congratulations, D," I exclaimed once the photographer had finally put the camera down. "I'm happy for you."

"Thanks, man," he answered. "I'm just glad it's over and we can finally party!"

Dalton was overjoyed to marry Piper, but I knew he was ready to just let loose on the dance floor. Being that this was his wedding, it was obvious that he was not going to hold back. I wouldn't have been surprised if Piper had to drag him out of the reception before the night was even over.

"Don't get too crazy," I joked, "or else you will have the shortest marriage known to man."

"You're right," he agreed. "My wife would kill me." He reveled in the ability to now refer to Piper as his wife.

It was different, Dalton being a husband now, but he was happy, and I knew he and Piper would last forever. They had always been one of the strongest couples I had ever known.

"Too bad Skylar couldn't come," Dalton continued on. "She's going to miss out on my awesome dance moves."

Dalton started to have a mini dance party with only himself. His moves were far from awesome, but his confidence made up for it.

"Actually, we just aren't together right now," I reluctantly admitted.

"What?" Dalton questioned in shock. "Didn't you guys just go on a trip together last weekend?

"Yeah, got in an argument on the flight back home," I explained.

Skylar and I had gone on a trip to Hawaii together. It was supposed to be a romantic vacation, but when I didn't propose to her at the end of our time there, she got upset. Unfortunately, she chose the plane ride home to discuss it and ended up switching seats with another passenger in order to not have to sit next to me for the duration of the flight. I didn't realize I was supposed to pop the question on a trip that she had planned all on her own, but I didn't get the memo and had to pay the price for it.

"Dang, man, I'm sorry to hear that," Dalton responded.

"It's okay. It happens all the time. We break up and make up. I'm sure we will be back together by the end of the week," I explained. "You know how it is."

Dalton forced a smile, but I could tell that he was concerned. He always supported me and my relationships and never once spoke badly about Skylar. However, I could tell he wasn't her biggest fan, either. Anytime I would tell him about our most recent fight, he would quickly change the subject. Whenever we would go on double dates, he would mostly just keep to himself, or only really talk to Piper and I. He didn't have anything nice to say about Skylar, so he just chose to not speak about her at all. I believed it was better that he just kept it to himself, anyway. There was no point in causing tension in our friendship because of a girl. He knew I would leave her when I was ready. For now, it was just best for him to let me live my life how I wanted to.

"As long as you're happy," Dalton noted. "Hopefully, your personal relationship hasn't affected your professional relationship."

"Oh, not at all," I affirmed. "We are still working well together."

"Good," Dalton commented. "We will have to celebrate once you complete your first sale."

"Absolutely," I acknowledged.

Skylar was still mentoring me and showing me the ropes of the real estate industry. I still had yet to sell a home, but she said it sometimes takes a real estate agent years to get one sale, so it wasn't like I was behind or anything. It was still a goal of mine to save up for an apartment of my own, but for now, I was satisfied staying at Skylar's.

My mom came over to have dinner one night to see where I had been living. She brought over a few pieces of home decor as a gift, and to have her motherly touch on the place. Unfortunately, Skylar refused to let her decorate the house, claiming it didn't fit with the aesthetic. My mom and Skylar got into a huge fight over a few pillow covers and paintings, and now they don't have a relationship at all. They can't even be in the same area as each other without getting upset. Their fight definitely put me in an awkward position. I was in the middle of an argument between my girlfriend and my mom. With all the time I spent living, dating, and working with Skylar, there wasn't a lot of time left over to see my mom. Skylar got angry anytime I would go over to my mom's house, anyway. Over time, I saw my mom less and less until eventually I just stopped seeing her altogether unless it was for a special occasion. It was a sad reality, but at least it felt like a short-term solution.

"Well, I'm going to take a few more pictures with Piper before the sun goes down. See you inside?" Dalton uttered.

"Yeah, D. I'll see you inside," I stated.

"Maybe this will be you next year," Dalton remarked before heading back to reunite with his new wife.

"Yeah, maybe," I whispered to myself.

I watched as Dalton lovingly kissed Piper, then grabbed her hand to take her to another location to take pictures. To be in love like that was something that I hoped was in my future. I knew it wasn't in the cards for Skylar and me, but her presence was still helping me move on from my ex. I still thought about Hailey a lot. I hadn't spoken to her since the last time

I had gone to her apartment and moved all my stuff out. Surprisingly, I also hadn't run into her, but she usually stayed inside, anyway. From her social media, she looked happy, so I didn't even bother reaching out to her. I had caused her enough pain.

I lived my life without regrets, but sometimes I wondered what it would've been like if Hailey and I hadn't broken up. Maybe I really would have been planning my own wedding soon if we had stayed together. If we hadn't gone our separate ways, maybe I wouldn't have been thrown on the roller coaster that Skylar was putting me through. I couldn't help but think that my life may have been in a better place right now if I had Hailey by my side instead of Skylar. However, Hailey appeared to be living a life that she was proud of, and she truly seemed happy. Therefore, even if I wasn't totally happy with where I was in life, at least Hailey was—which meant that the breakup was worth it. I just hoped that no matter how great her life turned out to be, she would never forget me. I wanted her to remember the good times we had, and all the laughs we shared. I wished nothing but the best for her, and if that meant that she would end up with someone other than me, then I was perfectly fine with that. I just wanted to see her happy. However, I did selfishly hope that Hailey still kept the thought of me in the back of her mind. I hoped that she had moved on with her life, but hadn't fully closed the chapter on us because I still loved her. I still had strong feelings for her. And, if she ever decided that she was open to exploring things and wanted to come back to me ... I'd be more than happy to welcome her back with open arms.

42

Hailey

Piper must have forgotten to invite me to her wedding, or Dalton overturned her vote in wanting me there, because I found out they got married from social media. I wasn't that surprised, though. My relationship with Dalton and Piper slowly faded over the year. They mostly hung out with Logan, and since he and I weren't together, I kind of just drifted out of their lives. Dalton did reach out to me one day, inviting me over to his house when Piper had gone out of town. In all honesty, I entertained the idea in my head for a little bit. I had always found Dalton attractive, and our flirty friendship was probably not as innocent as we had pretended it to be. It had also been a while since the last time I had any physical contact with a man, and it would have definitely given me the upper hand over Logan. There's nothing like getting back at your ex like sleeping with his best friend. Therefore, at first Dalton's offer was pretty tempting, but ultimately, I ended up denying him and then blocking his number.

I wish I had the morals to say that I didn't follow through with it because it would've hurt Logan, but I probably would have gone over if it hadn't been for Piper. Although we weren't that close, I knew it would have crushed her to know that Dalton reached out to me behind her back, especially since they were engaged. I even thought about showing her the text that her fiancé had sent me, but Piper was the type to blame the girl and then stick with her man. She was head over heels for Dalton, and I didn't want to bring any negative energy a few months before their wedding, so I just kept it to myself. Hopefully, Dalton was just asking me to come over as a friend and I was making a big deal out of nothing. If not, I hoped he had just caught himself in a weak moment and wasn't planning on betraying Piper ever again. Either way, that's all I could think of when I looked at their wedding pictures. They seemed so happy, and I hated knowing that the groom was possibly planning on cheating on his future bride shortly before their big day. I guess not everything was as it seemed.

I still had not taken the leap of faith of jumping back into another relationship, but I was happy on my own. I tried using dating apps, but apparently guys in Colorado were not looking for commitment. Actually, I didn't think they were looking for anything at all. Out of the few months that I was able to endure on the apps, I went on two dates. Both times we ended up splitting the bill, so I didn't even know if that really counted as a date. Maybe my person was just in a different state, but either way, I was fine being by myself. It was exhausting engaging in conversation with men who had more pictures of them holding a fish than actual words to say.

On the flip side, although my dating life was going downhill, my career was taking off. Shortly after meeting Bobby at the pet store, I quit my job and began working for him on his boot camp business. At first, I was just doing simple budgeting tasks, but after a couple months of that, I started leading a few classes. I actually enjoyed it more than I had originally thought, so although I still did the bookkeeping for the company, I was also one of the lead trainers. It was nice to be able to do a job that I was passionate about and also gave me a hefty paycheck. My parents even attended one of the classes I led. They struggled through it but had a blast in the process. Megan also joined in on a few sessions when she was in town, but that was a rare occurrence. She was loving school and stayed on campus even during holiday breaks. I believed she enjoyed Princeton more than she could have ever imagined, but I figured her extended stays there may have been motivated by another factor. I warned her about the complications of love, and I assumed she was finally realizing that for herself. I'd still pretend to be shocked when she was finally ready to admit that she was dating someone, even though I had called it from the beginning.

I finished scrolling through all of Piper's and Dalton's wedding photos when I heard a noise that sounded like paper shredding. I looked over the edge of my bed and saw Peanut Butter ripping a small notebook to shreds while Jelly watched. Fortunately, I managed to wrangle it out of his mouth. It wasn't completely destroyed, but it had a bunch of bite marks on it. I contemplated throwing it away until I realized it was the journal that I had used to try and heal from Logan. The first page was still intact, so I read the first entry I had written:

Dear Journal,
Logan and I broke up ... and I want him back.

I was hurting for the version of myself that wrote that only a year ago. I still had a long journey of healing in front of me, but I was definitely in a better place than I was when I initially made the entry. The pain that constantly tugged at my heart was no longer there, and I could go on about my life without the thought of Logan constantly popping in my head. I still had love for him, and I wasn't sure if that would ever go away, but I was still happy with how far I had come.

I opened the drawer to my nightstand and shuffled around inside until I found a pen. I wanted to make another entry in the journal to reflect my new mindset. I wasn't the hurting girl anymore that couldn't go a day without crying. I was turning my life around. The memories of Logan still weighed heavily on my heart, but all the growth I had done on my own was something that needed to be documented. I grabbed the pen and removed the cap to make a second entry.

Dear Journal,

I love Logan Tate ... but I love myself more.

I reread my note before putting the notebook and pen back inside the drawer of the nightstand. Maybe I'd find the journal again a year later, in an even more healed state, and make another entry. But for now, I was happy with where I was at. My life didn't end just because a relationship did.

I hadn't heard from or seen Logan since the day he moved out of the apartment. I figured he was happy with Skylar and didn't want to hear from me. Looking back, he probably did us both a huge favor by ending the relationship. We weren't headed in the right direction, and I didn't think we would have ever been able to recover. If he hadn't ended it, I probably would have ended up marrying him just for the sake of being married. On my wedding day, I would've been surrounded by people who weren't even my true supporters as Logan's mom didn't even like me, his best friend had been flirting with me, and Logan himself didn't even love me in the way that I needed to be loved. I still wanted the best for him and hoped that he had found love, but I kind of hoped that Skylar wasn't the one for him. I didn't really care for the other girls that would enter into his life, but the one Logan chose right after me felt more personal. It would be weird knowing that the girl he dated right after me was the one he would end up spending the rest of his life with. The unhealed part of me was wishing that Skylar would break his heart just like he broke mine. I always thought she was a rebound, but honestly, I was probably also a rebound from his first relationship with Ivy. The hurt side of me also hoped that he would never make it in real estate. He put so much emphasis on his career, that I hoped it ended up not working out for him and that he would have to admit to himself that he ended our relationship for nothing. I wanted him to still be thinking of me and regretting his decision to let me go. I hoped that he still loved me and one day would come running back to me, begging me to take him back ... I'd be more than happy to reject him like the way he rejected me.

A Note From The Author

Thank you for your support by reading, *You Should've Just Let Me Go*. This is my second self-published book that I have been able to share with the world. I had a lot of fun writing from two different perspectives, and I can't wait to continue to push myself in other realms as an author. It has been a pleasure to continue publishing works and creating stories from my wild imagination.

I encourage you to share this book with a friend and to sign up for my newsletter for updates regarding upcoming releases. I appreciate your love and support as I continue my writing journey.

Subscribe to my newsletter:
https://linktr.ee/authorbaileythomas

www.ingramcontent.com/pod-product-compliance
Lightning Source LLC
Chambersburg PA
CBHW022037240626
47154CB00007B/2442